Lucie Duff Gordon

Letters from Egypt, 1863-65

Lucie Duff Gordon

Letters from Egypt, 1863-65

ISBN/EAN: 9783337231675

Printed in Europe, USA, Canada, Australia, Japan

Cover: Foto ©Andreas Hilbeck / pixelio.de

More available books at **www.hansebooks.com**

LETTERS FROM EGYPT.

LETTERS FROM EGYPT,

1863-65.

BY

LADY DUFF GORDON.

London:
MACMILLAN AND CO.,
16, BEDFORD STREET, COVENT GARDEN.
1865.

PREFACE.

In the short introduction to Lady Duff Gordon's Letters from the Cape of Good Hope, published last year, I used some expressions which I am tempted to repeat here, because their description of the qualities which characterized those Letters, and the motives which prompted their publication, apply, and with still greater force, to those now submitted to the public.

"It is the entire absence of the exclusive and supercilious spirit which characterizes dominant races; the rare power of entering into new trains of thought, and sympathizing with unaccustomed feelings; the tender pity for the feeble and subject, and the courteous respect for their prejudices; the large and purely human sympathies,—these, far more than any literary or graphic merits, are the qualities which have induced the possessors of the few following Letters to give them to the public.

"They show, (what letters from Egypt, since received from the same writer, prove yet more conclusively,) that even among so-called barbarians are to be found hearts that open to every touch of kindness, and respond to every expression of respect and sympathy.

" If they should awaken any sentiments like those which inspired them, on behalf of races of men who come in contact with civilization only to feel its resistless force and its haughty indifference or contempt, it will be some con-solation to those who are enduring the bitter-ness of the separation to which they owe their existence."

When I wrote those words, many of the most interesting of the following letters were not yet in existence; nor had I the assurance I now have, that the character and spirit which pervade them would fall in with the tastes and opinions of the English public. Not only, however, are the qualities which distinguished the former letters still more remarkable in these, but those qualities have excited general sympathy and approbation.

They owe their existence to the same afflicting circumstances as those from the Cape. They were written under the influence of dangerous disease, and in the dreariness of solitary exile; far from all the resources which civilized society offers to the suffering body and the weary and dejected spirit; above all, far from all the objects of the dearest affections.

All the wonders and enchantments of Egypt would not have sufficed to fill so immense a void, even to a mind so alive to them. Nothing less than Humanity, in its most literal and its largest sense,—not circumscribed by race or religion, by opinions or customs, but the purely human sympathy which binds together those between whom no other tie exists,—could have made life under such conditions tolerable. But this expansive charity is twice blessed; for if the miserable objects of it have derived comfort from the pitiful and helpful hand of the Englishwoman, she, on her part, has found, in the interest they inspire and in the consciousness of mitigating their sufferings, some comfort under the privation of all her natural occupations and enjoyments. She has been requited by grateful affection and boundless confidence, and has had satisfactory proofs that the ascendancy acquired by kindness is far more complete than any that can be obtained by force.

It is to this large and tolerant humanity that the writer owes her power of understanding and interpreting thoughts and feelings unintelligible to most Europeans; to see the point at which the widely-severed but converging rays of truth meet; to feel those touches of nature which make the whole world kin. No doubt her admiration of her Arab friends will appear to many groundless or exaggerated, and the indulgence with which she regards some of their usages which are the least to our taste, excessive. But her object was not to blame, but to understand, and the first and most indispensable requisite for understanding is absolute impartiality. Nobody can understand that which he approaches with feelings of antipathy.

There are passages illustrative of the manners and morals of Arabs which I at first determined to omit; but further reflection convinced me that to do so would be to rob this little volume of much of its value. Of all the problems which society seeks in vain to solve, the most difficult by far are those which regard the relations between the sexes, and it is ridiculous to affect to treat of the condition of a people without endeavouring to discover in what way these most important problems present themselves to its moral sense. The task of civilizing and reforming (which we are so ready to undertake) requires above all things the power of regarding questions which lie at the root of all human society in a spirit equally remote from levity and antipathy. It may be, however, that any allusion to subjects which cynicism and corruption have given over to the jester and the libertine may shock some readers. To such, I have only to repeat that these Letters, like their predecessors, were written " to the two persons with whom of all others the writer felt the least necessity for reserve;" and that if anything were published that ought to have been withheld, the one to whom alone the selection was entrusted were alone to blame.

In justification of the enthusiastic interest with which the wretched condition of the Arabs has inspired Lady Gordon, it might be urged that she saw in them the relics of a most ancient and noble race, once the possessor of a high and distinct form of civilization, now crushed under the same barbarian force which destroyed the last remnants of the civilization of Greece. But it needed not the historical interest attached to Egypt or to Arabia to awaken her profound and passionate sympathy. It will hardly be imagined that the writer of these Letters is incapable of estimating the advantages, or enjoying the pleasures of cultivated society; but sympathy with the oppressed and indignation

against the oppressor are evidently more powerful with her than any of the tastes or wants
of civilized life.

Such a disposition unquestionably subjects
the possessor to mistakes and deceptions.
Making every allowance, however, for generous illusions in favour of the unfortunate, it
is clear, from the facts and conversations here
related, that qualities of a very high kind are
to be found among the Arabs, when they are
not debased and corrupted by contact with
cruel oppressors, or with the worst forms of
European civilization.

The Arabic proper names, and other words,
which occur in these Letters, have been corrected by an eminent oriental scholar, who is
no less intimately acquainted with the people,
than with the language of Egypt. To his cor-
dial sympathy with the sentiments of the writer
regarding them, I believe I owe much of the
kind interest with which he has watched the
book through the press.

Nobody will be surprised to learn that the
writer distrusts her power of reproducing

what made so powerful an impression on her own mind. "It was impossible," she says, "to express what I saw, and felt, and comprehended." And again, "All that can be said appears poor to one who knows, as I do, how curious, and interesting, and poetical the country is."

The publication of this volume has been somewhat delayed, in the hope that a letter might arrive relating the writer's departure from her Egyptian home, and her voyage down the Nile; but none has come, and it is not thought expedient to wait longer. We must, therefore, break off under the painful impression of the scenes which have thrown gloom and horror over the last days of her residence at El-Uksur.

Sarah Austin.

Weybridge, May 25, 1865.

LETTERS FROM EGYPT.

LETTER I.

Port of Leghorn, October 13, 1862.

I HEARD such reports of the dearness of Malta, and of the beauty of Cairo at this season, that I resolved to go at once to Cairo. We arrived here yesterday evening. I found there was time to go to Pisa, and had a delightful day. The weather was delicious. It was a *giorno di festa*, and the devices to extract more money on that plea were worth what they cost. The *vetturino* at Pisa assured me, "Ah, cara signora! siamo troppo sacrificati per il tarif." He called attention to his fine clothes, and told how he had intended to " divertirsi con la sua innamorata;—e lasciò tutto per mostrar la città alla signora,"—all with such a coaxing air that it was irresistible. The boatman who

B

brought me on board lamented that it was already dark—*bujo;* that he was frightened, and that the weather might change, and his *battello* be wrecked (in the port). " Per l'amor di Dio, datemi cinque o quattro franchi!" I sternly refused, and in the same breath he implored me to return with him next morning.

The Duomo, the Baptistery, and the Campo Santo were quite a new world to me, and the leaning tower is as lovely as it is odd. The pictures by Andrea del Sarto alone are worth the journey. I never was more delighted with anything; and the people are so handsome and pleasant.

I found the climate at Marseilles very trying. Since I have been at sea, I feel quite differently. I had no idea it was so warm; at sea now it is like the tropics,—not a chill in the air. A French artist has given me a letter to Lautner Bey, the Pasha's German doctor, and to a *ci-devant* St. Simonian, an old French painter turned Mussulman, and living in Old Cairo. I hope he will show me a good deal. We sail in an hour or two.

LETTER II.

October 27, 1862, Alexandria.

... I arrived here " all right," having lost a day by the *giorno di festa* at Leghorn, where we shipped a curious motley crew;—French singers and Italian dancers for Cairo; a Spanish grandee, like Don Quixote; Algerines, Egyptians, four Levantine ladies; and one poor Parisienne—a nice person, but so put out by the " méridionaux." I represented England. I was as comfortable in the boat as French want of order will permit. I had a cabin to myself, and the food was excellent, and beds clean, though hard. But I found the motion of the screw most distressing; it became like the slow torture of the drop of water.

I shall go on to Cairo in a few days. I am

dismayed at the noise and turbulence of the people here, after the soft voices and gentle ways of the Cape blacks. The weather is beautiful at present, but threatens rain. It is cool, but so bright after the dull South of France. The difference of atmosphere between Europe and Africa is wonderful; even Malta wants the clearness of Egypt, and this is far more misty than the Cape, but equally beautiful in a different way. I was delighted with Valetta, which seemed to me the most beautiful town I ever saw;—all so handsome and solid.

I am now going with the eldest Levantine girl to Sa-eed Pasha's harcem, where she is very intimate. She told the Princess that I had been very kind to her at sea when she was sick, and I was consequently invited to go to see the hareem.

I am frightened at the dearness of everything here. I found it quite impossible to get on without a servant able to speak English. The janissary of the American Consul-General recommended to me a youth called Omar (surnamed " the Father of sweets "), whom I have taken. He is an enthusiast about the

Nile; and if Cairo has a cheap boat, Omar will take it. I don't think I should get much good out of life in an Eastern town; the dust is intolerable, and the stuffiness in-doors very unwholesome. There is none of the out-doors existence which was so healthy at the Cape. My cough is bad, but Omar says I shall lose it and "eat plenty" as soon as I see a crocodile.

Yesterday I went with Mr. Thayer, the American Consul-General, who is equally kind and agreeable, and Hekekian Bey to see a few palaces; oh, what ignoble, shabby-genteel! One of them is merely a "Yankee notion" brought piecemeal from New York, and stuck up by the sea. I asked a poor lad at work there for a piece of the bread (filthy cakes, compounded of dirt, straw, and some grain quite unknown to me) which the labourers crouching about the half finished, half ruined palace were eating, and gave him sixpence. It was touching, the eagerness with which he threw more and more and more into the carriage to make up the value of such a coin. Contrary to my expectation, I find no begging here at all, only a great desire to be paid the uttermost penny. Nor could I blame even more than that in such a state of society. When I find myself fleeced by Christian and civilized men, shall not a poor Arab likewise scrape a few faddahs off me? Allah forbid!

Neither are the voices so bad as I expected. Every one bawls as loud as he can; but the *organe* is deeper and less screeching than the French or Italian. There is none of the pleasant *avenante* manner and smiling look to which I grew familiar at the Cape; but the people are prodigiously handsome;—lads like John of Bologna's Mercury, with divine legs, and young women so lovely in their dirt and scanty drapery; and among the Bedawee men I have seen simply the two handsomest men I ever beheld. Likewise the camels enchant me, and the date-palms.

But on the other hand, all is profoundly melancholy; the people's faces, the surface of the country, the dirt, the horrible wretchedness, the whacking of the little boys and girls who do all the work which Irish hodmen do with us. Such is my first impression of the land of Egypt; but Omar's eager description of Cairo and the Nile makes me expect something much more agreeable. If we reach

Nubia, we are to take a present of salt from Shaheen; J——'s nice red servant (for he is in form and colour the exact likeness of a hieroglyphic figure), to his parents; likewise to give them money on his account, should they need it. He has the dearest little brother, who is for ever in the hall here, and the Bowwáb's bench is the scene of incessant study. An old whitebearded man teaches reading and writing to Shaheen and a select circle of friends, and Shaheen's white slate looks very creditable indeed to my ignorant eye. The children are mostly hideous here, and cry incessantly. The donkey boy roared because Omar proceeded to change the saddle, but Shaheen tranquillized him with a cuff sufficient to fell an ox; whereupon every one was happy and pleased at once,—particularly the donkey boy, which seemed odd to me. But after cursing me and my saddle, he all at once became intensely loving, and would hug my feet and knees—an attention alike disinterested and undesired.

In the hut under the bedroom window, a poor woman is dying of consumption, which seems to be very common here, judging from the faces one sees and the coughs one hears; a baby, too, is ill. The anxious distress of the friends is very affecting, and quite contrary to the commonplace talk about Eastern apathy, hardness, etc. Their faces and behaviour show ten times the feeling of the common people in some parts of Europe; what is not pleasant, is the absence of all brightness or gaiety, even from young and childish faces. The very blacks here can't get up so much as a broad smile; a good laugh I have not yet heard. A stronger contrast than my present henchman, Omar, with his soft but anxious eyes and supple figure, and my last year's driver at the Cape, Choslullah, the world could not afford. The Malay's sturdy figure and beaming smile spoke independence as plainly as possible, while these young men, Omar and Shaheen, are more servile in look and gesture than is pleasant to me.

LETTER III.

Grand Cairo, 11th November, 1862.

I WRITE to you out of the real Arabian Nights. Well may the Prophet (upon whom be peace!) smile, when he looks down on Cairo. It is a golden existence, all sunshine and poetry, and, *I* must add, all kindness and civility. I came up last Thursday by railway with the American Consul-General, and had to stay at Shepherd's Hotel; but I do little but sleep there. Hekekian Bey, a learned old Armenian, takes care of me every day, and the American Consul is my sacrifice.

I went on Sunday to an Armenian christening, and heard Sáknch, " the restorer of hearts." She is wonderfully like Rachel in person and manner, and her singing is *hinreissend* from expression and passion. There was a

grand fantasia.   People feasted all over the
house, and in the streets.   Arab music clanged,
women cried the Zaghareet, black servants
served sweetmeats, pipes, and coffee, and behaved as if they belonged to the company, and
I was strongly under the impression that I was
at Noor-ed-Deen's wedding with the Wezeer's
daughter.   Yesterday I went to Heliopolis
with Hekekian Bey and his wife, and visited
an Armenian country lady close by.

My servant Omar turns out a jewel.   He
has discovered an excellent boat for the Nile
voyage; and I am to be mistress of a captain,
a steersman, eight men, and a cabin-boy, for
£25 a month.   I went to Boolák, the port of
Cairo, and saw various boats, and admired the
way in which English travellers pay for their
insolence and caprices.   Similar boats cost
people with dragomans from £50 to £65.
But then, "I shall lick the fellows," etc.   The
dragoman, I conclude, pockets the difference.
The owner of the boat, Seedee Ahmad el Ber-
beree, asked £30, whereon I touched my breast,
mouth, and eyes, and stated, through Omar,
that I was not, like other Inkeleez, made of
money, but would give £20.   He then showed

me another boat at £20, very much worse, and I departed (with fresh civilities) and looked at others, and saw two more for £20, but neither was clean, and neither had a little boat for landing. Meanwhile, Seedee Ahmad came after me, and explained that if I was not like other Inkeleez in money, I likewise differed in politeness, and had refrained from abuse, etc. etc., and I should have the boat for £25. It was so excellent in all its fittings, and so much larger than the others, that I thought it would make a great difference in health; so I said if he would go before the American Vice-Consul, and would promise all he had said to me before him, it should be well. The American Consul-General gives me letters to every consular agent depending on him, and two Coptic merchants of Girgeh and Kineh, whom I met at the fantasia, have already begged me to " honour their houses." I rather think the agents, who are all Copts, will think I am the Republic in person.

The weather has been all this time like a splendid English August. There is no cold here at night, as at the Cape; but the air is nothing like so clear or bright. It was pleasant to find that Hekekian Bey and the American Vice-Consul exactly confirmed all that Omar had told me about what I must take and what it would cost; they thought I might perfectly trust him. He put everything at just one-fourth of what the Alexandrian English told me, and even less. Moreover, he will cook on board; the kitchen, which is a hole in the bow where the cook must sit cross-legged, would be impossible for a woman to crouch down in. Besides, Omar will avoid everything unclean, and make the food such as he may lawfully eat. He is a pleasant, cheerful young fellow, and I think he rather likes the importance of taking care of me, and showing that he can do as well as a dragoman at £12 a month. It is characteristic that he turned his month's wages and the "£2 for a coat" into a bracelet for his little wife before leaving home. That is the Arab savings-bank.

I dined at Hekekian Bey's after the excursion yesterday. He is a most kind, friendly man, and very pleasant and cultivated. He dresses like an Englishman, speaks English like ourselves, and is quite like an uncle to me already.

Omar took S—— yesterday sight-seeing all day, while I was away, into several mosques. In one he begged her to wait a minute, while he said a prayer. They compare notes about their respective countries, and are great friends; but he is quite put out at my not having provided her with a husband long ago, as is one's duty towards a "female servant,"—which here always means a slave.

Of all the falsehoods I have heard about the East, the assertion that women are old hags at thirty is the greatest. Among the poor Felláh women it may be true enough, but not nearly so true as in Germany; and I have now seen a considerable number of Levantine ladies looking very handsome, or at least comely, till fifty. The lady we visited yesterday was forty-eight, and her daughter a good deal above twenty. The mother was extremely handsome, though very untidy; and the daughter, with two children, the eldest of whom is four years old, looked sixteen. I saw the same in four or five cases at the fantasia. Sákneh, the Arab Grisi, is fifty-five. Her face is ugly, I am told. She was veiled, and we only saw her eyes and glimpses of her mouth when she drank water; but she has the figure of a leopard, all grace and beauty, and a splendid voice of its kind—harsh, but thrilling, like Malibran's. I guessed her thirty, or perhaps thirty-five. When she improvised, the *finesse* and elegance of her whole manner were ravishing; and I was on the point of shouting out "Máshá-alláh!" as heartily as the natives. The eight younger "A'limeh" (*i.e.* "learned women," which we English call Almeh, and think it an improper word) were ugly, and screeched. Sákneh was treated with great consideration and quite as a friend by the Armenian ladies, with whom she talked between her songs. She is a Muslimeh, and very rich and charitable. She gets at least fifty pounds for a night's singing.

It would be very easy to learn colloquial Arabic, as they all speak with such perfect distinctness that one can follow the sentences and catch the words one knows as they occur. I think I know forty or fifty words already.

The reverse of the brilliant side of the medal in this country is sad enough;—deserted palaces and crowded hovels, scarce good enough for pigsties. "One day a man sees his dinner, and one other day he sees none," as

Omar observes; and the children are shocking to look at from bad food, dirt, and overwork; yet the little pot-bellied, blear-eyed wretches grow up into noble young men and women under all their difficulties. But the faces are all sad, and rather what the Scotch call *dour*, —not *méchantes* at all, but harsh, like their voices; all their melody is in walk and gesture. They are as graceful as cats, and the women have exactly the " breasts like pomegranates" of their poetry.

A tall Bedawee woman came up to us in the field yesterday, to shake hands and look at us. She wore a white sackcloth shirt and veil, and nothing else. She asked Hekekian a good many questions about me, looked at my face and hands, but took no notice of my rather smart gown which the village women admired so much, shook hands again with the air of a princess, wished me health and happiness, and strode off across the graveyard like a stately ghost. She was on a journey, all alone; and somehow it was very solemn and affecting to see her walking away towards the desert in the setting sun, like Hagar. All is so scriptural in the country here. S——

called out in the railroad, "There is Boaz sitting in the cornfield;" and so it was; and there he has sat for how many thousand years! And in one war-song Sákneh sang as Miriam, the prophetess, may have done when she took a timbrel in her hand and went out to meet the host.

Wednesday.—My contract was drawn up and signed by the American Vice-Consul to-day, and my Reyyis kissed my hand in due form; after which I went to the bazaar and sat on many a divan to buy the needful pots and pans. The transaction lasted an hour. The copper is so much per oka, the workmanship so much. Every article is weighed by a sworn weigher, and a ticket sent with it. More Arabian Nights. The shopkeeper compares notes with me about numerals, and is as much amused as I. He treats me to coffee and pipes from a neighbouring shop, while Omar eloquently depreciates the goods, and offers half the value. A waterseller offers a brass cup of water; I drink, and give the huge sum of twopence, and he distributes the contents of his skin to the crowd (there is always a crowd) in my honour. It seems I have done a pious act.

Finally, a boy is called to carry the *batterie de cuisine*, while Omar brandishes a gigantic kettle which he has picked up, a little bruised, for four shillings. The boy has a donkey, which I mount astride, *à l'Arabe*, while the boy carries all the copper things on his head. We are rather a grand procession, and quite enjoy the fury of the dragomans and other leeches who hang on the English, at such independent proceedings; and Omar gets reviled for spoiling the trade, by being cook and dragoman and all in one. We sail this day week, and intend to get to the Upper Cataract as soon as we can, and come leisurely back.

I went this morning with Hekekian Bey to the two earliest mosques. We were accosted most politely by some Arab gentlemen, who pointed out remarkable things, and echoed my lamentations at the neglect and ruin of such noble buildings (which Hekekian translated to them) most heartily. That of the Tooloon is exquisite, noble, simple, and what ornament there is, is the most delicate lacework and embossing in stone and wood. This Arab architecture is even more lovely than our Gothic. The mosque of the citadel (Mohammad Alee's) (where the English broke the lamps) is like a fine modern Italian church; but Abbas Pasha stole the alabaster columns, and replaced them by painted wood. The mosque of Sultan Hasan (early in our fourteenth century) is, I think, the most majestic building I ever saw, and the beauty of the details quite beyond belief to European eyes; the huge gates to his tomb are one mass of the finest enamel ornaments, as you may discover by rubbing the dirt off with your glove. No one has said a tenth part enough of the beauty of Arab architecture. The Hasaneeyeh is even grander than a Gothic cathedral, and all is in the noblest taste. The old Tooloon mosque is an absolute jewel of perfection and purity, perfectly simple and yet with details of *guipure* and embroidery in stone which one wishes to kiss—they are so lovely; but the roof has fallen in, and the great court is the dwelling of paupers.

The Tooloon is now a vast poor-house— "*quousque tandem?*" I went into three of their lodgings. Several Turkish families were in a large square room neatly divided into little partitions with old mats hung on ropes.

In each were as many bits of carpet, mat, and patchwork as the poor owner could collect, and a small chest, and a little brick cooking-place in one corner of the room, with three earthen pipkins, for I don't know how many people;—that was all. They possess no sort of furniture; but all was scrupulously clean, and no bad smell whatever. A little boy seized my hand, and showed where he slept, ate and cooked, with the most expressive pantomime. As there were women, Hekekian could not enter, but when I came out an old man told us they received three loaves (cakes as big as sailors' biscuits), four piastres a month (*i.e.* sixpence) per adult, a suit of clothes a year, and on festive occasions, lentil soup: such is the almshouse here. A little crowd belonging to that house had collected, and I gave sixpence to an old man to be *divided* (!) among them all, —ten or twelve people at least, mostly blind or lame. The poverty wrings my heart. We took leave with saláms and politeness, like people of the best society.

I then turned into an Arab hut, stuck against the lovely arches. I stooped low under the door, and several women crowded

in. This was still poorer than the last; for
there were no mats or rags of carpet, a still
worse cooking place, and a sort of dog-kennel,
piled up of loose stones to sleep in; it contained a small chest, and the print of human
forms on the stone floor. It was however
quite free from dirt, and perfectly sweet. I
gave the young woman who had led me in
sixpence, and here the difference between Turk
and Arab appeared. The division of this sum
created a perfect storm of noise, and we left
five or six Arab women outshrieking a whole
rookery. I ought to say, however, that no
one begged at all.

I suppose I shall be thought utterly para-
doxical when I deny the much talked-of dirt.
The narrow, dingy, damp, age-blackened, dust-
crusted, unpaved streets of Cairo are sweet as
roses compared to those of the " Centre of Civilization ;" moreover an Arab crowd does not
stink, even under this sun. I beg to say that
S —— will take her oath of this, contrary as it
is to our most cherished illusions. They are
ragged, utterly slovenly, and covered with dust,
but they do wash their bodies, and they don't
diffuse that disgusting human odour which of-

fends one in the most civilized countries of the continent. I have been in a poor boys' school, in the most miserable of workhouses, and in the huts of a village, and I declare that they are sweeter far than anything in Europe of that class, or even higher. The dirt is in fact dust, not foulness.

Friday.—I went to-day on a donkey to a mosque in the bazaar of what we call the "arabesque" style, like the Alhambra. The kibleh was very beautiful; and as I was admiring it, Omar pulled a lemon out of his breast and smeared it on the porphyry pillar on one side of the arch, and then entreated me to lick it. It cures all diseases. The old man who showed the mosque pulled eagerly at my arm to make me perform this absurd ceremony, and I thought I should have been forced to do it. The base of the pillar was clogged with lemon-juice.

I then went to the Tombs of the Memlook Sultans; one of the great ones had the most beautiful arches and wondrous cupolas, but all in ruins. There are scores of these noble buildings, any one of which is a treasure, falling to decay.

The next I went to, strange to say, was in perfect repair. I got off the donkey, and Omar fidgeted and hesitated a little, and consulted with a woman who had the key. As there were no overshoes, I pulled my boots off, and was rewarded by seeing the footprints of Mohammad in two black stones, and a lovely little mosque,—a sort of *sainte chapelle*. Omar prayed with ardent fervour, and went out backwards, saluting the Prophet aloud. To my surprise, the woman was highly pleased with sixpence, and did not ask for more. When I remarked this, Omar said that no Frank had ever been inside, to his knowledge. A mosque-keeper of the sterner sex would not have let me in.

I returned home through endless streets and squares of Muslim tombs, those of the Memlooks among them. It is very striking; and it was getting so dark that I thought of Noor-ed-Deen Alee, and wondered if a jinnee would take me anywhere if I took up my night's lodging in one of the comfortable little cupola-covered buildings.

I must now finish my letter, as the mail will close to-night. My Coptic friend has just called in, to say that his brother expects me at Kiné. I find nothing but civility and desire to please.

My boat is the Zeenet-el-Bahreyn, and I carry the English flag and a small American distinguishing pennant, as a signal to my consular agents. We sail next Wednesday.

LETTER IV.

Boat off Imbábeh, November 21, 1862.

WE embarked yesterday, and after the fashion of eastern caravans, are abiding to-day at a village opposite to Cairo. It is Friday, and therefore it would be improper and unlucky to set out on our journey. What one pays here on the exchange is frightful,—four shillings in the pound for Egyptian money; and no other is of any use for butter, milk, eggs, etc.

The scenes on the river are wonderfully diverting and curious; so much life and movement. But the boatmen are sophisticated. My crew have all sported new white drawers, in honour of the Sitt Inkeleezeeyeh. Of course compensation will be expected. Poor fellows they are very well mannered and quiet in their rags and misery, and their queer little humming song is rather pretty,—"Ei-yá Mohammad, ei-yá Mohammad," *ad infinitum*, except when one more energetic man cries " Yalláh !" (oh God!) Omar is gone to Cairo to fetch one or two more unconsidered trifles, and I have been explaining the defects to be remedied in the cabin door, broken window, etc. to my Reyyis, with the help of six words of Arabic and dumb show, which they understand and answer with wonderful quickness.

The air on the river is certainly quite celestial —totally unlike the damp chilly feeling of the hotel and Frank quarter of Cairo. The Ezbekeeyeh, or public garden, where all Franks live, was a lake, I believe, and is still very damp.

I shall go up to the Second Cataract as fast as possible, and return back at leisure. Hekekian Bey came and spent the day on board here yesterday, to take leave. He lent me several books. Pray tell Mr. Senior what a kindness his introduction to this excellent man has been. It would have been rather dismal in Cairo, if one could be dismal there, without a soul to speak to. I was sorry to know no Turks or Arabs, and have no opportunity of seeing any but the tradesmen of whom I bought my stores; but even that was very amusing. The young man of whom I bought my fingáns was so handsome, elegant, and melancholy, that I knew he must be the lover of the Sultan's favourite slave.

How I wish you were here to enjoy all this,—so new, so beautiful, and yet so familiar! And you would like the people, poor things! they are complete children, but amiable children. I went into the village here, where I was a curiosity, and some women took me into their houses and showed me their sleeping-place, cookery, poultry, etc., and a man followed me to keep off the children; but no baksheesh was asked for, which showed that Europeans were rare there. The utter destitution is terrible to see, though in this climate, of course, it matters less. But the much-talked-of dirt is simply utter poverty. The poor souls are as clean as Nile mud and water will make their bodies; and they have not a second shirt, or any bed but dried mud.

My cough has been better now for five days, without a bad return of it. It is the first reprieve for so long. The sun is so hot,—a regular broil (Nov. 21),—and all doors and windows open in the cabin,—a delicious breeze!

LETTER V.

Feshn, Monday, November 30, 1862.

I HAVE now been enjoying this most delightful way of life for ten days, and am certainly
better. I begin to eat and sleep, and cough
less.

My crew are a great amusement to me.
They are mostly men from the First Cataract
about Aswán,—sleek-skinned, gentle, patient,
merry black fellows. The little black Reyyis
is the very picture of good-nature, and full of
fun, " chaffing" the girls as we pass the villages,
and always smiling. The steersman is of
lighter complexion, also very cheery, but decidedly pious. He prays five times a day, and
utters ejaculations to the apostle " Rasool"
continually. He hurt his ankle on one leg
and his instep on the other, with a rusty nail,
and they festered. I dressed them with poul-

tices, and then with lint and strapping, with perfect success, to the great admiration of all hands, and he announced how much better he felt. "Praise be to God, and thanks without end, O lady!" and every one echoed the thanks. The most important person on board is the "weled" (boy), Ahmad—the most merry, clever, omnipresent little rascal, with an ugly pug-nosed face, a shape like an antique Cupid liberally displayed, and a skin of dark brown velvet. His voice, shrill and clear, is always heard above the rest; he cooks for the crew; he jumps overboard with the rope, and gives advice on all occasions; grinds the coffee with the end of a stick in a mortar, which he holds between his feet, and if I go ashore for a minute, uses the same large stick to walk proudly before me, brandishing it and ordering every one out of the way. " Yá Ahmad " resounds all day whenever anybody wants anything, and the " weled " is always ready and able. My favourite is Osmán, a tall, long-limbed black, who seems to have stepped out of a hieroglyphical drawing, shirt, skull-cap, and all. He has only those two garments, and how any one contrives to look so inconceivably

" neat and respectable," as S—— said, in that costume is a mystery. He is always at work, always cheerful, but rather silent; in short, the able seaman, and steady respectable " hand," *par excellence.* Then we have Ez-Zankalonee, from near Cairo,—an old fellow of white complexion, and a valuable person; an inexhaustible teller of stories at night and always ' *en train ;*' full of jokes, and remarkable for dry humour, much relished by the crew. I wish I understood the stories, which sound delightful, all about Sultans and Efreets, with effective " points," at which all hands exclaim " Máshá-alláh" or " ah !" (as long as you can drawl it out). The jokes perhaps I may as well be ignorant of. There is also a certain Shereef, who does nothing but laugh and work, and be obliging; helps Omar with one hand and S—— with the other, and looks like a great innocent black child. The rest of the dozen are of various colours, sizes, and ages, some quite old, but all very quiet and well behaved.

We have had either dead calms or contrary winds all the time, and the men have worked very hard at the towing-rope. On Friday I proclaimed a halt at a village in the afternoon at prayer-time, for the pious Muslims to go to mosque. This gave great satisfaction, though only five went,—the Reyyis, steersman, Zankalonee, and two old men. The up-river men never pray at all, and Osmán occupied himself by buying salt out of another boat and storing it to take to his family, as it is terribly dear high up the river. At Benee-Suweyf we halted to buy meat and bread. There is one butcher, who kills a sheep a day. I walked about the streets, escorted by Omar in front, and two sailors with huge staves behind, and created a sensation accordingly. It is a dull little country town, with a wretched palace of Sa-eed Pasha's.

On Sunday we halted at Bibeh, where I caught sight of a large Coptic church, and sallied forth to see whether they would let me in. The road lay past the house of the head man of the village, and there " in the gate," sat a patriarch surrounded by his servants and his cattle. Over the gateway were crosses, and queer constellations of dots more like Mithraic symbols than anything Christian; but Girgis was a Copt (Kubtee), though chosen head of the Muslim village. He rose as I came up, stepped out and salámed, then took my hand and said I must go into his house and enter the hareem before I saw the church. His old mother, who looked a hundred, and his pretty wife, were very friendly; but as I had to leave Omar at the door, our talk soon came to an end, and Girgis took me into the divan, without the sacred precincts of the hareem. Of course we had pipes and coffee, and he pressed me to stay some days, and to eat with him every day and to accept all his house contained. I took the milk he offered and asked him to visit me in the boat, saying I must return before sunset, when it gets cold, as I was ill. The house was a curious specimen of a wealthy man's house. I could not describe it if I tried; but I felt as if I were acting a passage in the Old Testament.

We went to the church, which looked like nine beehives in a box. Inside, the nine domes, resting on square pillars, were very handsome; Girgis was putting it into thorough repair at his own expense, and it will cost a good deal, I think, to repair and renew the fine old wood panelling of such minute and intricate workmanship. The church is divided by three

screens; one in front of the eastern three domes
is impervious, and conceals the Holy of Holies.
He opened the horse-shoe door for me to look
in, but explained that no hareem might cross
the threshold. All was in confusion, owing to
the repairs, which were actively going on, without the slightest regard to Sunday; but he
took up a large bundle, kissed it, and showed
it to me; what it contained I cannot guess, and
I scrupled to inquire through a Muslim interpreter. To the right of this sanctum is the tomb
of a Muslim saint, enclosed under the adjoin-
ing dome. Here we went in. Girgis kissed the
tomb on one side, while Omar salámed it on
the other;—a pleasant sight! They were much
more particular about our shoes than in the
mosques. Omar wanted to tie handkerchiefs
over my boots, as at Cairo, but the priest objected, and made me take them off and march
about in the brick and mortar rubbish in my
stockings. I wished to hear the service, but it
was not to be till sunset; and, as far as I could
make out, not different on Sunday to other
days. The hareem sit behind a third screen, the
furthest removed from the holy screen, where
also was the font, locked up, and shaped like

a Muslim tomb in little. ("Hareem" is used here, just like the German *Frauenzimmer*, to mean a respectable woman; Girgis spoke of me to Omar as "hareem.") The Copts have but one wife, but they shut her up even closer than the Arabs do. The children were sweetly pretty, so unlike the Arab brats, and the men very good-looking. They did not seem to acknowledge me at all as a *coréligionnaire*, and asked whether we of the English religion did not marry our brothers and sisters.

The priest asked me to drink coffee at his house, close by, and then I "sat in the gate," *i. e.* in a large sort of den, raised two feet from the ground and matted; to the left of the gate a crowd of Copts collected and squatted about. Presently we were joined by the mason who was repairing the church:—a fine, burly, rough-bearded old Muslim, who told how the Sheykh buried in the church of Bibeh had appeared to him three nights running at Cairo, and ordered him to leave his work and go to Bibeh and mend his church; how he came, and offered to do so without pay, if the Copts would find the materials. He spoke with evident pride, as one who had received a divine command, and the Copts all confirmed the story, and every one was highly gratified by the miracle.

I asked Omar if he thought it was all true, and he had no doubt of it; the mason he knew to be a man in full work, and Girgis added that for years he had tried to get a man to come for the purpose without success. It is not often that a dead saint contrives to be equally agreeable to Christians and Muslims, and here was the staunch old " true believer" working away, in the sanctuary which they would not allow an English fellow-christian to enter!

While we sat hearing these wonders, the sheep and cattle coming home at eve pushed in between us. The venerable old priest looked so like Father Abraham, and the whole scene was so pastoral and biblical, that I felt quite as if my wish to live a little while a few thousand years ago had been fulfilled. They wanted me to stay many days; and when I told them I could not do that, Girgis said I must stop at Feshn, where he had a fine house and garden, and he would go on horseback and meet me there, and would give me a whole troop of Fellaheen to pull the boat up quickly. Omar's eyes twinkled with fun as he translated this, and said he knew the Sitt would cry out, as she always did, about the Fellaheen, as if she were hurt herself. He told Girgis that the English customs did not allow people to work without pay, which evidently seemed very absurd to the whole party.

LETTER VI.

Tuesday, Gebel Sheykh Embarak.

I STOPPED last night at Feshn, but finding this morning that my Coptic friends were not expected till the afternoon, I would not spend the whole day there, and came on still against wind and stream. If I could speak Arabic, I should have enjoyed a few days with Girgis and his family immensely, in order to learn their ideas a little; but Omar's English is too imperfect to get beyond elementary subjects. The thing that strikes me most is the tolerant spirit that I find everywhere. They say, "Ah, it is your custom!" and express no sort of condemnation; and Muslims and Christians appear perfectly good friends, as my story of Bibeh goes to prove. I have yet to see the much-talked-of fanaticism; at present I have not met with a symptom of it. There were thirteen Coptic families at Bibeh, and also a considerable Muslim population who had elected Girgis their head man, and kissed his hand very heartily as our procession moved through the streets. Omar said he was a very good man and much liked.

The villages look like slight elevations in the mud banks, cut into square shapes. The best houses have neither paint, whitewash, plaster, bricks, nor windows, nor any visible roofs; at first they don't give one the notion of human dwellings at all, but soon the eye gets used to the absence of all that constitutes a house in Europe; the impression of wretchedness wears off, and one sees how picturesque they are with palm-trees, and tall pigeon-houses, and here and there the dome over a saint's tomb.

The men at work on the river-banks are of exactly the same colour as the Nile mud, with just the warmer hue of the blood circulating beneath the skin. Prometheus has just formed them out of the universal material at hand, and the sun breathed life into them. Poor fellows! even the boatmen, ragged crew as they are, say,

" Ah! Fellaheen!" with a contemptuous pity, when they see me watch the villagers at work.

The other day four huge barges passed us, towed by a steamer, and crammed with some hundreds of the poor souls, who had been torn from their homes to work at the Isthmus of Suez or some palace of the Pasha's for a nominal piastre (three halfpence) a day, finding their own bread and water and cloak. One of my crew, Abd-er-Rasool, a black savage whose function it is to jump overboard whenever the rope gets entangled or anything is wanted, recognized some relations of his own from a village close to Aswán. There was much shouting, and poor Abd-er-Rasool looked very mournful all day. It may be his turn next. Some of the crew disloyally remarked that they were sure the men there wished they were working for a Sitt Inkeleeych, as Abd-er-Rasool told them he was. Think, too, what splendid pay it must be that the boat-owner can give out of £25 a month to twelve men, after taking his own profits,—the interest of money being enormous!

When I call my crew black, don't think of negroes. They are elegantly-shaped Arabs, and all gentlemen in manners; and the black is transparent, with amber *reflets* under it in the sunshine; a negro looks blue beside them.

I have learned a great deal that is curious from Omar's confidences; he tells me his domestic affairs and talks about the women of his family, which he would not do to a man. He refused to speak to his brother, a very grand dragoman who was with the Prince of Wales. This man came up to us in the hotel at Cairo and addressed Omar, who turned his back on him. I asked the reason, and Omar told me how his brother had a wife, "an old wife,—been with him long time, very good wife." She had had three children, all dead; all at once the dragoman, who is much older than Omar, declared he would divorce her and marry a young woman. Omar said, "No, don't do that, keep her in your house as head of your household, and take one of your two black slave-girls as your hareem;" but the other insisted, and married a young Turkish wife; whereupon Omar took his poor old sister-in-law to live with him and his own young wife, and cut his grand brother dead.

See how characteristic! the urging his bro-

ther to take the young slave-girl "as his hareem," like a respectable man;—*that* would
have been all right; but what he did was "not
good." "I'll trouble you" (as Mrs. —— used
to say) to settle these questions to every one's
satisfaction.

Omar's account of the household of his
other brother, a confectioner, with two wives,
was very curious. He and his wife and they
all live together; one of the brother's wives
has six children; three sleep with their own
mother, and three with their other mother,
and all is quite harmonious.

LETTER VII.

Asyoot, December 10, 1862.

I could not send a letter from Minyeh, where we stopped and I saw a sugar manufactory, and visited a gentlemanly Turk who superintends the district,—the Mudeer. I heard a boy singing a Zikr to a party of·Darweeshes in a mosque, and I think I never heard anything more beautiful and affecting; ordinary Arab singing is harsh and nasal, but it can be wonderfully moving.

Since we left Minyeh we have suffered dreadfully from the cold. The chickens died of it, and the Arabs look blue and pinched. Of course it is *my* weather. Never were such cold or such incessant contrary winds known. To-day was better, and Wassef, a Copt here, lent me his superb donkey to go up to a tomb on the mountain. The tomb is a mere cavern, it is so defaced; but the view of beautiful Asyoot standing in the midst of a loop of the Nile was ravishing;—a green deeper and brighter than that of England, crowds of graceful minarets, a picturesque bridge, gardens, palm-trees, then the river encircling the picture, and beyond it, the barren yellow cliffs as a frame all round that. At our feet a woman was being carried to the grave, and the boys' voices rang out the Koran, full and clear, as the long procession, first white turbans and then black veils and robes, wound along.

It is all a dream to me; you can't think what an odd effect it produces to take up an English book and read it, and then to look up and hear the men cry "Yá Mohammad!" " Bless thee, Bottom, how art thou translated!" It is the reverse of all one's former life, when one sat in England and read of the East; and now I live in the real true Arabian Nights, and don't know whether "I be I, as I suppose I be," or not. I am afraid you will have to pay more for all this trash than it is worth, but I may not be able to write again.

LETTER VIII.

Thebes, December 20, 1862.

I HAVE had a long dawdling voyage up here, but I enjoyed it much, and have seen and heard many curious things. I have only stopped here for letters, and shall go on at once to Wadee Halfeh, as the weather is very cold still, and I shall be better able to enjoy the ruins when I return about a month hence; and shall certainly prefer the tropics just now. The oldest Nile traveller never know so cold a winter; it is like sharp English October weather, with interludes of hot days.

I can't describe the kindness of the Copts. The men whom, as I told you, I met at a party at Cairo, wrote to all their friends and relations to be civil to me. Wassef's attentions consisted, first, in lending me his splendid donkey, and accompanying me about all day. Next morning arrived a procession, headed by his clerk, a gentlemanly young Copt, and consisting of five black slaves, carrying a live sheep, a huge basket of the most delicious bread, a pile of cricket-balls of creamy butter, a large copper caldron of milk, and a cage of poultry. I was confounded, and tried to give a baksheesh to the clerk, but he utterly declined. At Girgeh one Mishrehgi was waiting for me, and was in despair because he had only time to get a few hundred eggs, two turkeys, a heap of butter, and a can of milk. At Kiné one Eesa (Jesus) also lent a donkey, and sent me three boxes of delicious Mecca dates, which Omar thought stingy. Such attentions are very agreeable here, where good food is hard to be had, except as gift. They all made me promise to see them again on my return, and to dine at their houses; and Wassef wanted to make a fantasia, and have dancing girls.

How you would love the Arab women in the country villages! I wandered off the other day alone while the men were mending the rudder, and fell in with a troop of them carrying jars. Such sweet, attractive beings, all smiles and grace. One beautiful woman pointed to the village, and made signs of eating, and took my hand to lead me. I went with her, admiring my companions as they walked. Omar came running after, and wondered I was not afraid. I laughed, and said they were much too pretty and kind-looking to frighten any one, which amused them exceedingly. They all wanted me to go and eat in their houses, and I had a great mind to it; but the wind was fair and the boat waiting, and I bade my beautiful friends farewell. They asked if we wanted anything,—milk or eggs,—for they would give it with pleasure; it was not their custom to sell things, they said. I offered a bit of money to a little naked child, but his mother would not let him take it. I shall never forget the sweet engaging creatures at that little village, or the dignified politeness of an old weaver whose loom I walked in to look at, and who also wished to " set a piece of bread before me." It is the true poetical pastoral life of the Bible in the villages where the English have not been, and happily they don't land at the little places. Thebes has become an English watering-place. There are now nine boats lying here, and the great object is to "do the Nile" as fast as possible. It is a race up to Wadee Halfeh or Aswán. All the English stay here "to make Christmas," as Omar calls it; but I shall go on, and do my Christmas devotions with the Copts at Esneh or Edfoo. I found that their seeming disinclination to let one attend their religious services, arose from an idea that we English would not recognize them as Christians.

I wrote home a curious story of a miracle. I find I was wrong about the saint being a Muslim (and so is Murray); he is no less than Mar Girgih, our own St. George himself. Why he selected a Muslim mason, I suppose he knows best. In a week I shall be in Nubia. Some year we must all make this voyage, you would revel in it.

If in the street I led thee, dearest,
Though the veil hid thy face divine,
They who beheld thy graceful motion
Would stagger as though drunk with wine.

Nay, e'en the holy Sheykh, while praying
For guidance in the narrow way,
Must needs leave off, and on the traces
Of thine enchanting footsteps stray.

O ye who go down in the boats to Dunnyat,
Cross, I beseech ye, the stream to Budallah,
Seek my beloved, and beg that she will not
Forget me,—I pray and implore her by Allah!

Fair as two moons is the face of my sweetheart,
And as to her neck and her bosom—Máshá-alláh!
And unless to my love I am soon reunited,
Death is my portion; I swear it by Allah!

So sings Alee Asleemee, the most *débraillé* of my crew, but a charming singer, and a good fellow; his songs are all amatory, except one comic one abusing the Sheykh-el-Beled, " May the fleas bite him!" Horrid imprecation! as I know to my cost; for, after visiting the Coptic monks at Girgeh, I came home to the boats with myriads. S—— said she felt like Rameses the Great, so tremendous was the slaughter of the active enemy.

LETTER IX.

Thebes, 11th February, 1863.

On arriving here last night, I found your letter. Pray write again forthwith to Cairo, where I hope to stay a few weeks on my return. A clever old dragoman whom I knew at Philæ, offers to lend me furniture for a lodging, or a tent for the desert; when I hesitated, he said he was very well off, and it was not his business to let things, but only to be paid for his services by rich people; that if I did not accept it as he meant it, he should be quite hurt. This is what I have met with from everything Arab,—nothing but kindness and politeness. I shall say farewell to Egypt with real regret; among other things, it will be a pang to part with Omar, who has been my shadow all this time, and for whom I have quite an affection, he is so thoroughly good and amiable.

We have had the coldest winter ever known in Nubia,—such bitter north-east winds; but when the wind, by great favour, did not blow, the weather was heavenly. If the millennium does come, I shall take out a good deal of mine on the Nile. At Aswán I had been strolling about, in that most poetically melancholy spot, the granite quarry of old Egypt, and burying-place of Muslim martyrs; and as I came homewards along the bank, a party of slave merchants, who had just loaded their goods for Sennár out of the boat upon the camels, were cooking, and asked me to dinner. And oh! how delicious it felt to sit on a mat among the camels, and strange bales of goods, and eat the hot, tough bread, and sour milk and dates, offered with such stately courtesy. We got quite intimate over our leather cup of sherbet (brown sugar-and-water); and the handsome jet-black men, with features as beautiful as those of the young Bacchus, described the distant lands in a way which would have charmed Herodotus. They proposed to me to join them, " they had food

enough;" and Omar and I were equally inclined to go.

It is of no use to talk of the ruins. Everybody has said, I suppose, all that can be said;
but Philæ surpassed my expectations. No
wonder the Arab legends of Anas-el-Wugood
are so romantic! and Aboo-Sembel, and many
more. The scribbling of names is quite in-
famous; beautiful paintings are defaced by
Tomkins and Hobson, but, worst of all, Prince
Pückler Muskau has engraved his and his
Ordenskreuz, in huge letters and size, on the
naked breast of that august and pathetic giant
who sits at Aboo-Sembel.

I have eaten many strange things with strange
people in strange places; dined with a respectable Nubian family (the castor-oil *was* trying);
been to a Nubian wedding (such a dance I
saw!); made friends with a man much looked
up to in his place—Kalabsheh,—inasmuch as
he had killed several intrusive tax-gatherers
and recruiting-officers. He was very gentlemanlike and kind, and carried me up a place so
steep I could not have reached it without his
assistance. By the bye, going up is nothing but
noise and shouting, but coming down is fine

fun. "Fantaseeyeh Keteer," as my excellent little Nubian pilot said. My sailors all prayed away manfully, and were horribly frightened. I confess my pulse quickened, but I don't think it was fear.

Below the Cataract I stopped for a religious fête, and went to the holy tomb with a remarkably handsome and graceful darweesh; —the true *feingemacht*, noble Bedawee type. He took care of me through the people, who never had seen a Frank woman before, and crowded fearfully. The holy man pushed the true believers unmercifully, to make way for me. He was particularly pleased at my not being afraid of the Arabs. I laughed, and asked if he was afraid of us. "Oh no! he would like to come to England. When there he would work to eat and drink, and then sit and sleep in the church." I was positively ashamed to tell my religious friend that, with us, the "house of God" is not the home of the poor stranger. I asked him to eat with me, but was holding a preliminary Ramadán (it begins next week), and could not; but he brought his handsome sister, who was richly dressed, and begged me to visit him, and eat of his bread, cheese, and milk. Such is the treatment one finds if one leaves the high-road and the baksheesh-hunting parasites. There are plenty of gentlemen, barefooted, and clad in a shirt and cloak, ready to pay attentions which you may return with a civil look and greeting, and if you offer a cup of coffee and a seat on the floor, you give great pleasure. Still more if you eat the durah and dates, or bread and sour milk, with an appetite.

At Kóm Omboo we met with a Rifáee darweesh, with his basket of tame snakes. After a little talk, he proposed to initiate me; and so we sat down and held hands like people marrying. Omar sat behind me and repeated the words as my " wakeel." Then the Rifáee twisted a cobra round our joined hands, and requested me to spit on it; he did the same, and I was pronounced safe, and enveloped in snakes. My sailors groaned, and Omar shuddered as the snakes put out their tongues; the darweesh and I smiled at each other like Roman augurs. I need not say the creatures were toothless.

It is worth while going to Nubia to see the girls. Up to twelve or thirteen, they are neatly dressed in a bead necklace, and a leather fringe, four inches wide, round their loins; and anything so absolutely perfect as their shapes, or so sweetly innocent as their look, cannot be conceived. The women are dressed in drapery, like Greek statues, and their forms are as perfect; they have hard, bold faces, but very handsome hair, plaited like the Egyptian sculptures and soaked with castor-oil. The colour of the skin is rich sepia-brown, as of velvet with the pile; very dark, and the red blood glowing through it,—unlike negro colour in any degree. My pilot's little girl came in the dress mentioned above, carrying a present of cooked fish on her head, and some fresh eggs. She was four years old, and so clever! I gave her a captain's biscuit and some figs; and the little pet sat with her little legs tucked under her, and ate it so daintily; she was very long over it, and when she had done, she carefully wrapped up some more biscuit in a little rag of a veil, to take home. I longed to steal her, she was such a darling. One girl of thirteen was so lovely, that even the greatest prude must, I think, have forgiven her sweet, pure beauty. But the women, though far handsomer, lack the charm of the Arab women; and the men, except at Kalabsheh, and those from far up the country, are not such gentlemen as the Arabs.

I shall stay here ten days or so, and then return slowly, to get to Cairo on the 20th of March, the last day of Ramadán. I have seen so much that, like M. de Conti, "Je voudrais être levée pour l'aller dire."

Pray write soon and tell me all about every one. Omar wanted to hear all that the "big gentleman" said about 'weled' and 'bint' (the boy and girl), and is much interested about Eton. He thinks that the Abu-l-Wiláid (father of the children) will send a sheep to the 'fikee' who teaches his son.

I long to bore you with travellers' tales. I have learned a new code of propriety altogether; "Cela a du bon et du mauvais," like our own. When I said "my husband," Omar blushed, and gently corrected me; when my donkey fell in the street, he cried with vexation, and on my mentioning it to Hekekian Bey, he was quite indignant. "Why you say it, ma'am? that shame!"—a *faux pas*, in fact. On the other hand, they mention with perfect satisfaction and pleasure all that relates to the great source of honour and happiness, the possession of children. A very handsome and modest young Nubian woman, wishing to give me the best present she could, brought a mat which she had made and which had been her marriage bed. It was a gift both friendly and honourable, and as such I received it.

Omar translated her message with equal modesty and directness. He likewise gave me a full description of his own marriage. I intimated that English people were not accustomed to some words he used, and might be shocked; upon which he said, " Of course I not speak my hareem to English gentleman, but to good lady, can speak it."

" Good bye, dear ——" No, that is improper, I must say, " Oh, my Lord," or " Father of my son ! "

LETTER X.

Luxor, February 17, 1863.

IT has been piercingly cold here for the last six or seven weeks, with only now and then a mild day. At Wadee Halfeh I longed to go on to Khartoom to get warm.

It is fine here now since yesterday, and here I shall stay till it is warm enough to venture down the river. In all other respects my journey has been most successful, and, to me, enchanting. My crew are dear, good, lazy fellows, or rather, children; their ways amuse me infinitely. Omar is one of the best servants I ever saw, and a *cordon bleu* of a cook, which is lucky, as I have taken to eating. I have sat on many divans and eaten many quaint things with many strange and pleasant hosts. Shaheen's family (who are quite great gentry in Nubia) gave me a dinner : first course, baked durah and dates ; second, leathery bread and sour milk ; third, durah and dates.   Shaheen's two sisters, Rayeh and Khadeegeh, are very handsome ; and his mother touched me by her anxiety to know "if her son was good." They shewed me his two black slaves and his baby, a very fine one. I presented a baksheesh, but was loaded with presents in return,—a lamb, dates, etc.

Today we had a fantasia on horseback ; the jereed-throwing and lance business are beautiful.   I·think Philæ a bit of paradise, and Aswán is beautiful ; the old burial-ground there charmed me more than I can express.

LETTER XI.

March 10, 1863.

I HAVE a superb illumination to-night, improvised by Omar in honour of the Prince of Wales's marriage, and consequently am writing with flaring candles, my lantern being on duty at the mast-head; and the men are singing an epithalamium, and beating the Darabukkeh as loud as they can. Omar wishes he could know exactly when the Prince " takes his wife's face," that we might shriek for joy, according to Arab fashion. I am all the better for the glorious air of Nubia and the high-up country. Already we are returning into misty weather. Even Nubia is not so clear and bright as the Cape, though the sun is more stingingly hot.

I dined with a Coptic friend in the harcem, and was pleased with their family life; poor

Waseef ate his boiled beans rather ruefully, while his wife and I had an excellent dinner, she being excused fasting on account of a coming baby. The Coptic fast is no joke, neither butter, milk, eggs, nor fish being allowed for fifty-five days. They made S—— dine with us, and Omar was admitted to wait and interpret. Waseef's younger brother waited on him, like those in the Bible, and his clerk, a nice young fellow, assisted. Black slaves brought the dishes in, and capital the food was. There was plenty of joking between the lady and Omar about Ramadán, which he has broken, and the Nasránce fast, and also about the number of wives allowed,—the young clerk hinting that he rather liked that point in Islám. I have promised to spend ten or twelve days at their house if ever I go up the Nile again. I can't describe how anxiously kind these people were to me; one gets such a wonderful amount of sympathy and real hearty kindness here.

A curious instance of the affinity of the British mind for prejudice is the way in which every Englishman I have seen scorns the Eastern Christians; and it is droll enough, that sinners like Mr. Kinglake and me should be the only people to feel the tie of " the common faith " (*vide* ' Eōthen '). A very pious Scotch gentleman wondered that I could think of entering a Copt's house; adding, that they were the publicans (tax-gatherers) of this country,—which is true. I felt inclined to mention that better company than he or I had dined with publicans, and even sinners. The Copts are evidently the ancient Egyptians,— the slightly aquiline nose and long eye are the very same as those in the profiles on the tombs and temples, and also like the very earliest Byzantine pictures. *Du reste*, the face is handsome, but generally sallow and rather inclined to puffiness, and the figure wants the grace of the Arabs; nor has any Copt the thorough-bred *distingué* look of the meanest man or woman of good Arab blood. Their feet are the long-toed, flattish foot of the Egyptian statue, while the Arab foot is classically perfect, and you could put your hand under the instep. The beauty of the Ababdeh, black, naked, and shaggy-haired, is quite marvellous; I never saw such delicate limbs and features, or such eyes and teeth.

LETTER XII.

A few miles below Girgeh, March, 1863.

I AM wonderfully better; the fine air of Nubia seemed to suit me as well as that of Caledon. It has the same merits, and the same drawback of violent winds. Fancy that meat kept ten and fourteen days, under a sun which even I was forced to cover my head before! In Cairo you must cook your meat in two days, and in Alexandria as soon as it is killed, —and the sun is nothing there. But in Nubia I walked till I wore out my shoes and roasted my feet, and was as dry as a chip; in Nubia, and as low down as Kiné, below Thebes some way; after that it alters, and, though colder, I perspire again. In Cairo the winter has been terribly cold and damp, as the Coptic priest told me yesterday at Girgeh.

He had been there, and suffered much from colds and coughs. So I don't repent the expense of the boat, for I am *all* the money the better, and really think of getting well.

Now that I know the ways of the country (which Herodotus truly says is like no other), I see that I might have gone and lived at Thebes, or at Kiné, or Aswán, on next to nothing; but then how could I know it? The English have raised a *mirage* of false wants and extravagance, which the servants of the country of course, some from interest, and some from mere ignorance, do their best to keep up. As soon as I had succeeded in really persuading Omar that I was not as rich as a Pasha, and had no wish to be thought so, he immediately turned over a new leaf as to what must be had, and said, " Oh, if I could have thought an English lady would have eaten and lived and done the least like Arab people, I might have hired a house at Kiné for you, and we might have gone up in a clean passenger-boat; but I thought no English could bear it." At Cairo, where we shall be on the 19th, Omar will get a lodging, and borrow a few mattresses and a table and chair, and, as he says, " keep the money in our pocket, instead of giving it to the hotel."

I hope you got a letter I wrote from Thebes, telling you that I had dined with the " blameless Ethiopians." I have seen all the temples in Nubia and down as far as I have come, and nine of the tombs of Thebes. Some are wonderfully beautiful,— Aboo-Sembel, Kalabsheh, Kóm Omboo,—a little temple at El-Káb, lovely,— all three at Thebes ; and most of all, Abydus. Edfoo and Dendarah are the most perfect, Edfoo *quite* perfect, but far less beautiful. But the most beautiful object my eyes ever saw is the island of Philæ; it gives one quite the supernatural feeling of Claude's best landscapes, only not the least like them. The Arabs say that Anas-el-Wugood, the most beautiful of men, built it for his most beautiful beloved, and there they lived in perfect beauty and happiness all alone. If the weather had not been so cold while I was there, I should have lived in the temple, in a chamber sculptured with the mystery of Osiris's burial and resurrection. Omar cleaned it out, and meant to move my things there for a few days, but it was too cold to sleep in a room without a door.

The winds have been extraordinarily cold this year, and are so still. We have had very little of the fine warm weather, and really have been pinched with cold most of the time. I had to wear all my thickest winter clothes and wraps; on the shore, away from the river, would be much better for invalids. Mustafa Agha, the consular agent at Thebes, has offered me a house of his up among the tombs, in the finest air, if ever I want it. He is very kind and hospitable indeed to all the English who come there. I went into his hareem, and liked his wife's manners very much. It was cheering to see that she hen-pecked her handsome old husband completely. They had beautiful children, and his boy, about thirteen or so, rode and played jereed one day, when Abdallah Pasha had ordered the people of the neighbourhood to shew that exercise to General Parker. I never saw so beautiful a performance. The old General and I were quite excited, and he tried it, to the great amusement of the Sheykh-el-Beled. The Sheykh and young Hasan, and old Mustafa, wheeled round and round like beautiful hawks, and caught the palmsticks thrown at them as they dashed round. It was superb; and the horses were good, although the bridles and saddles were rags and ends of rope, and the men tatterdemalions.

A little below Thebes I stopped, and walked inland to Koos, to see a noble old mosque falling to ruin. Few English had ever been there, and we were surrounded by a crowd in the bazaar. Instantly five or six tall fellows with long sticks, improvised themselves as a body-guard, and kept the people off, who however were perfectly civil, and only curious to see such strange " hareem ;" and after seeing us well out of the town, evaporated as quietly as they came, without a word. I gave about tenpence to buy oil, as it is Ramadán, and the mosque ought to be lighted ; and the old servant of the mosque kindly promised me full justice at the day of judgment, as I was one of those Nazarenes of whom the Lord Mohammad has said that they are not proud, and wish well to the Muslimeen. Mohammad Alee Pasha had confiscated all the lands belonging to the mosque, and allowed three hundred piastres (not two pounds a month) for all expenses. Of course the noble old building, with its beautiful carving and arabesque mouldings, must fall down. There was a smaller one beside it, where the servant declared that anciently forty women lived unmarried and recited Koran,—Muslim nuns, in fact. I intend to ask the Alim, for whom I have a letter from Mustafa Agha, about such an anomaly.

Some way above Belyeneh, Omar asked eagerly for leave to stop the boat, as a great sheykh had called to us, and we should inevitably have some disaster if we disobeyed. So we stopped, and Omar said, " Come and see the sheykh, ma'am." I walked off and presently found about thirty people, including all my own men, sitting on the ground round St. Simeon Stylites, without the column. A hideous old man, like Polyphemus, utterly naked, with the skin of a rhinoceros all cracked with the weather, sat there, and had sat night and day, summer and winter, motionless for twenty years. He never prays, he never washes, he does not keep Ramadán, and yet he is a saint. Of course I expected a good hearty curse from such a man; but he was delighted with my visit, asked me to sit down, ordered his servant to bring me sugar-cane, asked my name, and tried to repeat it over and over again; he was quite talkative and full of jokes and compliments, and took no notice of any one else. Omar and my crew smiled and nodded, and all congratulated me heartily. Such a distinction proves my own excellence (as the sheykh knows all people's thoughts), and is sure to be followed by good fortune. Finally, Omar proposed to say the Fat'hah, in which all joined except the sheykh, who looked rather bored by the interruption, and who desired us not to go so soon unless I were in a hurry. A party of Bedawees came up on camels, with presents for the holy man, but he took no notice of them and went on questioning Omar about me, and answering my questions. What struck me was the total absence of any sanctimonious air about the old fellow; he was quite worldly and jocose. I suppose he knew that his position was secure, and thought his dirt and nakedness were sufficient proofs of his holiness. Omar then recited the Fat'hah again, and we rose and gave the servant a few faddahs. The saint takes no notice of this part of the proceedings, but he asked me to send him twice my handful of rice for his dinner,—an honour so great that there was a murmur of congratulation through the whole assembly. I asked Omar how a man could be a saint who neglected all the duties of a Muslim, and I found that he fully believed that Sheykh Seleem could be in two places at once; that while he sits there on the shore, he is also at Mecca performing every sacred function, and dressed all in green. "Many people have seen him there, ma'am; quite true."

From Belyeneh we rode on pack donkeys without bridles, and only my saddle, to Abydus, six miles through the most beautiful crops ever seen. The absence of weeds and blight is wonderful, and the green of Egypt, where it is green, would make English green look black. Beautiful cattle, sheep, and camels were eating the delicious clover, while their owners camped in reed huts, during the time the crops are growing. Such a lovely scene, all sweetness and plenty! We ate our bread and dates in Osiris's temple, and a woman offered us buffalo milk on our way home, which we drank warm out of the huge earthen pan it had been milked in. At Girgeh I found my former friend Mishreghi absent, but his servants told some of his friends of my arrival, and about seven or eight big black turbans soon gathered in the boat.

A darling little Coptic boy came with his father, and wanted a "kitáb" (book) to write in. So I made one out of paper and the cover of my old pocket-book, and gave him a pencil. I also bethought me of showing him a picture-book, which was so glorious a novelty that he wanted to go with me to my town, "Beled el-Inkeleez," where more such books were to be found.

LETTER XIII.

Asyoot, March 8, 1863.

HERE I found letters telling me of Lord Lansdowne's death. Of course I know that his time was come; but the thought that I shall never see his face again,—that all that kindness and affection is gone out of my life, is a great blow. No friend could leave such a blank to me as that old and faithful one, though the death of younger ones might be more tragic; but so many things have gone with him into the grave. Many, indeed, will mourn that kind, wise, steadfast man. *Antiqua fides.* No one, nowadays, will be so noble, with such unconsciousness and simplicity. I have bought two Coptic turbans to make a black dress out of. I thought I should like to wear it for him—here, where " compliment " is out of the question.

I also had so bad an account of J—— that
I have telegraphed to Alexandria, and shall
go there if she is not much better. If she
is, I shall hold to my plan, and see Benee-
Hasan and the Pyramids on my way to Cairo.
I found my kind friend, the Copt Waseef,
who had the letters, kinder than ever. He
went off to telegraph to Alexandria for me,
and showed so much feeling and real kindness, that I was quite touched; it is such a
contrast to the hardness of colonial ways.

I feel very much better; can walk four or
five miles. All this in spite of really cold
weather, in a boat where nothing shuts within two fingers' breadth. I long to be back
again with my own people. Good Waseef
has just been here to see whether I did not
want money, or anything.

March 10.—No telegram, but Waseef has
just sent a letter now come with good news,
so I shall start at once with an easy heart. I
dined and spent the day with Waseef and his
hareem. Such an amiable, kindly household!
I was charmed with their manner to each
other, to the slaves and family. His brother,
as in patriarchal times, waited on us at table.

The slaves (all Muslims) told Omar what an excellent master they had.

Waseef lent me £10, as my captain wants money, and I am to repay it to his slave in Cairo, who does business for him. He had meant to make a dance fantasia for me, but as I had not good news, it was countermanded

LETTER XIV.

Cairo, March 19, 1863.

AFTER leaving Asyoot, I caught cold. The
worst of going up the Nile is that you must
come down again, and find horrid fogs and
cold nights, with sultry days; so I did not
attempt Sakkárah and the Pyramids, but came
a day before my appointed time to Cairo.
Here in the town it is much warmer and
drier. . . .

LETTER XV.

Cairo, Friday, April 9, 1863.

I HAVE had a very severe attack of bronchitis, and have gone through all the old long tedious story of cough and utter weakness. Omar wisely went for Hekekian Bey, who came at once, bringing Deleo Bey, the surgeon-in-chief to the Pasha's troops, and also the doctor to the Hareem. He has been most kind, coming two and three times a day. He won't take any fee, under the pretext that he is "*officier du Pacha.*" I must send him some present from England. As to Hekekian Bey, he is absolutely the good Samaritan; and these Orientals do their kindnesses with such an air of enjoyment to themselves, that it seems quite a favour to let them wait upon one. Hekekian comes in every day with his handsome old face and a budget of news,—all the gossip of the Sultan and his doings. I am up to-day for the second time. The weather has been chilly, and two days' rain! I am waiting for a warm day to go out. I hear the illuminations last night were beautiful. The Turkish bazaar was gorgeous. To-morrow the Mahmal goes. Think of my missing that sight

I have a black slave—a real one. I looked at her little ears, wondering they had not been bored for rings. She fancied I wished them bored. She was sitting on the floor, close at my side, and in a minute she stood up, and showed me her ear, with a great pin stuck through it, "Is that well, lady?" The creature is eight years old. The shock nearly made me faint. What extremity of terror had reduced that little mind to such a state? When she first came, she tells me, she thought I should eat her; now, her dread is that I shall leave her behind. She sings a wild song of joy at M——'s picture, and about the little Sitt. She was sent from Khartoom a present to the American Consul, who had no woman-servant in his house. He fetched me to look at her, and when I saw the terror-stricken creature roughly pulled about by his cook and groom, I said I would take her for the present. She sings quaint little Kurdufán songs all day. She had never seen a needle, and in a fortnight she sews very neatly and quickly. She wails aloud when Omar tells her she is not my slave. She is very quiet and gentle, poor little savage! but blacker than ebony. The utter slavishness of the poor little soul quite upsets me. She has absolutely no will of her own.

I am quite ready to do whatever is thought best in the summer. Deleo Bey can give no opinion, as he knows little but Egypt, and thinks England rather like Norway, I fancy. Only don't let me be put in a dreadful mountain valley to inhale those dismallest of vapours. I hear the drip, drip, drip of Eaux Bonnes when I am chilly and oppressed in my sleep.

LETTER XVI.

Cairo, April 13, 1863.

I HAVE been ill again. The fact is that the spring in Egypt is very trying, and I came down the river a full month too soon. People do exaggerate so about the heat. To-day is the first warm day we have had: till now I have been shivering.

I have been out twice for a drive, and saw the sacred Camel bearing the Holy Mahmal, rest for its first station outside the town. No words can describe the departure of the Holy Mahmal and the pilgrims for Mecca. I sat for hours in a Bedawee tent in a sort of dream. It is the most beautiful sight of man and beast, and colour and movement; and their first encampment is in a glorious spot, among the domes and minarets of the ruined tombs of the Memlook Sultans.

It is a deeply-affecting sight, when one thinks of the hardships all these men are prepared to endure. Omar's eyes were full of tears and his voice husky with emotion as he talked about it, and pointed out the Mahmal and the Sheykh-el-gemel who leads the Sacred Camel, naked to the waist, with flowing hair.

I loitered about a long time admiring the glorious "free people." The Bedawee and the Maghrabee and their noble-looking women are magnificent, and the irregular Turkish and Arab horsemen, so superior to the drilled cavalry, are wildly picturesque. To see a Bedawee and his wife walk through the streets of Cairo is superb. Her hand resting on his shoulder, and scarcely deigning to cover her haughty face, she looks down on the Egyptian veiled woman who carries the heavy burden and walks behind her lord and master.

Muslim piety is so unlike what Europeans think it: it is so full of tender emotions, so much more sentimental than we imagine, and it is wonderfully strong. I used to hear Omar praying outside my door while I was so ill, "O God, make her better!" "Oh, may God let her sleep!" as naturally as we should say,

" I hope she will have a good night." I found great kindness here, Hekekian Bey came to see me every day, and Deleo Bey, the doctor, attended me with the utmost care and tenderness. It had an odd, dreamy effect to hear old Hekekian Bey and my doctor discoursing in Turkish at my bedside. I shall always fancy the good Samaritan in a tarboosh and white beard and very long eyes.

The Sultan's coming is a kind of riddle. No one knows what he wants. The Pasha has ordered all the women of the lower classes to keep indoors while the Sultan is here. Arab women are outspoken, and might shout out their grievances to the Great Sultan. I fear I shall not see Sakkárah or the Pyramids, for strength returns very slowly after such an illness as I have had.

I am going to visit the old Muslim French painter's family. He has an Arab wife and grown-up daughters. He is a very agreeable old man, and has a store of Arab legends; I am going to persuade him to write them down, and let me translate them into English. The Sultan goes away to-day. He and his suite have eaten nothing but what came from Con-

stantinople; even water to drink was brought.
I heard that from Hekekian Bey, who formerly
owned the eunuch who is now Kislar Azi to
the Sultan himself; so Hekekian had the honour of kissing his old slave's hand.

If any one tries to make you believe any
nonsense about " civilization" in Egypt, laugh
at it. The real life and the real people are
exactly as described in that most veracious of
books, the 'Thousand and One Nights.' The
tyranny is the same, the people are not altered; and very charming people they are. If
I could but speak the language, I could get
into Arab society through two or three different
people, and see more than many Europeans
who have lived here all their lives. The Arabs
are deeply alive to the least prejudice against
them; but when they feel quite safe on that
point, they rather like the amusement of a
stranger.

Omar devised a glorious scheme, if I were
only well and strong, of putting me in a tahkt-
rawán and taking me to Mecca in the character of his mother, supposed to be a Turk.
To a European man of course it would be impossible, but an enterprising woman might do

it easily with a Muslim confederate. Fancy seeing the pilgrimage!

In a few days I must go down to Alexandria. Thus do Arabs understand competition; the owner of boats said that so few were wanted, times were so bad on account of the railway, etc. etc., that he must have double what he used to have. In vain Omar argued that this was not the way to get employment. Máleysh! (never mind.) Is not that Eastern? Up the river, where there is no railroad, I might have it at half that rate. All you have ever told me as most Spanish in Spain is in full vigour here; and also I am reminded of Ireland at every turn. The same causes produce the same effects.

To-day the Khamaseen is blowing, and it is decidedly hot: the heat is quite unlike that at the Cape: this is close and gloomy,—no sunshine. Altogether the climate is far less bright than I expected; very inferior to that of the Cape. Nevertheless I heartily agree to the Arab saying, "He who has drunk the Nile water will ever long to drink it again." S—— says all other water after that of the Nile is like bad small-beer compared to sweet ale.

When the Khamaseen is over, Omar insists on my going to see the tree and the well where Sittina Maryam (the Virgin Mary) rested with Seyyidna Eesa in her arms during the flight into Egypt. It is venerated by Christian and Muslim alike, and is a great place for feasting and holiday-making out of doors, which the Arabs so dearly love.

It would be delightful to have you at Cairo. Now I have pots and pans, and all things needful for a house but a carpet and a few mattresses, you could camp with me *à l'Arabe.* How you would revel in old Masr-el-Kahirah, peep up at lattice-windows, gape like a "Ghasheem" (green one) in the bazaar, go wild in the mosques, laugh at portly Turks and dignified sheykhs on their white donkeys, drink sherbet in the streets, ride wildly about on a donkey, peer under black veils at beautiful eyes, and feel generally intoxicated! I am quite a good *cicerone* now of the glorious old city. Omar is in rapture at the idea that ".Seedee-el-kebeer" (the great Master) might come. Máshá-alláh! how our hearts would be dilated!

It may amuse you to see what impression

Cairo makes. I ride along on my valiant donkey, led by the stalwart Hasan, and attended by Omar, and constantly say, " Oh, if our master were here, how pleased he would be !" (Husband is not a correct word). I went out again to the tombs yesterday. Omar witnessed the destruction of some of the most exquisite buildings; the tombs and mosques of the Memlook Sultans, which Saeed Pasha used to divert himself with bombarding, for practice for his artillery. Omar was then in the boy-corps of camel artillery, now disbanded. Thus the Pasha added the piquancy of sacrilege to barbarism.

Our street and our neighbours would divert you. Opposite lives a Christian dyer, who must be a seventh brother of the admirable Barber; he has the same impertinence, loquacity, and love of meddling with everybody's business. I long to see him thrashed, though he is a constant comedy. The Arabs next-door, and the Levantines opposite, are quiet enough; but how *do* they eat all the cucumbers they buy of the man who cries them every morning as " fruit gathered by sweet girls in the garden with the early dew"?

The more I see of the back slums of Cairo, the more in love I am with it. The dirtiest lane of Cairo is far sweeter than the best street of Paris. Here there is the dirt of negligence, and the dust of a land without rain, but nothing disgusting; and decent Arabs are as clean in their personal habits as English gentlemen. As to the beauty of Cairo, *that* no words can describe: the oldest European towns are tame and regular in comparison; and the people are so pleasant. If you smile at anything that amuses you, you get the kindest, brightest smiles in return; they give hospitality with their faces, and if one brings out a few words, "Máshá-alláh! what Arabic the Sitt Inkeleezeeyeh speaks!" The Arabs are clever enough to understand the amusement of a stranger, and to enter into it, and are amused in turn, and they are wonderfully unprejudiced. When Omar explains to me their views on various matters, he adds, "The Arab people think so; I not know if right." And the way in which the Arab merchants worked the electric telegraph, and the eagerness of the Fellaheen for steam-ploughs, are quite extraordinary. They are extremely clever and nice children, easily amused, and easily roused into a fury, which lasts five minutes and leaves no malice; and half the lying and cheating of which they are accused, comes from misunderstanding and ignorance. When I first took Omar he was by way of ten or twenty pounds being nothing for my dignity; but as soon as I told him that the Master was a Bey who had a salary but no baksheesh, he was as careful as for himself. The Arabs see us come here and do what only their greatest Pashas do,— hire a boat to ourselves,—and of course think our wealth boundless. The lying is mostly from fright. They dare not suggest a difference of opinion to a European, and lie to get out of scrapes which blind obedience has often got them into.

As to the charges of shopkeepers, that is the custom; and the haggling, a ceremony you must submit to. It is for the purchaser or employer to offer a price and fix wages,—the inverse of Europe. If you inquire the price, they ask for something fabulous at random. A few hundred pounds could be pleasantly spent in the bazaars here. Carpets, gay blankets, etc., are cheap and lovely. Cairo *is* the

Arabian Nights; there is a little Frankish var-
nish here and there, but the government, the
people, all are unchanged since that most faithful picture of manners was drawn.

The Christians are far more close and reserved and backward than the Arabs, and they
have been so repudiated by Europeans that they
are doubly shy of us. The Europeans resent
being called " Nasránce," as a genteel Hebrew
gentleman may shrink from the word " Jew."
But I said boldly, "I am a Nazarene, praise
be to God!" and found that it was much ap-
proved by the Muslims as well as the Copts.
Curious things are to be seen here in religion:
Muslims praying at the tomb of Mar Girgis
(St. George), and at the resting-places of Sittina Maryam and Seyyidna Eesa, and miracles
bran-new of an equally mixed description.

If you have any power over any artist, send
him to paint here; no words can describe
either the picturesque beauty of Cairo or the
splendid forms of the people in Upper Egypt,
and, above all, in Nubia. I was in raptures at
seeing how superb an animal man (and woman)
really is; my donkey-girl at Thebes, dressed
like a Greek statue, " Ward esh-Shám " (the

rose of Syria) was a feast to the eyes. And here too, what grace and sweetness! and how good is a drink of Nile water out of an amphora held to your lips by a woman as graceful as she is kindly! "May it benefit thee!" she says, smiling with her beautiful teeth and eyes.

The days of the beauty of Cairo are numbered: the superb mosques are falling to decay, the exquisite lattice-windows are rotting away and replaced by European glass and *jalousies;* only the people and the government remain unchanged.

LETTER XVII.

Alexandria, May 12, 1863.

I HAVE been here a fortnight, but the climate, although very warm, disagrees with me so much that I am going back to Cairo at once, by the advice of the French doctor of the Suez Canal. I fancy I can stay at Cairo a month perhaps, and then I hope to go home, or, if not well enough for that, to go somewhere in the south of Europe. I cannot at all shake off the cough here. The American Consul kindly lends me his nice little bachelor-house, and I take Omar back again for the job. It is very hot here, but with a sea-breeze which strikes me like ice. Strong people enjoy it, but it gives even J—— cold in the head.

I am terribly disappointed at not being as materially better as I hoped I should be, while in Upper Egypt. I cannot express the longing I have for home and my children, and how much I feel the sort of suspense my illness causes to you all. Perhaps Cairo will cure this cough, and then I may venture home in July. Next winter will cost very little, as all my cooking things and boat-furniture are safe at Cairo with my washerwoman, and Mustafa will lend me a house at Thebes, and there will be steamers up the Nile then; so I shall save all the boat expenses, which are so great, and shall live for nothing up there. When I went yesterday to deposit my goods at the worthy old woman's house, the neighbours seeing me arrive on my donkey, followed by a cargo of pots and pans, thought I was come to live there, and came running out. I was patted on the back and welcomed, and overwhelmed with offers of service to help to clean my house, etc. Of course all rushed upstairs, and my washerwoman was put to a great expense in pipes and coffee.

One must come to the East to understand absolute social equality. As there is no education, and no reason why the donkey boy who runs beside me may not become a great man, and as all Muslims are *ipso facto* brothers, money and rank are looked on as mere accidents; and my *savoir vivre* was highly thought of, because I sat down with Fellaheen, and treated every one alike, as they treat each other. In Alexandria all that is changed; the European ideas and customs have nearly extinguished the Arab, and those which remain are not improved by the contact. Only the Bedawee preserve their haughty *nonchalance*. I found the Maghrabee bazaar full of them when I went to buy a white cloak, and was amused at the way in which one splendid bronze figure, who lay on the shop-front, moved one leg to let me sit down. They grew interested in my purchase, and assisted in making the bargain and wrapping the long cloak round me, bedawee fashion; and they, too, complimented me on having the face of the "Arab," which means Bedawee. I wanted a little Arab dress for R——, but could find none, as at her age none are worn in the Desert.

I dined one day with Omar, or rather I ate at his house, for he would not eat with me. His sister-in-law cooked a most admirable dinner, and every one was delighted. It was an interesting family circle. There was a very respectable elder brother, a confectioner, whose elder wife was a black woman, a really remarkable person. She speaks Italian perfectly, and gave me a great deal of information, and asked very intelligent questions. She ruled the house, but as she had no children, he had married a fair gentle-looking Arab woman, who had five children, and all lived in perfect harmony. Omar's wife is a fine handsome girl of his own age, with very good manners, but close on her lying-in, and looking fatigued. She had been outside the door of the close little court which constituted the house *once* since her marriage. I now begin to understand the condition of the women, and the Muslim sentiments and maxims regarding them. There is a good deal of chivalry in some respects, and, in the respectable lower and middle classes, the result is not so bad. I suspect that among the rich, few are very happy, but I don't know them, or anything of the Turkish ways. I will go and see the black woman again, and hear more; her conversation was really interesting. I hope to see you all before very long.

LETTER XVIII.

Cairo, May, 1863.

I ONLY stayed a fortnight at Alexandria, and finding myself quite knocked up by the dampness of the air, I came back here. Mr. Thayer, the American Consul-General, who has been my earthly providence in this country, has lent me a little apartment which he has in Cairo and does not use except in winter; it is infinitely pleasanter than the hotel, and costs much less. I had a most successful voyage up to the Second Cataract, Wadee Halfeh, only the winter was the coldest ever known in Egypt, and I had many comfortless cold days in the Etesian wind. As to interest and enjoyment, I don't think Italy or Greece can equal the sacred Nile, the perfect freshness of the gigantic buildings, the beauty of the sculptures, and the charm of the people. Two beautiful young Nubian women visited me in my boat, with hair in the little plaits finished off with lumps of yellow clay, burnished like golden tags, soft deep bronze skins, and lips and eyes fit for Isis and Athor; their very dress and ornaments were the same as those represented in the tombs; and I felt inclined to ask them how many thousand years old they were. In their house, I sat on an ancient Egyptian couch with the semicircular head-rest, and ate and drank out of crockery which looked antique; and they brought me dates in a basket such as you see in the British Museum, and a mat of the same sort. At Aswán I dined on the shore with the " blameless Ethiopians," merchants from Soodán, black as ink and handsome as the Greek Bacchus. Most ancient of all, though, are the Copts; their very hands and feet are the same as those of the Egyptian statues. The bas-reliefs in the tombs are accurate representations of the country people of the present day,—especially the Nubians and Copts.

I was most kindly received by a Copt merchant at Asyoot, and am to spend a week at his hareem if ever I go up the Nile again; everywhere his relations welcomed me and gave me provisions. But generally they are a reserved people, and acknowledge no connection with other Christians.

Nothing is more striking to me than the way in which one is constantly reminded of Herodotus. Both the Christianity and the Islam of this country are full of the ancient practices and superstitions of the old worship. The sacred animals have all taken service with Muslim saints: at Minyeh, one of the latter reigns over crocodiles. I saw the hole of Æsculapius's serpent at Gebel Sheykh Haradee; and I fed the birds who used to tear the cordage of the boats that refused to feed them, and who are now the servants of Sheykh Nooneh, and still come on board by scores for the bread which no Reyyis dares to refuse them. Bubastis has not lost her influence, and cats are as sacred as ever: they are still fed in the Kádee's court, at Cairo, at public expense, and behave with singular decorum when the " servant of the cats " serves their dinner.

Among gods, Amun Ra, the god of the sun, and great serpent-slayer, calls himself Mar

Girgis (St. George), and Osiris holds his festivals twice a year as notoriously as ever at Tanta, in the Delta, under the name of Seyyid-el-Bedawce. The Fellah women offer sacrifices to the Nile, and walk round ancient statues, in order to have children.

These are a few of the ancient things, and in domestic life are numbers more. The ceremonies at births and burials are not Muslim, but ancient Egyptian. The women wail for the dead, as on the sculptures; a practice which is directly contrary to the injunctions of the Koran. All the ceremonies are pagan, and would shock an Indian Muslim as much as *his* objection to eat with a Christian shocks an Arab.

This country is a palimpsest, in which the Bible is written over Herodotus, and the Koran over that. In the towns the Koran is most visible; in the country, Herodotus. I fancy this is most marked and most curious among the Copts, whose churches are shaped like the ancient temples; but they are so much less accessible than the Arabs, that I know less of their customs.

In Cairo, of course, one is more reminded of

the beloved ' Arabian Nights,'—indeed Cairo *is* the ' Arabian Nights.' I knew that christian dyer who lives opposite to me, and is always wrangling, from my infancy; and my delightful servant Omar, Abu-l-Haláweh (the father of sweets), is the type of all the amiable *jeunes premiers* of the stories. I am privately of opinion that he is Bedr-ed-Deen Hasan,—the more, as he can make cream tarts, and there was no pepper in them. Cream tarts are not very good, but lamb stuffed with pistachio-nuts fulfils all one's dreams of excellence,—and dates and Nile water! they are excellent indeed, especially together, like olives and wine.

Next Friday the great Bairam begins, and every one is buying sheep and poultry in preparation for it: every poor Muslim eats meat at the expense of his richer neighbours. It is the day on which the pilgrims ascend Mount Arafat at Mecca, to hear the sermon which terminates the Hájj.

Next month is the Moolid-en-Nebbee, the feast of the Prophet, and I hope to see that too. I have been very fortunate in seeing a great deal here, and getting to know a good deal of the family life. I have been especially civilly treated by darweeshes and pious people, who might reasonably have cursed me. Even a tremendous saint, a naked Fakeer, treated me with the greatest distinction, and my crew were delighted, and prophesied great blessings for me. He had sat naked and motionless twenty years on one spot, and looked like the trunk of an old tree; but he had no pious airs, and was rather jocose.

I hope to go home next month, as soon as it gets too hot here, and is likely to be warm enough in England.

LETTER XIX.

Masr-el-Kahirah, (Cairo,) May 21, 1863.

I HAVE just received your letter and Mrs. K——'s, for which many thanks; but what she recommends is just what does not suit me. All those sea-coast places make me ill. Simon's Bay, Alexandria, and, in a less degree, Cape Town, all disagreed with me; while the dry heat of Caledon and of Nubia seemed to give me new life. Madeira, I am sure, would make me ill. It is curious that it should be so, while being at sea suits me so well; but it is the contest between land and sea air which is pernicious; and the warmer the climate, the more sensible that is. There are *poitrinaires* who thrive at Damietta even, but I am not one of them. Dr. Aubert Roche told me to go by the hygrometer, and I said I had discovered that already, and carried a most faithful one inside me;—worse luck!

I came here on Saturday night. To-day is Wednesday, and I am already much better. I have attached an excellent donkey and his master, a delightful Hasan, to my household. They live at the door, and Hasan cleans the stairs and goes errands during the heat of the day; and I ride out very early, at six or seven, and again at five. The air is delicious now: it is very hot for a few hours, but not stifling; and the breeze does not chill one, as it does at Alexandria. I live all day and all n̄ with open windows, and the plen̄ ȷ of fr⸍ warm air is the best of remedies. I can do ⸼ better than stay here till the heat becom⸍r too great. I left little Zeyneb, my slave, a⸍ Alexandria with J——'s maid, who quite loves her, and who begged to keep her " for company," and also to help in their removal to the new house. She clung about me, and made me promise to come back to her, but was content to stop with E——, whose affections she of course returns. It was a pleasure to see her so happy, and how she relished being " put to bed," with a kiss, by the maid. Her Turkish master, whom she pronounces to be "battál" (bad), called her "Salám-es-Seed" (the peace of her master), but she said that in her own village she used to be Zeyneb, and so we call her. She has grown fatter, and, if possible, blacker. The elder wife of Hegáb, the confectioner, was much interested in her, as her fate had been the same. She was bought by an Italian, who lived with her till his death, when she married Hegáb. She is a pious Muslimeh, and invoked the intercession of Seyyidna Mohammad for me, when I told her I had no intention of baptizing Zeyneb by force, as had been done to her.

The fault of my lodging here is the noise; we are on the road from the railway, and there is no quiet except in the few hot hours when nothing is heard but the cool tinkle of the Sakka's brass cups as he sells water in the street, or perchance "Erksoos"—liquorice water,— or Karroob and raisin sherbet. The "erksoos" is rather bitter, and very good; I drink it a good deal, for drink one must. A "gulleh" of water is soon gone. A "gulleh" is a wide-mouthed porous jar, and Nile water drunk out of it, without the intervention of a glass, is delicious. My lodging is very clean and nice, but quite like a French "appartement," except the kitchen and other domestic arrangements, which are Arab. Omar goes to market every morning with a donkey (I went too, and was much amused), and cooks, and in the evening goes out with me, if I want him. I told him I had recommended him highly, and hoped he would get good employment; but he declares that he will go with no one else so long as I come to Egypt, whatever the difference of wages may be. "The bread I eat with you is sweet!" said he; a pretty little unconscious antithesis to Dante. I have been advising his brother, Hajjee Alee, to set up a hotel at Thebes for invalids, and he has already set about getting a house there; there is *one*. Next winter there will be a steamer twice a week to Aswán,—Juvenal's distant Syene, where he died in banishment.

My old washerwoman sent me a fervent entreaty through Omar that I would dine with her one day, since I had made Cairo delightful by my return. If one will only devour these people's food they are enchanted,—they like that much better than a present; so I

will " honour her house " some day.   Good
old Hannah ! she is divorced for being too fat
and old, and replaced by a young Turk, whose
family sponge on Hajjee Alee, and are conde-
scending.

If I could afford it, I would have a sketch of
a beloved old mosque of mine, falling to decay, and with three palm-trees growing in the
middle of it ; indeed, I would have a book full,
for all is exquisite, and, alas ! all is going.   The
old Copt quarter is *entamé*, and hideous shabby
French houses, like the one I live in, are being ,
run up ; and in this weather how much better
would be the Arab courtyard, with its mastabah and fountain !

There is a quarrel now in the street ; how
they talk and gesticulate, and everybody puts
in a word !   A boy has upset a cake-seller's
tray.   " Nál-abook !" (curse your father !) he
claims six piastres damages, and every one
gives an opinion, *pro* or *contra*.   We all look
out of the windows.   My opposite neighbour,
the pretty Armenian woman, leans out (baby
sucking all the time), and her diamond head-
ornaments and earrings glitter as she laughs
like a child.   The Christian dyer is also very

active in the row, which, like all Arab rows, ends in nothing,—it evaporates in fine theatrical gestures and lots of talk. Curious! in the street they are so noisy; and set the same men down in a coffee-shop, or anywhere, and they are the quietest of mankind. Only one man speaks at a time,—the rest listen and never interrupt; twenty men do not make the noise of three Europeans.

—— is my near neighbour, and he comes in, and we discuss the government. His heart is sore with disinterested grief for the sufferings of the people. " Don't they deserve to be decently governed,—to be allowed a little happiness and prosperity? they are so docile, so contented; are they not a good people?" Those were his words as he was recounting some new iniquity. Of course, half these acts are done under pretext of improving and civilizing, and the Europeans applaud and say, "Oh, but nothing could be done without forced labour," and the poor Fellaheen are marched off in gangs like convicts, and their families starve, and (who would have thought it?) the population keeps diminishing. No wonder the cry is, " Let the English Queen come and take us." You know that I don't see things quite as our countrymen generally do, for mine is another *Standpunkt*, and my heart is with the Arabs. I care less about opening up the trade with the Soodán, or about all the new railways, and I should like to see person and property safe, which no one's is here,—Europeans of course excepted.

Ismaeel Pasha got the Sultan to allow him to take 90,000 feddans of uncultivated land for himself as private property. Very well. But the late Viceroy granted, eight years ago, certain uncultivated lands to a good many Turks, his *employés*,—in hopes of founding a landed aristocracy, and inducing them to spend their capital in cultivation. They did so; and now Ismaeel takes their improved land, and gives them feddan for feddan of his new land (which will take five years to bring into cultivation) instead. He forces them to sign a *voluntary* deed of exchange, or they go off to Feyzóghloo,—a hot Siberia, whence none return. I saw a Turk, the other day, who was ruined by the transaction.

The Sultan also left a large sum of money for religious institutions and charities, Muslim,

Jew, and Christian. None have received a faddah. It is true, the Sultan and his suite plundered the Pasha and the people here; but, from all I hear, the Sultan really wishes to do good. What is wanted here, is, hands to till the soil; wages are very high; food, of course, gets dearer, the forced labour inflicts more suffering than before, and the population will decrease yet faster. This appears to me to be a state of things in which it is of no use to say that public works *must* be made at any cost. I dare say the wealth will be increased, if, meanwhile, the people are not exterminated. The nevery new Pasha builds a huge new palace, whilst those of his predecessors fall to ruin. Mohammad Alee's sons even cut down the trees of his beautiful botanical garden, and planted beans there; so money is constantly wasted more utterly than if it were thrown into the Nile, for then the Fellaheen would not have to spend the time, so much wanted for agriculture, in building hideous barrack-like so-called palaces. What chokes me is, to hear Englishmen talk of the stick being "the only way to manage Arabs," as if there could be any doubt that it is the easiest way to manage anybody, where it can be used with impunity.

Sunday, May 24.—I went to a large unfinished new Coptic church this morning. Omar went with me up to the women's gallery, and was discreetly going back, when he saw me in the right place; but the Copt women began to talk to him, and asked questions about me all the time I was looking down on the strange scene below.

I believe they celebrate the ancient mysteries still. The clashing of cymbals, the chanting or humming, unlike any sound I ever heard, the strange yellow copes covered with stranger devices;—it was *wunderlich*. At the end, every one went away, and I went down and took off my shoes to go and look at the church. While I was doing so, a side-door opened and a procession entered: a priest, dressed in the usual black robe and turban of all Copts, carrying a trident-shaped sort of candlestick, another with cymbals, a number of little boys, and two young ecclesiastics of some sort in the yellow satin copes (contrasting queerly with the familiar tarboosh of common life, on their heads); each of these carried a little baby and a huge wax taper. They marched round and round three times, beating the cymbals furiously, and chanting a jig-tune; the dear little tiny boys marched just before the priest, with a pretty little solemn consequential air. Then they all stopped in front of the sanctuary, and the priest untied a sort of broad coloured tape which was round each of the babies, reciting something in Coptic all the time, and finally touched their foreheads and hands with water. This is a ceremony subsequent to baptism, after I don't know how many days; but the priest ties and unties the bands. Of what is this symbolical?—I am at a loss to divine.

Then an old man gave a little round cake of bread, with a cabalistic-looking pattern on it, both to Omar and to me. A group of closely-veiled women stood on one side of the aisle, and among them the mothers of the babies, who received them from the men in yellow copes at the end of the ceremony. One of these young men was very handsome, and as he stood looking down and smiling on the baby he held, with the light of the torch sharpening the lines of his features, he would

have made a lovely picture. The expression
was sweeter than that of St. Vincent de Paul,
because his smile told that he could have
played with the baby as well as prayed for it.
In this country, one gets to see how much
more beautiful a perfectly natural expression
is than even the finest mystical expression
given by painters; and it is so refreshing that
no one tries to look pious. The Muslim looks
serious, and often warlike, as he stands at
prayer. The Christian just keeps his every-
day face. When the Muslim gets into a state
of devotional frenzy, he is too much in ear-
nest to think of making a face; it is quite
tremendous. I don't think the Copt has any
such ardours. But the scene of this morning
was all the more touching, that no one was
"behaving him or herself" at all. A little
acolyte peeped into the sacramental cup and
swigged off the drop left in it with the most
innocent air, and no one rebuked him, and
the quiet little children ran about in the sanctuary. Up to seven, they are privileged; only
they and the priests and acolytes enter it. It
is a pretty commentary on the words, " Suffer
little children," etc.

I am more and more annoyed at not being able to ask questions for myself, as I do not like to ask through a Muslim, and no Copts speak any foreign language, or very, very few. Omar and Hasan had been at five this morning to the tomb of Sittina Zeyneb, one of the granddaughters of the Prophet, to "see her" (Sunday is her day of reception), and say the Fat'hah at her tomb.

Yesterday I went to call on pretty Mrs. W. She is an Armenian, of the Greek faith, and was gone to pray at the convent of St. George (Mar Girgis), for the cure of the pains which a bad rheumatic fever has left in her hands.

Now I have filled such a long letter, I hardly know whether it is worth sending, and whether you will be amused by my commonplaces of Eastern life. To-day is Monday, 25th May, and very hot. I doubt whether I shall stay more than a fortnight longer here. I am better as to my cough. I kill a sheep next Friday, and Omar will cook a stupendous dish for the poor Fellaheen, who are lying about the railway-station waiting for work. That is to be my Beyram, and Omar hopes great benefit for me from the process.

LETTER XX.

On board the ' Venetian,' June 15, 1863.

WE shall be at Malta to-morrow, Inshallah !
I feel much better since I have been at sea.
We left Alexandria on Thursday, and are very
comfortable, having the whole spacious ladies'
cabin to ourselves, and a very pleasant captain.　But we are laden to the water's edge,
and a gale in " the Bay " would be very wet,
rough work.　We have had a breeze in our
teeth ever since we left, but very fine weather.
Omar shed some " manly tears," like a great
baby, as he kissed my hand on board ship, and
prayed for me to " the Preserver."

LETTER XXI.

Marseilles, September, 1863.

I WRITE quite in the dark, as there is a tremendous thunderstorm going on, which I hope will end the gale of wind. We sail to-morrow, and only touch at Messina, so I shall not write again till I arrive at Alexandria. We are drowned here; what must it be on the Rhône? Floods seem the order of the day, even with old Father Nile. I hope Omar will meet me, and see our luggage through the custom-house and turbulent hammáls at Alexandria. It is quite winter here now, though not very cold, but so damp. I am glad I have not delayed going back to Egypt any longer.

LETTER XXII.

Alexandria, Monday, October 19, 1863.

WE had a wretched voyage; good weather, but such a *pétaudière* of a ship. I am competent to describe the horrors of the middle-passage,—hunger, suffocation, dirt, and such *canaille*, high and low, on board. The only gentleman was a poor Moor going to Mecca, who stowed his wife and family in a spare boiler on deck. I saw him washing his children in the morning. "Que c'est dégoûtant!" exclaimed a French spectator. If an Oriental washes, he is a *sale cochon*. No wonder! A delicious man who sat near me on deck, when the sun came round to our side, growled between his clenched teeth, "Voilà un tas d'intrigants à l'ombre, tandis que le soleil me grille, moi."

But I was consoled, on arriving at noon on Friday, by seeing J—— come in a boat to meet me, looking as fresh and bright and merry as ever she could look, and the faithful Omar radiant with joy and affection. He has refused an offer of a place as messenger with the mails to Suez and back; and also to go with an English lady at very high pay, which his brother wanted him to do. But Omar said he could not leave me. "I think my God give her to me to take care of her; how then I leave her? I can't speak to my God if I do bad things like that." He kisses your hand, and is charmed with the knife you sent him, but far more that my family should know his name and be satisfied with my servant. Omar is gone to try to get me a Dahabeeyeh, to go up the river, as I hear the half-railway, half-steamer journey is dreadfully inconvenient and fatiguing, and the sight of the overflowing Nile is said to be magnificent; so we shall be five or six days *en route*, instead of eight hours.

Zeyneb is much grown, and seems extremely active and quick, but has grown rather loud and rough, from being allowed to associate with the Nubian man and boy, and to go out without a veil, which I won't allow in my hareem. However, she is as affectionate as ever, and delighted at the idea of going with us.

Tuesday, October 20.

Omar has got a boat for £12, all ready furnished, which is not more than the railway would cost, now that half must be done per steamer and a bit on donkeys or on foot. Two and a half hours to sit grilling at noon on the bank, and two miles to walk carrying one's baggage, is no joke. I shall take Haggeh Hannah in my boat, for the poor old soul was *moulue* by her journey. I have bought blankets here, but they are much dearer than last year. Everything is almost doubled in price, owing to the cattle murrain and the high Nile. Such an inundation as this year's was never known before. Does the blue god resent Speke's intrusion on his privacy? it will be a glorious sight, I believe. But the damage to crops, and even to the last year's stacks of grain and beans, is frightful,—one sails away among the palm-trees, over the submerged cotton-fields.

Ismaeel Pasha has been very active, but

there have been as many calamities in his short reign as during Pharaoh's, and ill-luck makes a man unpopular. The cattle murrain is fearful, and is now beginning in Cairo and Upper Egypt. I hear the loss reckoned at twelve millions sterling in cattle. The gazelles in the desert have it too, but not horses, asses, or goats.

Omar apologized for the stupidity of the Arabs in thinking that the dearness of all necessaries was the fault of the government, and was astonished to hear that many Europeans were no wiser.

LETTER XXIII.

Alexandria, Monday, October 26, 1863.

I AM much the worse for the damp of this place. On Thursday I shall get off, as the boat will be clean. I have a funny little dahabeeyeh, barely big enough to hold us; but I am lucky to get that for twelve pounds.

I went to two hareems the other day, with a little boy of Mustafa Agha's, and was much pleased. A very pleasant Turkish lady pulled out all her magnificent bedding and dresses for me and was most amiable. At another, a superb Arab, dressed in white cotton, with most *grande dame* manners and unpainted face, received me statelily. Her house would drive you wild,—such enamelled tiles, covering the panels of the walls, all divided by carved wood, and such carved screens and galleries, all very

old and rather dilapidated, but magnificent,—
and the lady worthy of her house. A bold-eyed
slave-girl with a baby, put herself forward for
admiration, and was ordered to bring coffee,
with cool though polite imperiousness. None
of our great ladies can half crush a rival
in comparison; they do it too coarsely. The
quiet scorn of the beautiful pale-faced, black-
haired Arab was beyond any English powers.
Then it was fun to open the lattice and make
me look out on the "*place*," and to wonder
what the neighbours would say at the sight of
my face and European hat. She asked about
my children, and blessed them repeatedly, and
took my hand very kindly in doing so, for
fear I should think her envious and fear her
eye, as she is childless.

I shall go to ——'s house; it is very bad,
but the hotel is worse, and I may find a better
on the spot. I heard of a good house at Boolak for two pounds a month, but I don't think
that place is healthy with the receding Nile.
I am anxious to get up the river.

LETTER XXIV.

Kafr ez-Zeiyát, Saturday, October 31, 1863.

We left Alexandria on Thursday about noon, and sailed with a fair wind along the Mahmoodeeyeh canal. My little boat flies like a bird, and my men are a capital set of fellows, bold and careful sailors. I have only seven in all, but they work well, and at a pinch Omar leaves the pots and pans, and handles a rope or pole manfully. We sailed all night, and passed the locks at Fum el-Mahmoodeeyeh at four yesterday, and were greeted by old Nile tearing down like a torrent. The river is magnificent,—"seven men's height," my Reyyis says, above its usual pitch; it has gone down five or six feet, and left a sad scene of havoc on either side. However, what the Nile takes, he repays with threefold interest, they say. The women are at work rebuilding their mud huts, and the men repairing the dykes. A Frenchman told me he was on board a Pasha's steamer, and they passed a flooded village where two hundred people stood on their roofs crying for help: would you, could you believe it? they passed on and left them to drown! Nothing but an eye-witness could have made me believe such frightful cruelty.

All to-day we sailed in heavenly weather,— a sky like nothing but its most beautiful self. At the bend of the river, just now, we had a grand struggle to get round, and got entangled with a big timber-boat. My crew became so vehement that I had to come out with an imperious request to every one to bless the Prophet. Next the boat nearly dragged the men into the stream, and they pulled, and hauled, and struggled, up to their waists in mud and water; and Omar brandished his pole, and shouted "Islám, el Islám!" which gave a fresh spirt to the poor fellows, and round we came with a dash and caught the breeze again. Now we have put up here for the night, and shall pass the railway bridge to-morrow. The railway is all under water from hence up to Tanta, eight miles, and in many places higher up.

LETTER XXV.

Cairo, Saturday, November 14, 1863.

HERE I am at last in my old quarters at Mr. Thayer's house, after some trouble. The very morning I landed, I was seized with violent illness; however, I am now better. I arrived at Cairo on Wednesday night, the 4th of November, slept in the boat and went ashore next morning.

The passage under the railway bridge at Tanta (which is only opened once in two days) was most exciting and pretty. Such a scramble and dash of boats,—two or three hundred at least! Old Zeydán, the steersman, slid under the noses of the big boats with my little cangia, and through the gates before they were well open, and we saw the rush and confusion behind us at our ease, and headed the whole fleet for a few miles. Then we stuck, and Zeydán raged, but we got off in an hour, and again overtook and passed all; and then we saw the spectacle of devastation,—whole villages gone, submerged and melted, mud to mud; and the people, with their beasts, encamped on spits of sand or on the dykes, in long rows of ragged makeshift tents, while we sailed over the places where they had lived; cotton rotting in all directions, and the dry tops crackling under the bows of the boat. When we stopped to buy milk, one poor woman exclaimed, " Milk! from where? Do you want it out of my breasts?" However, she took our saucepan and went to get some from another family. No one refuses it if they have a drop left, for they all believe the murrain to be a punishment for churlishness to strangers;—by whom committed, no one can say. Nor would they fix a price, or ask more than the old rate. But here everything has doubled in price: meat was $4\frac{1}{2}$ guroosh, now it is 8; eggs, etc., the same, and cotton 12 guroosh the pound. Yesterday I had to buy mattresses for Omar and Zeyneb, and loud were Omar's lamentations at the expense;

he was quite minded to sleep on the stones
rather than cost three napoleons for a bed;
that included, however, the pillow and bed-
stead, made of palm sticks,—very light and
comfortable.

Zeyneb has been very good ever since she
has been with us. I think the little Nubian
boy led her into idleness and mischief. She
will soon be a complete "drago-woman," for
she is fast learning Arabic from Omar and English from us. At Alexandria she only heard
a sort of *lingua franca* of Greek, Italian, Nubian, and English. She asked me, "How pic-
colo bint?" (how is the little girl?)—a fine
specimen of Alexandrian.

On Thursday evening I rode up to the Ab-
báseeyeh, and met all the schoolboys going
home for their Friday. Such a pretty sight!
The little Turks on grand horses with velvet
housings, and two or three Sáises running by
their side; and the Arab boys fetched, some
by proud fathers on handsome donkeys, some
by trusty servants on foot, some by poor mothers astride on shabby donkeys, and taking
up their darlings before them, some two and
three on one donkey, and crowds on foot,—

such a number of lovely faces! They were all dressed in white European-cut clothes and red tarbooshes.

Last night, we had a wedding opposite. The bridegroom, a pretty little boy of thirteen or so, with a friend of his own size—dressed, like him, in a scarlet robe and turban,—on each side, surrounded by men carrying tapers and singing songs, and preceded by cressets flaring, stepped along like Agag, slowly and mincingly, and looked very shy and pretty.

My poor Hasan (donkey-driver) is ill. His father came with the donkey for me, and kept drawing his sleeve over his eyes, and sighing so heavily, " Ya Hasan meskeen! ya Hasan Ibnee !" (O my son, my son !) and then in a resigned tone, " Allah kereem " (God is merciful)! I will go and see him this morning, and have a doctor to him, "by force," as Omar says he is very bad. There is something heart-rending in the patient helpless suffering of these people.

Sunday.—Aboo Hasan reported his son so much better that I did not go after him, having several things to do, and Omar being deep in cooking a *festin de Baltazar*, as I have people to dinner. The weather is delicious, much like what we had at Bournemouth in the summer; but there is a great deal of sickness, and I fear will be more, from people burying dead cattle in their premises inside the town. It costs a hundred guroosh to bury an ox out of the town. All labour is rendered scarce too, as well as food dear, and the streets are not cleaned, and water is hard to get. My Sakka comes very irregularly, and makes quite a favour of supplying us with water. All this must tell heavily on the poor. Hekekian's wife had seventy-four head of cattle on her farm; now one wretched bullock is left; of the seven to water the house in Cairo, also one only is left, and that is expected to die.

I have just been leaning out of the window to see two Coptic weddings, very gay and pretty, with lots of tapers and mesh'als (cressets). The bride dressed in white, veiled, and blazing with diamonds, was led by two men, and preceded by very pretty music,—abyatees, with harp, sackbut, and dulcimer, singing before her; and attended by little girls, in scarlet habarahs, as bridesmaids. It is gayer and less stately than the Muslim wedding.

Monday, November 16.

I am much better since I have been in a dry house. I have bought such a pretty cupboard for my clothes for seven dollars (45 francs), all painted over like the old Arab ceilings, in the colours and patterns of an Indian shawl. They make chests of the same work for from four to six dollars,—very handsome and effective, and not ill put together.

Haggee Alee has just been here, and offers me his tents if I like to go up to Thebes, and not live in a boat, so that I may not be dependent on the houses there, in case of any hitch. I fancy I might be very comfortable among the tombs of the kings, or in the valley of Assaseef, with good tents. It is never cold at all among the hills at Thebes, quite the contrary; on the sunny side of the valley, you are broiled and stunned with heat in January, and in the shade it is heavenly. I shall rather like the change from a boat life to a Bedawee one, with my own sheep and chickens and horses about the tent, and a small following of ragged retainers. Moreover, it will be cheaper.

LETTER XXVI.

Cairo, November 21, 1863.

I AM very comfortably installed here, and much better for the Cairo climate, after being damaged by staying a fortnight at Alexandria. There is terrible distress here, owing to the cattle-disease, which makes everything nearly double the usual price, and many things very hard to get at all. The weather is lovely, much like English summer, but finer; I shall stay on till it gets colder, and then go up the Nile, either in a steamer or a boat.

My poor donkey-driver, Hasan, is ill, and his old father takes his place; he gave me a fine illustration of Arab feeling towards women to-day. I asked if Abd-el-Kádir were coming here, as I had heard; he did not know, and asked me if he were not "Akhul-Benát" (a brother of girls)? I prosaically said, I did not know if he had sisters. "The Arabs, O Lady! call that man a 'brother of girls,' to whom God has given a clean heart to love all women as his sisters, and strength and courage to fight for their protection." Omar suggested a " thorough gentleman " as the equivalent of Aboo Hasan's title. European galimatias about "the smiles of the fair," etc., looks very mean beside " Akhul-Benát." Moreover they do carry it somewhat into common life. Omar told me of some little family tribulations, showing that he is not a little henpecked.

Here is another story. A man married at Alexandria and took home the daily provisions for the first week; after that, he neglected it for two days, and came home with a lemon in his hand. He asked for some dinner, and his wife placed the stool and the tray and the washing-basin and napkin, and on the tray the lemon cut in half. " Well, and the dinner ?" " Dinner!—you want dinner!—where from ? What man are you to want women, when you don't keep them! I am going now to the Kádee, to be divorced from you;" and she did. The man must provide all necessaries for his hareem, and if she has money or earns any, she spends it in dress. If she makes him a skull-cap or a handkerchief, he must pay for her work. All is not roses for these Eastern tyrants,—not to speak of the unbridled license of tongue allowed to women and children. Zeyneb hectors Omar, and I can't persuade him to check her. "How I say anything to it, that one child?" Of course the children are insupportable,—and, I fancy, the women little better.

A poor neighbour of mine lost his little boy yesterday, and came out into the street, as usual, for sympathy. He stood under my window, leaning his head against the wall, and sobbing and crying till literally his tears wetted the dust. He was too much grieved to tear off his turban or to lament in form, but clapped his hands and cried, " Oh, my boy! oh, my boy!" The bean-seller opposite shut his shop ; the dyer took no notice, but smoked his pipe. Some people passed on, but many stopped and stood round the poor man, saying nothing, but looking concerned. Two were well-dressed Copts on handsome donkeys, who dismounted, and all waited till he went home, when about twenty men accompanied him with a respectful air. How strange it seems to us to go out into the street, and call on the passers-by to grieve with one!

I was at the house of Hekekian Bey the other day, when he received a parcel from Constantinople from his former slave, now the Sultan's chief eunuch. It contained a very fine photograph of Shureyk Bey (that is his name), whose face, though negro, is very intelligent and of a charming expression; a present of illustrated English books, and some printed music composed by the Sultan Abdel-Azeez himself. *O tempora! O mores!* one was a waltz! Shureyk Bey was dressed in European clothes too, all but the tarboosh.

The very ugliest and scrubbiest of street-dogs has adopted me, like the Irishman who wrote to Lord Lansdowne that he had selected him as his patron; and he guards the house, and follows me in the streets. He is rewarded with scraps; and S—— cost me a new tin mug by letting the dog drink out of the old one, which is used to scoop the water from the jar; forgetting that Omar and Zeyneb could not drink after the poor beast.

Monday.—I went yesterday to the port of Cairo, Boolak, to see Hasaneyn Efendi about boats. He was gone up the Nile, and I sat with his wife,—a very nice Turkish lady, who speaks English to perfection,—and heard all sorts of curious things. The Turkish ladies are taking to stays! and the fashions of Constantinople are changing with fearful rapidity. Like all Eastern women that I have seen, my hostess complained of indigestion, and said she knew she ought to go out more and to walk,—but custom! "È contro *il nostro* decoro."

I have seen Deleo Bey, who advises me not to live in a tent; it is too hot by day, and too cold by night. So I will take a boat conditionally, with leave to keep it four months, or to discharge it at Thebes if I find a lodging. It is now a little fresh in the early morning, but like fine English summer weather. I ride on my donkey in a thin gown, and a thin white cloak; but about the middle of next month it will begin to get cold.

Tuesday evening.—Since I have been here, my cough is nearly gone, and I am the better for having good food again. Omar manages to get good mutton, and as he is an excellent cook, I have a good dinner every day, which I find makes a great difference. I have also discovered that some of the Nile fish is excellent: the bayád, which is sometimes as much as six or eight feet long and very fat, is delicious, and I am told there are still better kinds; the eels are very delicate and good too. The worst is, that everything is just double last year's price, as of course no beef can be eaten at all; and the draught oxen being dead, labour is become dear as well. The high Nile was a small misfortune compared to the murrain.

There is a legend about it, of course. A certain Sheykh-el-Beled (*bürgermeister*) of some place not named, lost his cattle, and being rich, defied God; said he did not care, and bought as many more. They died too, and he continued impenitent and defiant, and bought on till he was ruined; and now he is sinking into the earth bodily, though his friends dig and dig around him without ceasing, night and day.

It is curious, how like the Arab legends are to the German; all those about wasting bread wantonly are almost identical. If a bit is dirty, Omar carefully gives it to the dog; if clean, he keeps it in a drawer for making bread-crumbs for cutlets; not a bit must fall on the floor. In other things they are careless enough; but *das liebe Brod* is sacred; (*vide* Grimm's 'Deutsche Sagen'). I am constantly struck with resemblances to German customs. A Fellah wedding is very like a German *Bauernhochzeit,*—the firing of guns, and the display of household goods, only on a camel instead of a cart.

I have been trying to find a teacher of Arabic, but it is very hard to find one who knows any European language, and the consular dragomans ask four dollars a lesson! I must wait till I get to Thebes, where I think a certain young Saeed can teach me. Meanwhile, I am beginning to understand rather more, and to speak a little.

LETTER XXVII.

Cairo, December 1, 1863.

IT is beginning to be cold, comparatively cold, here; and I only await the result of my inquiries about possible houses at Thebes, to hire a boat and depart.

Yesterday I saw a camel go through the eye of a needle, *i. e.* the low-arched door of an enclosure. He must kneel and bow his head to creep through, and thus the rich man must humble himself. See how a false translation spoils a good metaphor, and turns a familiar simile into a ferociously communist sentiment.

I went to see poor Hasan, who is better, but very weak. The whole family were much pleased, and all had excellent manners. Hasan himself is one of the most winning persons I ever saw,—so gentle and courteous He is going to give a great Khatmeh for his recovery, and to kill the sheep for God and the poor, which his father had bought for his wedding.

There are rumours of troubles at Jeddah, and a sort of expectation of fighting somewhere next spring. Even here, I think, people are buying arms to a great extent; the gunsmiths' bazaar looks unusually lively.

Zeyneb has turned sulky, in consequence of the association at Alexandria with the Berber servants, who have instilled religious intolerance into her mind, poor child! I shall place her in a respectable Muslim family before I go. She is very clever, and may rise in life, with all the accomplishments of sewing, washing, etc., which she has now acquired. But we are Christian dogs, and she despises us, and Omar still more, I believe, for loving me. She pretends not to be able to eat, because she thinks everything is "pig." There is no conceit like *black* conceit. I am sorry her head has been so turned, but I see it is incurable. I suppose the Nubians thought it right to preach Islám to her, and to neutralize our evil teaching. I will offer her to Hekekian Bey, and if she does not do there in a household of black Muslim slaves, they must pass her on to a Turkish house. To keep a sullen face about me is more than I can endure, as I have shown her every possible kindness. How much easier is it to instil the bad part of religion than the good! It is really a curious phenomenon in so young a child. She waits capitally at table, and *can* do most things, but she won't move, if the fancy takes her, except when ordered, and spends her time on the terrace. One thing is, that the life is dull for a child, and I think she will be happier in a larger and more bustling house.

Omar performs wonders of marketing and cooking. I have excellent dinners—soup. fish, a *petit plat* or two, and a *rôti*, every day. But butter and meat and milk are horribly dear. I never saw so good a servant as Omar, and such a nice creature,—so pleasant and good. When I hear and see what other people spend here in travelling and in living, and what trouble they have, I say, " May God favour Omar and his descendants!"

Wednesday, 3rd.—I stayed in bed yesterday for a cold, and, I think, cured it. My next-door neighbour, a Coptic merchant, kept me awake all night by auditing his accounts with his clerk. How would you like to chant rows of figures? He had just bought lots of cotton, and I had to get into my door on Monday over a camel's back—the street being filled with bales.

I have sent a request to the French Consul-General, M. Tastu, to let me live in the French house over the temple at Thebes. It is quite empty, and would be the most comfortable, indeed the only comfortable one there. M. Tastu is the son of the charming poetess of that name, whom my mother knew at Paris.

LETTER XXVIII.

Cairo, December 17, 1863.

At last, I shall be off in a few days. I have had one delay after another. M. Tastu, the French Consul, has very kindly lent me the house at Thebes.

Boats are at a frightful price; nothing under £35 to Thebes alone. But M. M——, the agent to Haleem Pasha, is going up the Nile to Esneh, and will let me travel in the steamer which is to tow his dahabeeyeh. It will be dirty, but it will cost nothing, and take me out of this cold weather in five or six days. I have brought divans, tables, prayer carpets, blankets, a cupboard, a lovely old copper handbasin and ewer, and shall live in Arab style. The tables and four chairs are the only concession to European infirmity.

December 22.

I wrote the above five days ago, since when I have had no end of troubles. M. M—— is waiting in frantic impatience to set off, and so am I; but Ismaeel Pasha keeps him from day to day. The worry of depending on any one in the East is beyond belief. To-morrow morning, I am to know definitively whether I am to sail in three or four days. It feels very cold to me, though you would think it warm; much like an English September. But the want of fires makes one very chilly. For four hours in the day the sun is hot, but the nights are cold and sometimes damp.

You would have laughed to hear me buying a carpet yesterday. I saw an old broker with one on his shoulder in the Hamzawee bazaar, and asked the price. Eight napoleons. Then it was unfolded and spread in the street, to the great inconvenience of passers-by, just in front of a coffee shop. I look at it superciliously, and say, "Three hundred piastres, O uncle!" The poor old broker cries out in despair to the gentlemen sitting outside the coffee shop: "O Muslims, hear that, and look at this excellent carpet; three hundred piastres!

by the faith, it is worth two thousand!" But the gentlemen take my part, and one mildly says, "I wonder that an old man as thou art should tell us that the lady, who is a traveller and a person of experience, values it at three hundred. Thinkest thou we will give thee more?" Then another suggests that "if the lady will consent to give four napoleons, he had better take them;" and that settles it. Everybody gives an opinion here, and the price is fixed by a sort of improvised jury.

Christmas Day, Evening.

At last my departure is fixed. I embark to-morrow afternoon at Boolák, and we sail, or steam rather, on Sunday morning quite early, and expect to reach Thebes in eight days.

I heard a curious illustration of Arab manners to-day. I met Hasan, the janissary of the American Consulate, a very respectable, good man. He told me had married another wife since last year. I asked, What for?

It was the widow of his brother, who had always lived in the same house with him, like one family, and who died, leaving two boys.

She is neither young nor handsome, but he considered it his duty to provide for her and the children, and not let her marry a stranger. So you see that polygamy is not always sensual indulgence; and a man may thus practise greater self-sacrifice than by talking sentiment about deceased wives' sisters. I said, laughing, to Omar, as we went on, that I did not think the two wives sounded very comfortable. " Oh no! not comfortable at all for the man, but he take care of the woman; that is what is proper. That is the good Muslim."

I shall have the company of a Turkish Efendi on my voyage,—a Commissioner of Inland Revenue, in fact,—going to look after the tax-gatherers in the Saeed. I wonder whether he will be civil. An Englishman bred at Constantinople is immensely astonished at the civility of the Arabs, and at their not abusing Christians. He says that it is not so at Constantinople, where " unwashed infidel dog " is a common salutation. He quite stared at Omar buttoning my boots. Such a prodigious condescension from a "True Believer" to a Christian woman! His eating too with my maid is more than a Turk would do, it seems.

S—— is gone with a party of English servants to the Virgin's tree, the great picnic frolic of Cairene Christians, and, indeed, of Muslims also at some seasons.

Omar is gone to a Khatmeh (a reading of the Koran), at Hasan the donkey-boy's house. I was asked, but am afraid of the night air. A good deal of religious celebration goes on now, the middle of the month of Regeb, six weeks before Ramadán. I rather dread Ramadán, as Omar is sure to be faint and ill, and everybody else cross during the first five days or so; then their stomachs get into training.

The new passenger-steamers have been promised ever since the 6th, and will not now go till after the races, the 6th or 7th of next month. Fancy, the Cairo races! It is growing dreadfully cockney here; I must go to Timbuctoo.

And we are to have a railway to Mecca, and take return tickets for the Haj—from all parts of the world.

LETTER XXIX.

Boolák, evening, December 27, 1863.
On board a River steamboat.

After infinite delays and worries, we are at last on board and shall sail to-morrow morning. After all was comfortably settled, Ismaeel Pasha sent for *all* the steamers up to Er-Ródah, near Minyeh; and, at the same time, ordered a Turkish general to come up instantly somehow. So Lateef Pasha, the head of the steamers, had to turn me out of the best cabin; and if I had not come myself and taken rather forcible possession of the forecastle cabin, the servants of the Turkish general would not have allowed Omar to embark the baggage. He had been waiting on the bank all the morning in despair. But at four I arrived, and ordered the hammáls to carry the goods into the fore-cabin, and walked on board myself, where the Arab captain pantomimically placed me in his right eye and on the top of his head. Once installed, my cabin has become a hareem, and I may defy the Turkish Efendi with success. I have got a good-sized cabin, with clean divans round three sides for S—— and myself. Omar will sleep on deck, and cook where he can. A poor Turkish lady is to inhabit a sort of dust-hole by the side of my cabin. If she seems decent, I will entertain her hospitably. There is no furniture of any sort but the divan; and we cook our own food, bring our own candles, jugs, basins, beds, everything. If I were not such a complete Arab, I should think it very miserable; but, as things stand this year, I think myself lucky it is no worse.

The promised passenger-boats go on being promised, and that is all. They asked me £35 for a bad dahabeeyeh only to Thebes. The rush of travellers is enormous. Luckily it is a very warm night, and we can make our arrangements unchilled. There is no door to the cabin, so we nail up an old plaid; and as no one ever looks into a hareem, it is quite enough. The boat is not so clean as an

English, but very much less dirty than a French one. All on board are Arabs; captain, engineer, and men. An English Sitt is a novelty on board, and the captain is unhappy that things are not *à la Franca* for me. We are to tow two dahabeeyehs. Only fancy the Queen ordering all the river steamers up to Windsor! At Minyeh the Turkish general leaves us, and we shall have the boat to ourselves; so the captain has just been down to tell me.

See what a strange combination of people float on old Father Nile: two Englishwomen, one Levantine (Madame M——), one Frenchman, Turks, Arabs, Negroes, Circassians, and men from Darfoor,—all in one party; perhaps the other boats contain some other strange element. There are seven women in the engine room, among them a Bey's wife, who wanted to share my cabin, but our good old captain would not let her. The Turks are from Constantinople, and can't speak Arabic, and make faces at the muddy river-water, which, indeed, I would rather have filtered.

I must now leave off and go to bed, for I am tired with my day's scuffle, and with writing on my knees.

LETTER XXX.

On board the steamer, near Asyoot,
Sunday, January 3, 1864.

WE left Cairo last Sunday morning, and a wonderfully queer company we were. I had been promised all the steamer to myself; but owing to Ismaeel Pasha's caprices, our little steamer had to do the work of three; *i. e.* to carry passengers, to tow M. M——'s dahabee-yeh, and to tow the oldest, dirtiest, queerest Nubian boat, in which the young son of the Sultan of Darfoor, and the Sultan's envoy, a handsome black of Dongola (not a negro), had visited Ismaeel Pasha. The best cabin was taken by a sulky old one-eyed Turkish Pasha, so I had the fore-cabin, luckily a large one, where I slept on one divan, S—— on the other, and Omar at my feet. He tried sleeping on deck, but the Pasha's Arnaouts were too bad company, and the captain begged me to "cover my face," and let my servant sleep at my feet. Besides, there was a poor old asthmatical Turkish Efendi going to collect the taxes, and many women and children in the engine-room. It would have been insupportable, but for the hearty politeness of the Arab captain, a regular "old salt;" and, owing to his attention and care, it was only very amusing. At Benee-Suweyf, the first town above Cairo—about seventy miles—we found no coals; the Pasha had been up, and had taken them all. So we kicked our heels on the bank all day, with the prospect of doing so for a week.

The captain brought H.R.H. of Darfoor to visit me and begged me to make him hear reason about the delay; as I, being English, must know that a steamer could not go without coals. H. R. H. was a pretty imperious little nigger, about eleven or twelve, dressed in a yellow silk kaftán and a scarlet burnus, who cut the good old captain short by saying, "Why, she is a woman, she can't talk to me!"

"Wallah! wallah! What a way to talk to

English Hareem!" shrieked the captain, who was about to lose his temper. But I had a happy idea, and produced a box full of French sweetmeats, which altered the young prince's views at once. I asked him if he had brothers;—"Who can count them? they are like mice." He said that the Pasha had given him only a few presents, and was evidently not pleased. Some of his suite are the most formidable-looking wild beasts in human shape I ever beheld; bull-dogs and wild boars, black as ink, red-eyed, and, ye gods! such jaws and throats and teeth! others like monkeys, with arms down to their knees. The Illyrian Arnaouts on board our boat are revoltingly white, like fish or drowned people,—no red in the tallowy skin at all. There were Greeks also, who left us at Minyeh (the second large town), and the old Pasha left us this morning at Er-Ródah.

The captain at once ordered all my goods into the cabin he had left, and turned out the Turkish Efendi, who wanted to stay with us. He said he was an old man and sick, and my company would be agreeable to him; then he said he was ashamed before the people to be turned out by an Englishwoman. So I was very civil, and begged him to pass the day and to dine with me, which set all right; and now, after dinner, he has gone off quite pleasantly to the fore-cabin, and left me here. I have a stern cabin, a saloon, and an anteroom; and we are comfortable enough,—only the fleas! Never till now did I know what fleas could be. I send a dish from my table every day henceforth to the captain; as I take the place of the pasha, it is part of my dignity to do so; and as I occupy the kitchen, and burn the ship's coals, I may as well let the captain dine a little at my expense. In the day I go up and sit in his cabin on deck, and we talk as well as we can without an interpreter. The old fellow says he is sixty-seven, but does not look more than forty-five. He has just the air and manner of a seafaring man with us, and has been wrecked four times,—the last, in the Black Sea, during the Crimean war, when he was taken prisoner by the Russians and sent to Moscow, where he remained for three years, until the peace. He has a charming boy of eleven with him, and he tells me he has twelve children in all, but only one wife, and is as strict a monogamist as Dr. Primrose; he told me he should not marry again if she died; nor, he believed, would she give him a successor.

There are a good many Copts on board of a rather low class, and not pleasant. The Christian gentlemen are very pleasant, but the low are low indeed, compared to the Muslims; and one gets a feeling of dirtiness about them, when one sees them eat all among the coals, and then squat down there and pull out their beads to pray, without washing their hands even. It does look nasty, when compared to the Muslim coming up clean washed, and standing erect and manly-looking to his prayers. Besides, they are coarse in their manners and conversation, and have not the Arab respect for women. I only speak of the common people, not of educated Copts. The best fun is to hear the Greeks abusing the Copts,—rogues, heretics, schismatics from the Greek Church, ignorant, rapacious, cunning, impudent, etc. etc.; in short, they narrate the whole fable about their own sweet selves.

I am quite surprised to see how well the men manage their work. The boat is nearly

as clean as an English boat, equally crowded,
could be kept, and the engine in beautiful order.
The head engineer, Ahmad Efendi, and indeed
the captain and all the crew, wear English
clothes, and use the universal "all right," " turn
her head," "*forreh* (full) speed," " half speed,"
" stop her," etc.   I was diverted to hear " All
right, go ahead, el Fat'hah !" in one breath.
Here we always say the Fat'hah (first chapter
of the Koran, nearly identical with the Lord's
Prayer) on starting on a journey, concluding
a bargain, etc. etc.   The combination was very
quaint.

Already the climate has changed: the air
is sensibly drier and clearer, and the weather
much warmer; and we are not yet at Asyoot.
I remarked last year that the climate changed
most at Kiné, forty miles below Thebes.   The
banks are terribly broken and washed away
by the inundation; the Nile is even now far
higher than it was six weeks earlier last
year.   At Benee-Suweyf, which used to be the
great cattle place, not a buffalo was left, and
we could not get a drop of milk; but since
we left Minyeh, we see them again, and I hear
the disease is not spreading up the river.

Omar told me that the poor people at Bence-Suweyf were complaining of the drought and of the prospect of scarcity, as they could no longer water the land for want of oxen.

I paid ten napoleons passage-money, and shall give four or five more as baksheesh, as I have given a good deal of trouble with all my luggage, bedding, furniture, provisions, etc., for four months, and the boat's people have been more than civil—really kind and attentive to us; but a bad dahabeeyeh would have cost £40, so I am greatly the gainer. Nothing can exceed the muddle, uncertainty, and carelessness of the "administration" at Cairo: no coals at the depôts; boats announced to sail, and dawdling on for three weeks; no order, and no care for anybody's convenience but the Pasha's. But the subordinates on board the boats do their work perfectly well. We go only half as quickly as we ought, because we have two very heavy dahabeeyehs in tow instead of one; but no time is lost. As long as the light lasts on we go, and start again as soon as the moon rises.

The people on board have promoted me in rank, and call me " El-Emeereh," an obsolete

Arab title, which the engineer thinks is the equivalent for " Ladysheep;" Sittee, he said, was the same as "Missees." I don't know how he acquired his ideas on the subject of English precedence.

Omar has just come in with coffee, and begs me to give his best salám to his big master and his little master and lady ; and not to forget to tell them he is their servant, and my memlook (slave) " from one hand to the other" (*i.e.* the whole body).

At Kiné we must try to find time to buy two filters and some gullehs (water-coolers). They are made there: at Thebes nothing can be got.

LETTER XXXI.

January 5, 1864.

WE left Asyoot this afternoon. The captain had announced that we should start at ten o'clock (four, Arab time), so I did not go into the town, but sent Omar to buy food. But the men of Darfoor all went off, declaring that they would stop, and promising to cut off the captain's head if he went without them. Hasan Efendi, the Turk, was furious, and threatened to telegraph his complaints to Cairo if the boat did not go directly, and the poor captain was in a sad predicament. He appealed to me, peaceably sitting on the trunk of a palm-tree with some poor Fellaheen (of whom more anon). I uttered the longest sentence I could compose in Arabic, to the effect that he was captain, and while on the boat we were all bound to obey him.

" Máshá-alláh ! one English hareem is more than ten men for sense ; these Inkeleez have only one word both for themselves and for other people,—dughree-dughree (Right is right). This Emeereh is ready to obey like a memlook, and when she has to command— whew !" with a most expressive toss back of the head.

The bank was crowded with poor Fellaheen, who had been taken for soldiers, and sent to await the Pasha's arrival at Girgeh. Three weeks they lay there, and were then sent down to Soohay. (The Pasha wanted to see them himself, and pick out the men he liked.) Eight days more at Soohay, then to Asyoot ; eight days more, and meanwhile Ismaeel Pasha has gone back to Cairo, and the poor souls may wait indefinitely, for no one will venture to remind the Pasha of their trifling existence ; Wallah ! wallah !

While I was walking on the bank with Monsieur and Madame M——, who joined me, a person came up, whose appearance puzzled me, and saluted them. Don't call me a Persian, when I tell you it was an eccentric Bedawee young lady. She was eighteen or twenty at most, dressed like a young man, but small and feminine, and rather pretty, except that one eye was blind. Her dress was handsome, and she had women's jewels, and a European watch and chain; her manner was excellent, quite *ungenirt*, yet not the least impudent or swaggering; and I was told—indeed I could hear—that her language was beautiful,—a thing much esteemed among Arabs. She is unmarried, and fond of travelling, and of men's society, being very intelligent; so she has her dromedary and goes about quite alone. No one seemed astonished, no one stared; and when I asked if it was proper, our captain was surprised. "Why not? If she does not wish to marry, she can go alone; if she does, she can marry. What harm? She is a virgin, and free." She expressed her opinions pretty freely, as far as I could understand her. Madame M—— had heard of her before, and said she was much respected and admired. Monsieur M—— had heard she was a spy of the Pasha's; but the people on board the boat here say that the truth is, that she went before Saeed Pasha herself to complain of some tyrannical Mudeer, who ground and imprisoned the Fellaheen,—a bold thing for a girl to do. Anyhow she seemed to me far the most curious thing I have yet seen.

The weather is already much warmer; it is nine in the evening, and we are steaming along, and I sit with the cabin-window open. To-day, for the first time, I pulled my cloak over my head in the sun,—it was so stinging hot,—quite delicious, and it is the 5th of January. Our captain declares that during the three years he was prisoner at Moscow and at Bakshi Serai, he never saw the sun at all;—hard lines for an Egyptian. Luckily we left all the fleas behind us in the fore-cabin, for the benefit of the poor old Turk, who, I hear, suffers severely. The divans are all bran-new, and the fleas must have come in the cotton stuffing, for there are no live things of any sort in the rest of the boat.

Girgeh, Thursday, January 7.

We have just put in here for the night. To-day we took on board three convicts in chains, two bound for Feyzóghloo,—one for calumny and perjury, and one for manslaughter;—hard labour for life in that climate will soon dispose of them; the third is a petty thief from Kiné, who has been a year in chains in the custom-house of Alexandria, and is now being taken back to be shown in his own place in his chains. The *causes célèbres* of this country would be curious reading; their manner of doing their crimes is so different from ours. If I can get hold of any one who can relate a few cases well, I will write them down; Omar has told me a few, but he may not know the details accurately.

I made further inquiry about the Bedawee lady, who is older than she looks, for she has travelled constantly for ten years. She is rich, and much respected, and received in all the best houses, where she sits with the men all day and sleeps in the hareem. She has been into the interior of Africa and to Mecca, and, I hear, speaks Turkish, and is extremely agreeable,—full of interesting information about all the countries she has visited. As soon as I can talk, I must try to find her out; she likes the company of Europeans.

Here is a contribution to "folklore," new even to Lane, I think. When the coffee-seller lights his stove in the morning he makes two cups of coffee of the best, and nicely sugared, and pours them out, all over the stove, saying, "God bless, or favour, Sheykh Shádhilee and his descendants." The blessing on the saint who invented coffee of course I knew, and often utter, but the libation is new to me. You see the ancient religion crops up, even through the severe faith of Islam. If I could describe all the details of an Arab, and still more, of a Coptic wedding, you would think I was relating the mysteries of Isis. At one house I saw the bride's father looking pale and anxious, and Omar said, "I think he wants to hold his stomach with both hands till the women tell him if his daughter makes his face white;"—it was such a good phrase for the sinking at heart of anxiety! It certainly seems more reasonable that a woman's misconduct should blacken her father's face than her husband's.

There are a good many things about "hareem" here, which I am barbarian enough to think extremely good and rational. I heard from an ear-witness a conversation which passed between an old Turk of Cairo, and a young Englishman, who politely chaffed him about Muslim license. Upon this the venerable Turk, who had been in Europe, asked some questions as to the nature and number of the Englishman's relations to women, which the latter was wholly unable to answer.

" Well, young man," said the Turk, " I am old, and was married at twelve; and I have *seen*, in all my life, seven women; four are dead, and three are happy and comfortable in my house. *Where are all yours?*" (As a woman is never seen but by her husband or possessor, the word has acquired another meaning.)

I find that the criminal convicted of calumny, accused (together with twenty-nine others, not in custody) the Sheykh-el-Beled of his village, of murdering his servant, and produced a basketful of bones as proof; but the Sheykh produced the living man, and his detractor gets hard labour for life. The proceeding is characteristic of the childish *ruse* of this country. I inquired whether the thief who was dragged in chains through the streets would be able to find work, and was told, " Oh, certainly,—is he not a poor man? for the sake of God every one will be ready to help him."

An absolute uncertainty of justice naturally leads to this result. Our captain was quite shocked to find that in my country we did not like to employ a returned convict.

Luxor, Monday.

We spent all the afternoon of Saturday at Kiné, where I dined with the English consul, a worthy old Arab, who also invited our captain, and we sat round his copper tray on the floor, and ate with our fingers, the Captain, who sat next me, picking out the best bits with his brown fingers and feeding me with them. After dinner, the French consul, a Copt, sent to invite me to a fantasia at his house, where I found the M——s, the Mudeer and some other Turks, and an ill-bred Italian. I was glad to see the dancing-girls, but I liked old Seyyid Ahmad's patriarchal ways much better than the tone of the Frenchified Copt. At first I thought the dancing queer and dull. One girl was very handsome, but cold and uninteresting; one who sang was also pretty and engaging; but the dancing consisted of contortions, more or less graceful,—very wonderful as a gymnastic feat, but no more. But the captain called out to one Lateefeh, an ugly, clumsy-looking wench, to show the Sitt what she could do, and then it was revealed to me. The ugly girl started on her feet, and became the " serpent of old Nile,"—the head, shoulders, and arms eagerly bent forward, waist in and haunches advanced on the bent knees,— the posture of a cobra about to spring. I could not call it voluptuous, any more than Racine's 'Phèdre;' it is "Vénus toute entière à sa proie attachée," and to me seemed tragic. It is far more realistic than the fandango, and far less coquettish, because the thing represented is *au grand sérieux,*—not travestied, *gazé,* or played with ; and like all such things, the Arab men don't think it the least improper. Of course the girls do not commit any indecorums before European women, except the dance itself.

Seyyid Ahmad would have given me a fantasia, but he feared I might have men with me ; he had had great annoyance from two Englishmen, who behaved in such a manner to the girls that he was obliged to turn them out of his house, after hospitably entertaining them.

Our procession home to the boat was very

droll: Madame M—— could not ride on an Arab saddle, so I lent her mine and *enfourchéd* my donkey; and away we went, with men running before us with mesh'als (fire-baskets on long poles) and lanterns, and the captain shouting out " full speed " and such English phrases all the way, like a regular old salt as he is.

We got here last night, and this morning Mustafa Agha and the Názir came down to conduct me up to my palace. I have such a big rambling house, all over the top of the temple of Khem; how I wish I had you and the children to fill it! We had about twenty fellahs to clean the dust of three years' accumulation, and my room looks quite handsome with carpets and a divan. Mustafa's little girl found her way here when she heard I was come, and it was so pleasant to have her playing on the carpet with a doll and some sugar-plums, and making a feast for Dolly on a saucer, arranging the sugar-plums Arab fashion; such a quiet little brown tot, curiously like R——, with the addition of walnut juice. She was extremely pleased with R——'s picture and kissed it.

The view all round my house is magnificent

on every side; across the Nile in front, facing N.W., and over a splendid expanse of green and a range of distant orange-buff hills to the S.E., where I have a spacious covered terrace. It is rough and dusty in the extreme, but will be very pleasant. Mustafa came in just now to offer me the loan of a horse, and to ask me to go to the mosque a few nights hence, to see the illumination in honour of a great sheykh, a descendant of Seedee Hoseyn or Hasan. I asked whether my presence might not offend any Muslim, but he would not hear of such a thing. The sun set while he was there, and he asked if I objected to his praying in my presence; on my replying in the negative, he went through his four rek'ahs very comfortably on my carpet.

My next-door neighbour (across the court-yard, all filled with antiquities) is a nice little Copt, who looks like an antique statue himself; I shall *voisiner* with his family. He sent me coffee as soon as I arrived, and came to help. I am invited to El-Mutáneh, a few hours up the river, to visit the M——s, and to Kiné to visit Seyyid Ahmad, and also the head of the merchants there, who settled the price of a carpet for me in the bazaar, and seemed to like me. He was just one of those handsome, high-bred, elderly merchants, with whom a story always begins in the Arabian Nights. A very nice English couple gave me a breakfast in their boat.

When I can talk, I will go and see an Arab hareem. I asked Mustafa about the Arab young lady; he spoke very highly of her, and is to let me know if she comes here, and to offer her hospitality from me; he did not know her name. She is called " El Hajjeeyeh," the pilgrimess.

Thursday.

Now I am settled in my Theban palace it seems more and more beautiful, and I am quite melancholy that you cannot be here to enjoy it. The house is very large, and has good thick walls, the comfort of which we feel to-day, for it blows a hurricane, but in-doors it is not at all cold. I have glass windows and doors to some of the rooms; it is a lovely dwelling. Two funny little owls, as big as my fist, live in the wall under my window, and come and peep in, walking on tiptoe and looking inquisitive, like the owls in the hieroglyphics, and barking at me like young puppies; and a splendid horus (the sacred hawk) frequents my lofty balcony. Another of my contemplar gods I sacrilegiously killed last night,—a whip snake. Omar is rather in consternation, for fear it should be "the snake of thè house;" for Islam has not dethroned the "Dii Lares et tutelares."

Some men came to mend the staircase, which had fallen in, and which consists of huge solid blocks of stone. One man crushed his thumb, and I had to operate on it. It is extraordinary how these people bear pain; he never winced in the least, and went off thanking God and the lady quite cheerfully. I have been "sapping" at the "Alif Bay"—A B C —to-day, under the direction of Sheykh Yoosuf, a graceful, sweet-looking young man, with a dark-brown face, and such fine manners in his fellah dress,—a coarse brown woollen shirt, a libdeh or felt skull-cap, and a common red shawl round his head and shoulders. Writing the wrong way is very hard work.

It was curious to see Sheykh Yoosuf blush from shyness when he came in first;

it shows quite as much in the coffee-brown
Arab skin as in the fairest European,—quite
unlike that of the much lighter coloured mulatto or Malay, who never change colour at all.
A photographer, who is living here, showed
me photographs done high up the White
Nile. One negro girl is so splendid, that I
must get him to do me a copy to send you.
She is not perfect like the Nubians, but so superbly strong and majestic. If I can get hold
of a handsome Fellaheh here, I will get her
photographed, to show you in Europe what a
woman's breast can be, for I never knew it
before I came here; it is the most beautiful
thing in the world, and gloriously independent of stays or any support.

LETTER XXXII.

January 20, 1864.

WE have had a week of piercing winds, and I have been obliged to stay in bed. To-day was fine again, and I mounted old Mustafa's cob pony and jogged over his farm with him, and lunched on delicious sour cream and fateerch at a neighbouring village, to the great delight of the fellaheen. It was more biblical than ever; the people were all relations of Mustafa's, and to see Seedee Omar, the head of the household, and the young men coming in from the field, and the flocks and herds and camels and asses, was like a beautiful dream. All these people are of good blood, and a sort of "roll of Battle" is kept for the genealogies of the noble Arabs who came in with Amr, the first Arab conqueror and lieutenant of Omar. Not one of these brown men who do not own a second shirt, would give his brown daughter to the greatest Turkish Pasha. This country *noblesse* is more interesting to me by far than the town people, though Omar, who is quite a cockney and piques himself on being " delicate," turns up his nose at their beggarly pride, as Londoners used to do at " barelegged Highlanders." The air of perfect equality (except as to the respect due to the head of the clan) with which the villagers treated Mustafa, and which he fully returned, made it all seem so very gentlemanlike. They are not so dazzled by a little show, and are far more manly than the Cairenes. I am already on visiting terms with the " county families " resident near Luxor. The Názir (magistrate) is a very nice person, and my Sheykh Yoosuf, who is of the highest blood (being descended from Abu-l-Hajjáj himself), is quite charming.

There is an intelligent German here as Austrian consul, who draws nicely. I went into his house, and was startled by hearing a pretty little Arab boy, his servant, say, " Soll ich den Kaffee bringen ?" What next ? They are all mad to learn languages, and Mustafa begs me and S—— to teach his little child, Zeyneb, English.

Friday, January 22.

Yesterday, I rode over to Karnac with Mustafa's Sais running by my side; glorious hot sun and delicious air. To hear the Sais chatter away, his tongue running as fast as his feet, made me deeply envious of his lungs. Mustafa joined me, and pressed me to go to visit the sheykh's tomb for the benefit of my health, as he and Sheykh Yoosuf wished to say a Fat'hah for me; but I must not drink wine that day. I made a little difficulty on the score of difference of religion, but Sheykh Yoosuf, who came up, said he presumed I worshipped God and not stones, and that sincere prayers were good anywhere. Clearly the bigotry would have been on my side if I had refused any longer, so in the evening I went with Mustafa.

It was a very curious sight: the little dome illuminated with as much oil as the mosque could afford, over the tombs of Abu-l-Hajjáj and his three sons. A magnificent old man, like Father Abraham himself, dressed in white, sat on a carpet at the foot of the tomb; he was the head of the family of Abu-l-Hajjáj. He made me sit by him, and was extremely polite. Then came the Názir, the Kádee, a Turk travelling on government business, and a few other gentlemen, who all sat down round us, after kissing the hand of the old sheykh. Every one talked; in fact, it was a *soirée* in honour of the dead sheykh. A party of men sat at the further end of the place, with their faces to the kibleh, and played on a darabukkeh (sort of small drum stretched over an earthenware funnel, which gives a peculiar sound), a tambourine without bells, and little tinkling cymbals(seggal), fitting on thumb and finger (crotales), and chanted songs in honour of Mohammad, and verses from the Psalms of David. Every now and then, one of our party left off talking, and prayed a little or counted his beads. The old sheykh sent for coffee and gave me the first cup,—a wonderful concession; at last the Nazir proposed a Fat'hah for me, which the whole group round me repeated aloud, and then each said to me: —"Our Lord God bless thee, and give thee health and peace, to thee and thy family, and take thee back safe to thy master and thy children;" every one adding "Ameen" and giving the salám with the hand. I returned it and said, "Our Lord reward thee and all people of kindness to strangers," which was considered a very proper answer.

After that we went away, and the worthy Názir walked home with me to take a pipe and a glass of sherbet and enjoy a talk about his wife and eight children, who are all in Fum-el-Bahr, except two boys at school in Cairo. Government appointments are so precarious, that it is not worth while to move his family up here, as the expense would be too heavy on a salary of £15 a month, with the chance of recall any day.

I ought to add that in Cairo or Lower Egypt, it would be quite impossible for a Christian to enter a sheykh's tomb at all,—above all on his birthday festival, and on the night of Friday.

Friday, January 29.

The last week has been very cold here, the thermometer 59° and 60°, with a nipping wind and bright sun. I was obliged to keep my bed for three or four days, as a palace without doors or windows to speak of was very trying, though far better than a boat. Yesterday and to-day are better,—not much warmer, but a different air. The Moolid (festival) of the sheykh terminated last Saturday with a procession, in which the new cover of his tomb, and the ancient sacred boat, were carried on men's shoulders; it all seemed to have walked out of the royal tombs, only dusty and shabby instead of gorgeous. These festivals of the dead are such as Herodotus alludes to as held in honour of " him whose name he dares not mention ;"—" him who sleeps in Philæ," only the name is changed, and the mummy is absent. For a fortnight every one who had a horse and could ride, came and "made fantasia" every afternoon for two hours before sunset, and very pretty it was. The people here show their good blood in their riding.

For the last three days, all strangers were entertained with bread and cooked meat, at the expense of the Luxor people. Every house killed a sheep and baked bread. As I could not do that for want of servants enough, I sent

100 piastres (about twelve shillings) to the servants of Abu-l-Hajjáj at the mosque, to pay for the oil burnt at the tomb, etc. I was not well, and in bed, but I hear that my gift gave great satisfaction, and that I was again well prayed for.

The Coptic bishop came to see me, but he is a tipsy old monk. He sent for tea, alleging that he was ill, so I went to see him, and quickly perceived that his disorder was too much arakee. He has a very nice black slave, a Christian, who is a friend of Omar's, and sent him a handsome dinner, all ready cooked; among other things, a chicken stuffed with green wheat was excellent. Omar constantly gets dinners sent him,—bread, some dates, and cooked fowls or pigeons, and fatcereh with honey, all tied up hot in a cloth. I gave an old fellow a pill and dose some days ago, but his *dura ilia* took no notice, and he came for more and got castor oil. I have not seen him since, but his employer, Fellah Omar, sent me some delicious butter in return. I think it shows great intelligence in these people that none of them will any longer consult an Arab hakeem, if they can get a European to physic

them.   They now ask directly whether the
government doctors have been to Europe to
learn " hekmeh," and, if not, they don't trust
them.   For poor " savages " and " heathens "
this is not so stupid.   I had to interrupt my
lessons from illness, but Sheykh Yoosuf came
again last night.   I have mastered some things.
Oh, dear! what must poor Arab children suffer
in learning A, B, C! it is a terrible alphabet,
and the shekel, or points, are distracting.

You may conceive how much we are natu-
ralized, when I tell you I have received a serious
offer of marriage for S———.   Mustafa Agha, the
richest and most considerable person here, has
requested me to " give her to him " for his
eldest son, Seyyid, a nice lad of nineteen or
twenty at most.   He said, that of course, she
would keep to her own religion and her own
customs.   I said she was too old, but they
think that no objection at all.   She will have
to say that her father would not allow it, for
a handsome offer deserves a civil refusal.
S———'s proposals would be quite an ethnolo-
gical study.   Mustafa asked what I should require as dowry for her.

The young Englishmen to whom my mother

gave letters met me yesterday in the street. I knew Mr. S—— from his likeness to his mother. They were drawing the ruins. They go up the river to-morrow, and I will give them a dinner when they come down again, Arab fashion, and let them eat with their fingers. I have not knives and forks enough for more than two people, so I will borrow a copper tray and serve *à l'Arabe*.

I should like to give them a fantasia, but it is not proper for a woman to send for the dancing-girls; and as I am the friend of the Mamoor Maohn (the police magistrate), the Kádee, and the respectable people here, I cannot do what is indecorous in their eyes. It is quite enough that they tolerate my unveiled face and my associating with men; that is " my custom," and they think no harm of it.

I am so charmed with my house that I begin seriously to contemplate staying here all the time; Cairo is so dear now, and so many dead cattle are buried there, that I think I should do better in this place. There is a huge hall here, so large and cold now as to be uninhabitable, which in summer would be glorious. I could only afford a very poky lodging in Cairo, and here I shall live for a trifle in comfort and save the expense of boat hire; moreover, the complete quiet would suit me better than travelling. My dear old captain of steamer No. 12 will bring me up coffee and candles, and if I " sap," and learn to talk to the people, I shall have plenty of company.

The cattle disease has not extended above Minyeh to any great degree, and here there has not been a case. Food is very good here, at rather less than half Cairo prices even now; in summer it will be half that. Mustafa urges me to stay, and proposes picnics of a few days over in the tombs, with his hareem, as a diversion.

I send you a photograph of my two beloved lonely palm-trees on the river-bank just above Philæ. I send you also the seal and names of Abraham and all the family buried in the tomb of Machpelah. It is, of course, a " hegáb " (talisman).

LETTER XXXIII.

Sunday, February 7, 1864.

WE have had our winter pretty sharp for three weeks, and everybody has had violent colds and coughs,—the Arabs I mean. I have been a good deal ailing, but have escaped any violent cold altogether, and now the thermometer is up to 64°, and it feels very pleasant. In the sun it is always very hot, but that does not prevent the air from being keen, and chapping lips and noses, and even hands. It is curious how a temperature which would be summer in England makes one shiver at Thebes; El-hamdu-lilláh, it is over now!

My poor Sheykh Yoosuf is in great distress about his brother, also a young sheykh (*i. e.* one learned in theology, and competent to preach in the mosque). Sheykh Mohammad

N

is come home from studying in El-Azhar at
Cairo,—I fear, to die. I went with Sheykh
Yoosuf, at his desire, to see if I could help
him, and found him gasping for breath, and
very, very ill; I gave him a little soothing
medicine, and put mustard plasters on him,
and as they relieved him, I went again and repeated them. All the family and a number
of neighbours crowded in to look on. There
he lay in a dark little den with bare mud-
walls, worse off, to our ideas, than any pauper
in England; but these people do not feel the
want of comforts, and one learns to think it
quite natural to sit with perfect gentlemen in
places inferior to our cattle-sheds. I pulled
some blankets up against the wall, and put
my arm behind Sheykh Mohammad's back, to
make him rest while the poultices were on
him; whereupon he laid his green turbaned
head on my shoulder, and presently held up
his delicate brown face for a kiss, like an affectionate child. As I kissed him, a very pious
old moollah said " Bismilláh!" (In the name
of God!) with an approving nod, and Sheykh
Mohammad's old father (a splendid old man
in a green turban) thanked me with " effu-

sion," and prayed that my children might always find help and kindness. I suppose if I
confessed to kissing a " dirty Arab " in a hovel,
civilized people would execrate me ; but it
shows how much there is in "Muslim bigotry,"
" unconquerable hatred of Christians," etc. ; for
this family are Seyyids (descendants of the Prophet), and very pious. Sheykh Yoosuf does not
even smoke, and he preaches on Fridays.

I rode over to a village a few days ago, to
see a farmer named Omar; of course I had
to eat, and the people were enchanted at my
going alone, as they are used to see the English
armed and guarded. Seedee Omar, however,
insisted on accompanying me home, which is
the civil thing here. He piled a whole stack
of green fodder on his little nimble donkey,
and hoisted himself atop of it without saddle
or bridle, (the fodder was for Mustafa Agha,)
and we trotted home across the beautiful green
barley-fields, to the amazement of some European young men who were out shooting.
We did look a curious pair certainly, with
my English saddle and bridle, habit, and hat
and feather, on horseback, and Seedee Omar's
brown shirt, bare legs, and white turban, guid-

ing his donkey with his chibouque; we were laughing very merrily, too, over my blundering Arabic.

To-morrow or next day, Ramadán begins, at the first sight of the new moon; it is a great nuisance, because everybody is cross. Omar did not keep it last year, but this year he will; and if he spoils my dinners, who can blame him?

There was a wedding close by my house last night, and about ten o'clock all the women passed under my window, with cries of joy —"El Zaghareet,"—down to the river. I find on inquiry, that in Upper Egypt, as soon as the bridegroom has "taken the face" of his bride and left her, the women take her down to "see the Nile;" they have not yet forgotten that the old god is the giver of increase, it seems.

I have been reading Miss Martineau's book; the descriptions are excellent, and it is true as far as it goes; but there is the usual defect;— to her, as to most Europeans, the people are not real people, only part of the scenery. She evidently knew and cared nothing about them, and had the feeling of most English travellers, that the differences of manners are a sort of impassable gulf;—the truth being that their feelings and passions are just like our own. It is curious that all the old books of travels that I have read mention the natives of strange countries in a far more natural tone, and with far more attempt to discriminate character, than modern ones,—*e. g.* Carsten Niebuhr's Travels here and in Arabia, Cook's Voyages, and many others. *Have* we grown so *very* civilized since a hundred years, that outlandish people seem to us like mere puppets, and not like real human beings? Miss Martineau's bigotry against Copts and Greeks is droll enough, compared to her very proper reverence for "Him who sleeps in Philæ," and her attack upon the hareems is outrageous. She implies that they are scenes of debauchery. I must admit that I have not seen a Turkish hareem, and she apparently saw no other, and yet she fancies the morals of Turkey to be superior to those of Egypt. Very often a man marries a second wife, out of a sense of duty, to provide for a brother's widow and children, or the like. Of course licentious men act loosely here as elsewhere. "We are all sons of Adam," as Sheykh Yoosuf says constantly, "bad-bad and good-good;" and modern travellers show strange ignorance in talking of foreign nations *in the lump*, as they nearly all do.

Monday.—I have just heard that poor Sheykh Mohammad died yesterday, and was, as usual, buried at once. I had not been well for a few days, and Sheykh Yoosuf took care that I should not know of his brother's death. He went to Mustafa Agha, and told him not to tell any one of my house till I was better, because he knew " what was in my stomach " towards his family, and feared I should be made worse by the news. And how often have I been advised not to meddle with sick Arabs, because they are sure to suspect a Christian of poisoning those who die! I do grieve for the graceful handsome young creature and his old father. Omar was vexed at not knowing of his death, because he would have liked to help to carry him to the grave. These Saeedees are much nicer than the Lower Egypt people; they have good Arab blood in their veins, keep pedigrees, and are more manly and independent, and more liberal in religion. You would like them much, they are such thorough gentlemen.

I am beginning to stammer out a little Arabic, but find it horribly difficult; the plurals are bewildering, and the verbs quite heart-rending. I have at last learnt the alphabet, and can write it quite tidily, but now I am in a fix for want of a dictionary; I have written to Hekekian Bey to buy me one in Cairo. Sheykh Yoosuf knows not a word of English, and Omar can't read or write, and has no notion of grammar or of " word for word" interpretation, and it is very slow work. When I walk through the court of the mosque, I give the customary coppers to the little boys who are spelling away loudly under the arcade, with a keen sympathy with their difficulties and well-smudged tin slates. An additional evil is, that the Arabic books printed in England, and at English presses here, require a forty-horse power microscope to distinguish a letter. The ciphering is like ours, but with other figures; and I felt very stupid when I discovered how I had reckoned Arab fashion, from right to left all my life, and never observed the fact. However, it must be remarked that they cast *down* a column of figures from top to bottom.

I am just called away by some poor men who want me to speak to the English travellers about shooting their pigeons. It is very thoughtless, but it is in great measure the fault of the servants and dragomans, who think they must not venture to tell their masters that pigeons are private property; I have a great mind to put a notice on the wall of my house about it. Here, where there are never less than eight or ten boats lying for full three months, the loss to the Fellaheen is serious, and our Consul, Mustafa Agha, is afraid to say anything. I have given my neighbours permission to call the pigeons mine, as they roost in flocks on my roof; and to go out and say that the Sitt objects to her poultry being shot, —especially as I have had them shot off my balcony as they sat there.

I got a note from M. M—— yesterday, inviting me to go and stay at El Mootaneh, Haleem Pasha's great estate near Edfoo, and offering to send his dahabeeyeh for me. I certainly will go as soon as the weather is decidedly hot; it is now very warm and

pleasant.   If I find Thebes too hot as summer
advances, I must drop down and return to
Cairo, or try Suez, which I hear is excellent
in summer,—bracing desert air. But it is very
tempting to stay here ;—a splendid cool house,
food extremely cheap,—about a pound a week
for fish, bread, butter, meat, milk, eggs, and
vegetables ;—all grocery, of course, I brought
with me :—no trouble, rest and civil neighbours.   I feel very much disinclined to move
unless I am baked out, and it takes a good deal
to bake me.   The only fear is the Khamaseen wind.   I do not feel very well ; I don't
ail anything in particular, and have much less
cough ; but I am so weak, and good for nothing.   I seldom feel able to go out, or do
more than sit in the balcony, on one side or
other of the house.   I have no donkey here,
the hired ones are so very bad and so dear
but I have written to M. M—— to try and
get me one at El Mootaneh, and send it down
in one of Haleem Pasha's corn-boats. There is
no comfort like a donkey always ready.   If I
have to send for Mustafa's horse, I feel lazy,
and fancy it is too much trouble, unless I can
go just when I want.

What dreadful weather you have had! We felt the ghost of it here in our three weeks of cold. Sometimes I feel as if I *must* go back to you all, *coûte qui coûte;* but I know it would be of no use to try it this summer. I long for more news of you and my chicks.

LETTER XXXIV.

February 12, 1864.

WE are in Ramadán now, and Omar really enjoys a good opportunity of " making his soul." He fasts and washes vigorously, prays his five times a day, and goes to mosque on Fridays and is quite merry over it, and ready to cook infidels' dinners with exemplary good humour. It is a great merit in Muslims that they are not at all grumpy over their piety. Weather like that of Paradise has set in since five or six days ! I sit on my lofty balcony and drink the sweet northerly breeze, and look at the glorious mountain opposite, and think if only you and the children were here, it would be " the best o' life." The beauty of Egypt grows on one, and I think it far more lovely this year than I did last.

My great friend the Maohn (he is not the názir, who is a fat little pig-eyed Turk) lives in a house which also has a superb view in another direction, and I often go and sit " on the bench," *i. e.* the mastabah in front of his house, and do what little talk I can, and see the people come with their grievances. I don't understand much of what goes on, as the *patois* is broad and doubles the difficulty, or I would send you a Theban police-report; but the Maohn is very pleasant in his manner to them, and they don't seem frightened.

We have appointed a very small boy our bowwáb or porter, or rather he has appointed himself, and his assumption of dignity is quite delicious; he has provided himself with a huge staff, and he behaves like the most tremendous janissary. He is about the size of a child of five, and as sharp as a needle, and possesses the remains of a brown shirt and a ragged kitchen duster as turban. I am very fond of little Ahmad, and like to see him doing *tableaux vivants* from Murillo, with a plate of broken victuals. The children of this place have become so insufferable about baksheesh, that I have complained to the Maohn, and he will assemble a committee of parents and enforce better manners. It is only here, and just where the English go. When I ride into the little villages, I never hear the word, but am always offered milk to drink ; I have taken it two or three times and not offered to pay, and the people always seemed quite pleased.

Yesterday Sheykh Yoosuf came again, the first time since his brother's death ; he was evidently deeply affected, but spoke in the usual way, " It is the will of God, we must all die." I wish you could see Sheykh Yoosuf ; I think he is the sweetest creature in look and manner I ever beheld,—so refined and so simple, and with the animal grace of a gazelle. A high-bred Arab is as graceful as an Indian, but quite without the feline *Geschmeidigkeit*, or the look of dissimulation ; the eye is as clear and frank as a child's. The Austrian consular agent here, who knows Egypt and Arabia well, tells me that he thinks many of them quite as good as they look, and said of Sheykh Yoosuf, "*Er ist so gemüthlich !*"

There is a German here deciphering hiero-glyphics, Herr Dümmichen, a very agreeable man, but he has gone across the river to live at El-Kurneh. He has been through Ethiopia in search of temples and inscriptions. I am to go over and visit him, and see some of the tombs again in his company, which I shall enjoy, as a good interpreter is sorely wanted in those mysterious regions.

I have just heard that a good donkey is *en route* in a boat from El Mootaneh; he will cost between four and five pounds, and will enable me to be about far more than I could by merely borrowing Mustafa's horse, about which I have scruples, as he lends it to other lady-travellers. Little Ahmad will be my Sáis as well as my doorkeeper, I suppose.

Mustafa Agha has acted as English consular agent here for something like thirty years, and is really the slave of the travellers. He gives them dinners, mounts them, and does all the disagreeable business of wrangling with the Reyyis and dragomans for them, takes care of their letters, makes himself a postmaster, sends them out to the boats, and does all manner of services for them, and, lastly, lends his house for infidels to pray in on Sundays when a clergyman is here. For this he has no remuneration at all, except such presents as the

English think fit to make him, and I have seen enough to know that they are not often large, nor always gracefully given. The old fellow at Kiné, who has nothing to do, gets regular pay, and I think Mustafa ought to have something; he is now old and somewhat infirm, and has to keep a clerk to help him, and at least his expenses ought to be covered. Please say this to Mr. Layard from me, as my message to him.

Tell my friends who desire to hear from me that I have no news to send from hence; I only know what wheat, barley, lentils, and sesame fetch per ardebb, and how sugar-cane rules. By the bye, I hear meat is ten piastres (1*s.* 3*d.*) a pound in Cairo. Of course everything will have risen in proportion.

February 14, 1864.

Yesterday we had a dust-storm from the desert; it made my head heavy and made me feel languid, but did not affect my chest at all. To-day is a soft, grey day; there was a little thunder this morning and a few, very few, drops of rain, hardly enough for even Herodotus to consider portentous. My donkey came down last night and I tried him to-day, and he is very satisfactory, though alarmingly small, as the real Egyptian donkey always is; the big ones are from the Hejaz. But it is wonderful how the little creatures run along under one, as easy as possible, and they have no will of their own. I rode mine out to El-Karnak and back, and he did not seem to think me at all heavy. I could put him in my pocket, but his vigour and spirit are amazing. When they are overworked and over-galloped, they become bad on the legs and easily fall. All those for hire are quite stumped up, poor beasts! they are so willing and docile that every one overdrives them.

I have a letter for the Comte de Rougé, the great Egyptologist, whose steamer has just come down here; Mariette Bey is with him. I hope they will turn out good company. I have seen Lord and Lady S——, and several other English travellers. One never hears people's names here; so unless they like to call on me, the boats come and go, and I don't know who is in them. The Arab servants never know their English masters' names, and never ask.

I am getting on with Arabic, but it is very

difficult; Sheykh Yoosuf is bent on making an Alimeh of me, and teaching me to speak elegantly with inflections, which are only used by the learned. Meanwhile my vocabulary increases slowly. Omar has not an idea of translating; he learned English too young to remember the process of learning, and he can give no help because he talks too quick, and rattles out such a heap of illustrative sentences that one is bewildered.

February 18, 1864.

We have had strange weather; first a whole wet day—not known for ten years—and three days of hurricane from the south-west, with an atmosphere of sand and dust—horrid!

I went the other day to a fantasia which Mustafa Agha gave to young S—— and Co., and was much amused; there was one very good dancer. Mariette Bey and M. de Rougé came in with some dear old-fashioned English people, whose *naïve* wonder was irresistibly comic. A lady wondered how the women here could wear clothes " so different from English females, poor things!" but they were not *malveillants*, only pitying and wonderstruck. What surprised them most was to see me going through the saláming ceremonies with Seleem Efendi, the maōhn, and our sitting down together on his carpet.

Mustafa told Omar that he expected Fadl Pasha, the Governor of all Upper Egypt, to dinner, and asked him to go and help to arrange the entertainment.   Did not Omar bristle up?   "What! could his lady be left for some hours without her servant, on account of a Turkish pasha?   Did not Mustafa know that this was an Emeereh of the Inkeleez?   No, not for Efendeena (the Viceroy) himself would he do such a thing! Wallah!"   There is nothing like an Arab servant for asserting his master's or mistress's greatness, and I suspect a little sly pleasure in defying a big Turk from behind the protection of my dignity; for Omar muttered something about high English people not "making themselves big;" which sounded like a covert reflection on those who do.

A characteristic trait of manners was that last night, Sheykh Yoosuf having stayed till dark over my lesson, I asked him to "breakfast" at my dinner; being now Ramadán, he said quite simply, " Oh yes, but he could not eat on a table with forks, so he would go and eat with Omar, and come back to enjoy my society." This was not at all the slavish feeling which made the chaplain of old prefer the steward's room, but the genuine *fraternité et égalité* of this people. "All Muslims are brothers," says the Koran, and they behave as such. Catch a Frenchman or American doing such a thing so simply!

This weather is so depressing I hardly have courage to write at all ; it has been quite as bad as a Cape south-easter. I never saw such an atmosphere of sand and dust ; no one could stir out. Some women who tried to fetch water had their pitchers blown off their heads. I was very glad to be in a good house, and not on a boat.

LETTER XXXV.

El-Uksur, February 19, 1864.

I HAVE only time for a few lines, to go down by Mr. S—— and his companions to Cairo. They are very good specimens of young Englishmen, and are quite recognized here as "belonging to the higher people," because they "do not make themselves big."

We had a whole day's rain (which Herodotus says is a portent here), and a hurricane from the south, worthy of the Cape. I thought we should have been buried under the drifting sand. To-day is again heavenly. I saw Abd-el-Azeez, the chemist, in Cairo; he seemed a very good fellow, and was a pupil of my old friend M. Chevreul, and highly recommended by him. Here I am out of all European ideas.

The Sheykh-el-Arab (of the Ababdeh tribe), who has a sort of town-house here, has invited me out into the desert to the black tents, and I intend to make a visit with old Mustafa Agha. The Sheykh is identical in face with A—— A——, if the latter were painted dark mahogany colour. There is a Roman well in his yard, with a ghool in it. I can't get the story from Mustafa, who is ashamed of such superstitions, but I'll find it out.

I begin to feel all the time before me to be away from you all very long indeed, but I do think my best chance is a long spell of real heat. I have got through this winter without once catching cold at all to signify, and now the fine weather is come. All my Egyptian friends have such a great idea of the good to be done by the summer, which they consider the healthy season.

I am writing in Arabic, from Sheykh Yoosuf's dictation, the dear old story of the Barber's Brother, with the basket of glass. The Arabs are so diverted at hearing that we all know the Elf Leyleh wa-Leyleh, the 'Thousand Nights and a Night.' The want of a dictionary, with a teacher knowing no word of

English, is terrible; I don't know how I learn at all.

The post is pretty quick up to this place; I got your letter within three weeks, you see, but I get no newspapers; the post is all on foot, and can't carry anything so heavy. One of my men of last year, Asgalanee, the steersman, has just been to see me; he says his journey was happier last year.

We have slain two snakes here, at several times. A jackal was caught in the garden, but let go again by fear and clumsiness. No one here has the faintest idea of " pets."

The thermometer in the cold antechamber now is 67°, where no sun ever comes, and the blaze of the sun is prodigious.

11 Ramadán.

LETTER XXXVI.

El-Uksur, February 26, 1864.

I HAVE your letter of the 3rd instant. You would be amused to see Omar bring me a letter, and sit down on the floor till I tell him the family news; and then, "El-hamdu-lilláh!" we are so pleased, and he goes off to his pots and pans.

Lord and Lady S—— are here. The English *milord*, extinct on the continent, has revived in Egypt, and is greatly reverenced, and usually much liked. "These high English have mercy in their stomachs," said one of my last year's sailors, who came to kiss my hand;—a pleasing fact in natural history. "Fee wáhed lord!" (Here's a lord!) was Ahmad's announcement of Lord S——.

I heard of ice at Cairo, and meat at famine

prices; so I will e'en stay here and grill at Thebes. Marry come up, with your Thebes and savagery! what if we do wear ragged brown shirts! 'tis manners make the man; and we defy you to show better breeding. We are now in the full enjoyment of summer weather; there has been no cold for fully a fortnight, and I am getting better every day. If the heat does not overpower me, I feel sure it will be very healing to my lungs. I sit out on my glorious balcony, and drink the air from early morning till noon, when the sun comes upon it and drives me under cover. The thermometer has stood at 64° for a fortnight or three weeks, rising sometimes to 67°; but people in the boats tell me it is still cold at night on the river; up here, only a stone's throw from the Nile, it is warm all night. I fear the loss of cattle has suspended irrigation to a fearful extent, and that the harvests of Lower Egypt of all kinds will be sadly scanty. The disease has not spread above Minyeh, or very slightly; but, of course, cattle will rise in price here also. Already food is getting dearer here; meat and bread have risen considerably,—I should say corn, for no baker exists here   1 pay a woman to grind and bake my wheat, which I buy; and delicious bread it is.

It is impossible to say how exactly like the early parts of the Bible every act of life is here; and how totally new it seems when one reads it on the spot here. Old Jacob's speech to Pharaoh really made me laugh (don't be shocked), because it is so exactly like what a Fellah says to a Pasha, " Few and evil have been my days," etc. (Jacob being a most prosperous man); but it is manners to say all that. I feel quite kindly now towards Jacob, whom I used to think ungrateful and discontented. And when I go to Seedee Omar's farm does he not say, " Take now fine meal and bake cakes quickly," and want to kill a kid? Fateereh, with plenty of butter, is what the " three men" who came to Abraham ate; and the way in which Abraham's chief memlook, acting as wekeel, manages Isaac's marriage with Rebecca, is precisely what a man in his position would now. All the vulgarized associations with Puritanism, and abominable little " Scripture tales and pictures,"—peel off here, and the inimitably truthful representation of life and character comes out; as, for example, Joseph's tears, and his love for the brother *born of the same mother*, which are perfectly lifelike. Leviticus and Deuteronomy are very heathenish, compared to the law of the Koran, or to the early days of Abraham.

Don't think that Sheykh Yoosuf has " proposed Islám " to me. He and M. de Rougé were here last evening, and we had quite an Arabic *soirée*. M. de Rougé speaks Arabic admirably, quite like an Alim ; and it was charming to see Sheykh Yoosuf's pretty look of grateful pleasure at finding himself treated like a " gentleman and a scholar," by two such eminent Europeans (for by comparison with Arab hareem I, of course, am a Sheykhah). It is very interesting to see something of Arabs who have read, and have the " gentleman " ideas. Yoosuf is however superstitious; he told me how some one down the river cured his cattle with water poured over a " mus-haf " (a copy of the Koran), and has hinted at writing out a chapter for me to wear as a " hegáb," or amulet, for my health. (Yet he thinks the Arab doctors of no use at all, who also give verses of the Koran as charms.) He is interested in the antiquities, and in M. de

Rougé's work; and is quite up to the connection between ancient Egypt and the books of Moses. He was anxious to know if M. de Rougé had found anything about Moosa (Moses) or Yoosuf (Joseph). He produced a bit of old Cufic manuscript, and consulted M. de Rougé as to its meaning,—a pretty little bit of flattery in an Arab alim to a Frenchman, to which the latter was not quite insensible, I saw.

Yoosuf's brother, the Imám, has lost his wife, to whom he had been married twenty-two years, and won't hear of taking another. I was struck with the sympathy he expressed with the English Sultana, since all the uneducated people say, Why does she not marry again? It is curious how refinement brings out the same feelings under all "dispensations." If I go down to Cairo again I will get letters to some of the Alim there, from Abd-el-Waris, the Imám here, and I shall see what few Europeans but Lane have seen. I think things have altered since his days, and that men of that class would be less inaccessible now than they were then; and a woman who is old (Yoosuf guessed me at sixty) and educated, does not shock, and does interest them. All the Europeans here are traders, and don't care to know educated Arabs; if they see anything above their servants, it is only Turks or Arab merchants. Don't fancy I can speak at all decently yet, but I understood a good deal, and stammer out a little.

El-Uksur, March 1, 1864.

The glory of the climate now is beyond description, and I feel better every day. I go out as early as seven or eight o'clock on my tiny black donkey, come in to breakfast at about ten, and go out again at four. The sun is very hot in the middle of the day, and the people in boats say it is still cold at night. In this large house I feel neither heat nor cold.

An English traveller who brought a letter to me came in while I was reading with Sheykh Yoosuf, and persisted in ignoring his existence in a manner which led me to draw odious comparisons.

I want to photograph Yoosuf for you; the feelings and prejudices and ideas of a cultivated Arab, as I get at them little by little, are curious beyond compare. It won't do to generalize from one man, of course, but even one gives some very new ideas. The most striking thing is the sweetness and delicacy of feeling, the horror of hurting any one (this must be individual, of course; it is too good to be general). I apologized to him two days ago for inadvertently answering the " Salám aleykum," which he of course said to Omar on coming in, and which is sacramental to Muslims. Yoosuf blushed crimson, touched my hand and kissed his own, and looked quite unhappy.

Yesterday evening he walked in, and startled me by a " Salám aleykee," addressed to me; he had evidently been thinking it over,—whether he ought to say it to me, and came to the conclusion that it was not wrong. " Surely it is well for all the creatures of God to speak peace (*Salám*) to each other," said he. Now, no uneducated Muslim would have arrived at such a conclusion. Omar would pray, work, lie, do anything for me,—sacrifice money even; but I doubt whether he could utter " Salám aleykum" to any but a Muslim. I answered as I felt,—" Peace, O my brother, and God bless thee!" It was almost as if a Catholic priest had felt impelled by charity to offer the communion to a heretic.

I observed that the story of the Barber was new to him, and asked if he did not know the Thousand and One Nights. No, he studied only things of religion; no light amusements were proper for an Alim of the religion. Europeans did not know that, of course, as *our* religion was to enjoy ourselves; but *he* must not make merry with diversions, or music or droll stories. (See the mutual ignorance of all ascetics!) He has a little girl of six or seven, and teaches her to write and read. No one else, he believes, thinks of such a thing, out of Cairo; there many of the daughters of the Alim learn,—those who desire it.

His wife died two years ago, and six months ago he married again a wife twelve years old! (Sheykh Yoosuf is thirty, he tells us; he looks twenty-two.) What a stepmother, and what a wife! He can repeat the whole Koran without book; it takes twelve hours to do it. He has read the Towrat (the Old Testament), and the Gospels (el Engeel), of course. "Every Alim should read them : the words of Seyyidna

Eesa are the true faith: but Christians have altered and corrupted their meaning. So we Muslims believe. We are all the children of God." (I ask, if Muslims call themselves so, or only the slaves of God?) "It is all one—children or slaves. Does not a good man care for both tenderly alike?" (Pray observe the oriental feeling here. *Slave* is a term of affection, not contempt; and remember the Centurion's "*servant* (slave), whom he loved.") As he acts as clerk to Mustafa, our consular agent, and wears a shabby brown shirt or gown, and speaks no English, I dare say he not seldom encounters great slights from sheer ignorance.

In answer to the invariable questions about all my family, I once told him that my father had been a great Alim of the law, and that my mother had got ready his written book, and put his lectures in order, that they might be printed. He was amazed first that I had a mother, as he told me he thought I was fifty or sixty, and immensely delighted at the idea. "God has favoured your family with understanding and knowledge. I wish I could kiss the sheykhah your mother's hand. May God favour her!" M——'s portrait (as usual) he admired fervently, and said one saw his good qualities in his face ;—a compliment I could have fully returned, as he sat looking at the picture with affectionate eyes, and praying *sotto voce* for " el ged'a, el gemeel" (the youth, the beautiful), in the words of the Fat'hah, " Oh, give him guidance, and let him not stray into the paths of the rejected !" Altogether something in Sheykh Yoosuf reminds me of Worsley.* There is the same *Seelenreinheit*, with far less thoughtfulness, and an additional childlike innocence. I suppose some mediæval monks may have had the same look, but no Catholic I have ever seen looks so peaceful or so unpretending. I see in him that easy familiarity with religion which characterizes all people who don't know what doubt means. I hear him joke with Omar about Ramadán, and even about Omar's assiduous prayers, and he is a frequent and hearty laugher. I wonder whether this gives you any idea of a character new to you; it is so impossible to describe manner, which gives so much of the impression of novelty.

* Philip Stanhope Worsley, Esq., translator of the Odyssey.—S.A.

My conclusion is the heretical one, that to dream of converting here is absurd, and, I will add, wrong. All that is wanted is more general knowledge and education, and the religion will clear and develope itself; the elements are identical with those of Christianity, encumbered, as that has been, with asceticism and intolerance. The creed is simpler, and there are no priests. I think the faith has remained wonderfully rational, considering the extreme ignorance of those who hold it. I will add my maid's practical remark,—" The prayers are a fine thing for a lazy people; they must wash first, and the prayer is a capital drill." You would be amused to hear her, when Omar does not wake in time to wash, pray, and eat before daybreak now in Ramadán. She knocks at his door, and acts as Muezzin, —" Come, Omar, get up and pray, and have your dinner." (The evening meal is " breakfast," the morning one "dinner.") Being a light sleeper, she hears the Muezzin, which Omar often does not, and passes on the " Prayer is better than sleep,"—in a prose version.

Ramadán is a dreadful business; everybody is cross or lazy—no wonder. The camel-men

quarrelled all day under my window yesterday, and I asked what it was about: "All
about nothing, it is Ramadán with them,"
said Omar laughing,—"I want to quarrel with
some one myself, it is hot to-day and thirsty
weather." Moreover, I think it injures the
health of numbers permanently. But of course
it is the thing of most importance in the eyes
of the people; there are many who never pray
at ordinary times, but few fail to keep Ramadán. It answers to the Scotch Sabbath.

Friday.—My friend Seleem Efendi has just
been here talking about his own affairs and a
good deal of theology; he is an immense talker,
and I just put in "yes," and "no," and "very
true," and learn "manners and customs."

He tells me he has just bought two black
slave women, mother and daughter, from a
Copt, for about £35. 10s. the two. The mother is a good cook, and the daughter is "for
his bed," as his wife does not like to leave
Cairo and her boys at school there. He had
to buy the mother too, as the girl refused to
be sold without her. What would a 'South-
erner' say to a slave with such a will of her
own? Poor Seleem! how the old body will

bully him if her daughter is lucky enough to have a child! It does give one a sort of start to hear a most respectable magistrate tell one such a domestic arrangement. He added, that it would not interfere with the " Sitt Kebeereh" (the great lady), the black girl being only a slave; and these people never think they have children enough. Moreover, he said he could not get on with his small pay without women to keep house for him, which is quite true here, and women are not respectable in a man's house on any other terms. Seleem was full of his purchase, and told it over again to Omar, who remarked to me afterwards that it was "rude" of him to talk *to men* so. To me it was quite proper.

Seleem has a high reputation, and is said " not to eat the people." He is a hot Muslim, and held forth much as a very superficial Unitarian might do; evidently feeling considerable contempt for the absurdities, as he thinks them, of the " Copts" (he was too civil to say " Christians"), but no hatred (and he is known to show no partiality); only he cannot understand how people can believe such nonsense. He is a good specimen of the good, honest, steady-going, man-of-the-world Muslim,—a strong contrast to the tender piety of dear Sheykh Yoosuf, who has all the feelings which we call Christian charity in the highest degree, and whose face is like that of " the beloved disciple," but no inclination whatever for doctrinal harangues like worthy Seleem.

There is a very general idea among the Arabs that Christians hate the Muslims; they attribute to us the old Crusading spirit. It is only lately that Omar has let us see him at prayers, for fear of being ridiculed; but now he is sure that is not so, I often find him praying in the room where S—— sits at work, which is a clean, quiet place; and Yoosuf went and joined him there yesterday evening, and gave him some religious instruction, quite undisturbed by S—— and her needlework. I am continually complimented on *not hating* the Muslims. Yoosuf promises me letters to some Alim, in Cairo, when I go there again, that I may be shown the Azhar (the great college). Omar had told him that I refused to go with a janissary from the Consul, for fear of giving offence to any very strict Muslims, which astonished him much. He says his friends shall dress me in their women's clothes and take me in. I asked whether as a concealment of my religion? and he said no, only there were hundreds of young men, and it would be more " delicate,"—that they should not stare and talk about my face.

Seleem told me a very pretty grammatical quibble about "son" and "prophet" (*à propos* of Christ), on a verse in the Gospel depending on the reduplicative sign ּ (*sheddeh*) over one letter. He was just as much put out when I reminded him that the original was written in Greek, as some of our amateur theologians are if you say the Bible was not composed in English. However, I told him that many Christians in England, Germany, and America, did not believe that Seyyidna Eesa is God, but only the greatest of prophets and teachers. He at once declared that that was sufficient; that all such had " received guidance," and were not " among the rejected." How could they be, since such Christians only believed the teaching of Eesa, which was true, and not the falsifications of the priests and bishops (the bishops always " catch it," as schoolboys say)?

I was curious to hear whether, on the strength of this, he would let out any further intolerance against the Copts; but he said far less, and far less bitterly, than I have heard certain Christians say of each other, and *débitait* the most usual commonplace, common-sense arguments on the subject. I fancy it would not be very palatable to many Unitarians to be claimed, " mir nichts, dir nichts," as followers of El Islám. But if people really wish to convert, in the sense of improving, they must insist on what the two religions have in common, and not on the most striking points of difference. That door is open, and no other.

March 7.

We have now settled into quite warm-weather ways; no more going out at midday. It is now broiling, and I have been watching eight tall blacks swimming and capering about, with their skins shining like otter's fur when wet. They belong to a Gelláb, a slave-dealer's boat, I see. The beautiful thing is to see men and boys at work among the green corn. In the sun their brown skins look like dark clouded amber,—semi-transparent, so fine are they.

I have a friend, a farmer in a neighbouring village, and am much amused at seeing country life. It cannot be rougher, as regards material comforts, in New Zealand or Central Africa, but there is no barbarism or lack of refinement in the manners of the people.

The fine sun and clear air are delicious and reviving, and I mount my donkey early and late, with little Ahmad trotting beside me. In the evening comes my dear Sheykh Yoosuf, and I blunder through an hour's dictation and reading of the story of the Barber's fifth brother. I presume that Yoosuf likes me, for I am constantly greeted with immense cordiality by graceful men in green turbans belonging, like him, to the holy family of Sheykh Abu-l-Hajjáj. They inquire tenderly after my health, and pray for me, and hope I am going to stay among them.

I received an 'Illustrated News,' with a print of a ridiculous Rebekah at the well, from a picture by Hilton. With regard to Eastern subjects, two courses are open; to paint like mediæval painters, white people in European clothes, or to come and see. Mawkish Misses, in fancy dress, are not " benát el-Arab," like

Rebekah; nor would a respectable man go on his knees like an old fool before the girl he was asking in marriage for the son of his master.

Of all comical things, though, Victor Hugo's 'Orientales' is the funniest. *Elephants* at Smyrna! Why not at Paris and London? *quelle couleur locale!* Sheykh Yoosuf had a good laugh over Hilton's Rebekah, and the camels, more like pigs, as to their heads. He said we must have strange ideas of the books of Towrát (the Pentateuch) in Europe.

I rejoice to say that next Wednesday is Bairam, and to-morrow Ramadán "dies." Omar is very thin and yellow and head-achy, and every one cross. How I wish I were going, instead of my letter, to see you all; but it is evident that this heat is the thing that does me good, if anything will.

LETTER XXXVII.

El-Uksur, March 10, 1864.

YESTERDAY was Bairam, and on Tuesday evening everybody who possessed a gun or a pistol banged away, every drum and darabukkeh
was thumped, and all the children hallooed
Ramadán mat! Ramadán mat! " Ramadán is
dead," about the streets. At daybreak Omar
went to the early prayer, a special ceremony
of the day; there were crowds of people;
so, as it was useless to pray and preach in
the mosque, Sheykh Yoosuf went out upon
a hillock in the burying-ground, where they
all prayed and he preached. Omar reported
the sermon to me as follows (it is all extem-
pore):—

First Yoosuf pointed to the graves,—
" Where are all those people?" and to the an-

cient temples, "Where are those who built them? Do not strangers from a far country take away their very corpses to wonder at? What did their splendour avail them? etc. etc. What, then, O Muslims, *will* avail that you may be happy when that comes which will come for all? Truly God is just, and will defraud no man, and he will reward you if you do what is right; and that is, to wrong no man, neither in his person, nor in his family, nor in his possessions. *Cease then to cheat one another, O men!* and to be greedy; and do not think that you can make amends by afterwards giving alms or praying or fasting, or giving gifts to the servants of the mosques. *Benefits come from God; it is enough for you if you do no injury to any man, and, above all, to any woman or little one!*"

Of course it was much longer, but this was the substance, Omar tells me, and pretty sound morality too methinks, such as might be preached with advantage even in Exeter Hall. There is no predestination in Islam, and every man will be judged upon his actions. "Even unbelievers God will not defraud," says the Koran. Of course a belief in meritorious works leads to the same sort of superstition as among Catholics;—the endeavour to "make one's soul," by alms, fastings, endowments, etc.; therefore Yoosuf's stress upon doing no evil seems to me very remarkable, and really profound. After the sermon, all the company assembled rushed on him to kiss his head and his hands and his feet, and mobbed him so fearfully that he had to lay about him with the wooden sword which is carried by the officiating Alim. Yoosuf came to wish me the customary good wishes of the season soon after, and looked very hot and tumbled, and laughed heartily about the awful kissing he had undergone. All the men embrace on meeting at the festival of Bairam. The kitchen is full of cakes, ring-shaped, which all my friends have sent me, just such as we see offered to the gods (Bairar) in the temples and tombs, and such as my Malay friends at Capetown gave me at "Labunan."

I went to call on the Maohn in the evening, and found a number of people all dressed in their best. Half were Copts,—among them a very pleasing young priest, who carried on a religious discussion with Seleem Efendi,—

strange to say, with perfect good humour on both sides.

A Copt came up with his farm labourer, who had been beaten and the field robbed. The Copt stated the case in ten words, and the Maohn sent off a kawás with him to apprehend the accused persons, who were to be tried at sunrise and beaten, if found guilty, and forced to make good the damage.

General —— called yesterday, a fine old blue-eyed soldier; he found a group of Fellaheen sitting with me, enjoying coffee and pipes hugely. They all started up in dismay at the entrance of such a grand-looking Englishman, and got off the carpet, and they were much gratified at our pressing them not to move or disturb themselves. So we told them that in our country the business of a farmer was looked upon as very respectable, and that the General would ask his farmers to sit and drink wine with him. " Máshá-alláh, teiyib keteer!" (it is the will of God, and most excellent !) said Omar, my Fellah friend, and kissed his hand to the General, quite affectionately.

We English are certainly liked here. Seleem said yesterday evening, "that he had often had to do business with them, and found them always 'dughree' (straight); men of one word and of no circumlocutions, and unlike all the other Europeans." The fact is, that few but decent English come here, I fancy; our scamps go to the colonies, whereas Egypt is the sink for all the iniquity of the south of Europe.

A worthy Copt here, one Todoros, took " a piece of paper" for £20, in payment for antiquities sold to an Englishman, and after the Englishman was gone, brought it to me to ask what sort of paper it was, and how he could get it changed ; or was he perhaps to keep it till the gentleman sent him the money? It was a circular note, which I had difficulty in explaining; but I offered to send it to Cairo to the bankers, and get it cashed; as to when he would get the money, I could not say, as they must wait for an opportunity to send up gold. I told him to put his name on the back of the note, and Todoros thought I wanted it as a receipt for the money, *which was yet to come,* and was going cheerfully to write me a receipt for the £20 he was entrusting to me. Now a Copt is not at all green where his pocket is concerned ; but they will take anything from the English.

Mr. Close told me, that when his boat sank in the cataract, and he remained half dressed on the rock without a farthing, four men came and offered to lend him anything. While I was in England last year, an Englishman, to whom Omar acted as *laquais de place*, went away, owing him seven pounds for things bought for him. Omar had money enough to pay all the tradespeople, and kept it secret, for fear any of the other Europeans should say " shame for the English ;" he did not even tell his own family. Luckily, the Englishman sent the money by the next mail from Malta, and the sheykh of the dragomans proclaimed it, and so Omar got it ; but he never would have mentioned it otherwise.

This concealing of evil is considered very meritorious, and where women are considered, positively a religious duty. *Le scandale est ce qui fait l'offense,* is very much the notion in Egypt, and I believe that very forgiving husbands are commoner here than elsewhere. The whole idea is founded on the verse in the Koran, incessantly quoted, " The woman is made for the man, but the man is made for the woman." *Ergo,* the obligations to chastity are equal; and, as the men find it difficult, they argue that the women do the same. I have never heard a woman's misconduct spoken of without a hundred excuses: perhaps her husband had slave-girls; perhaps he was old or sick, or she did not like him, or she could not help it;—violent love comes " by the visitation of God," as our juries say. A poor young fellow is now in the madhouse of Cairo, owing to the beauty and sweet tongue of an English lady, whose servant he was. " How could he help it? God sent the calamity."

If a dancing-girl repents, the most respectable man may and does marry her, and no one blames or laughs at him. I believe all this leads to a good deal of irregularity, but certainly the feeling is amiable. It is impossible to conceive how startling it is to a Christian, to hear the rules of morality applied with perfect impartiality to both sexes, and to hear Arabs who know our manners, say that Europeans are " hard upon their women," and do not fear God and conceal their offences. I asked Omar, who is very correct in his notions, whether, if he saw his brother's wife do anything wrong, he would tell her husband.

(N.B., he can't endure her.)   " Certainly not,"
he said, " I must cover her with my cloak."
Of course any unchastity is wrong and "harám,"
but equally so in men and women. Seleem
Efendi talked in this strain, and seemed to in-
cline to greater indulgence towards women, on
the score of their ignorance and weakness.
Remember, I only speak of Arabs; I believe
the Turkish ideas are different, as is their
whole hareem system, and Egyptian manners
are not the rule for all Muslims.

Saturday, March 12, 1864.

I dined last night with Mustafa, who again
had the dancing-girls for some Englishmen to
see. Seleem Efendi got the doctor, who was
of the party, to prescribe for him all about his
ailments, as coolly as possible. He as usual
sat by me on the divan, and during the pause
in the dancing, called " El Maghribeeyeh," the
best dancer, to come and talk to us. She
kissed my hand, sat on her heels before us,
and at once laid aside the professional *gaillar-
dise* of manner, and talked very nicely in very
good Arabic, and with perfect propriety, more
like a man than a woman; she seemed very

intelligent. What a thing we should think it, for a worshipful magistrate to call up a girl of that character to talk to a lady!

Yesterday, we had a strange and unpleasant day's business. The evening before, I had my pocket picked in El-Karnak by two men who hung about me, one to sell a bird, the other one of the regular "loafers" who hang about the ruins to beg, and sell water or curiosities, and who are all a lazy bad lot, of course. I went to Seleem, who wrote at once to the Sheykh-el-Beled of El-Karnak, to say that we should go over next morning at eight o'clock (two, Arab time), to investigate the affair, and to desire him to apprehend the men.

Next morning Seleem fetched me, and Mustafa came to represent English interests, and as we rode out of El-Uksur, the Sheykh-el-Abab'deh joined us with some of his tribe, with their long guns or lances; he was a volunteer, furious at the idea of a lady and a stranger being robbed. It is the first time it has happened here, they say, and the desire to beat was so strong, that I went to act as counsel for the prisoners. Every one was peculiarly savage that it should have happened to me, a person well known to be so friendly to "El-Muslimeen."

When we arrived, we went into a square inclosure, with a sort of cloister on one side, spread with carpets, where we sat, and the wretched fellows were brought in chains; to my horror, I found they had been beaten already. I remonstrated,—"What if you have beaten the wrong men?" "Máleysh, we will beat the whole village until your purse is found." I said to Mustafa, "This won't do; you must stop this." So Mustafa ordained, with the concurrence of the Maohn, that the Sheykh-el-Beled and the "Gefieh," the keeper of the ruins, should pay me the value of the purse. As the people of El-Karnak are very troublesome in begging and worrying, I thought this would be a good lesson to the said sheykh to keep better order, and I consented to receive the money, promising to return it and to give a napoleon over, if the purse comes back with its contents ($3\frac{1}{2}$ napoleons). The Sheykh-el-Abab'deh harangued the people on their ill behaviour to "Hareemát," and called them "Harámee" (rascals), and was very high and mighty to the Sheykh-el-Beled.

Hereupon, I went away on a visit to a Turkish lady in the village, leaving Mustafa to settle. After I was gone, they beat eight or ten of the boys who had mobbed me and begged with the two men; Mustafa, who does not like the stick, stayed to see that they were not hurt, and so far it will be a good lesson to them. He also had the two men sent over to the prison here, for fear the Sheykh-el-Beled should beat them again; and will keep them here for a time.

So far so good; but my fear now is, that innocent people will be squeezed to make up the money, if the men do not give up the purse. I have told Sheykh Yoosuf to keep watch how things go, and if the men persist in the theft, and don't return the purse, I shall give the money to those whom the Sheykh-el-Beled will assuredly squeeze, or else to the mosque of El-Karnak. I cannot pocket it, though I thought it quite right to exact the fine as a warning to the El-Karnak *mauvais sujets*.

As we went home, the Sheykh-el-Abab'deh (such a fine fellow he looks!) came up and rode beside me and said, " I know you are a person of kindness,—do not tell this story in this country; if Efendéena (Ismael Pasha) comes to hear it, he may ' take a broom and sweep away the village.'" I exclaimed in horror, and Mustafa joined in at once in the request, and said, "The Sheykh-el-Arab says quite true; it might cost many lives." I shall not mention it to any travellers.

The whole thing distressed me horribly. If I had not been there, they would have been beaten right and left, and if I had shown any desire to have any one punished, evidently they would have half killed the two men.

Mustafa behaved extremely well; he showed sense, decision, and more humanity than I at all expected of him. Pray do not forget my request about him. It is he who has all the trouble and work of the Nile boats, and he is boundlessly kind and useful to the English, and a real protection against cheating. Most of the English to whom I have spoken are of the same opinion.

LETTER XXXVIII.

El-Uksur, March 22, 1864.

THE whole of the European element has now departed from Thebes, save one lingering boat on the opposite shore, belonging to two young Englishmen,—the same who lost their photographs and all their goods by the sinking of their boat in the cataract last year. They are an excellent sample of our countrymen, kind, well-bred, and straightforward.

I am glad my letters amuse you. Sometimes I think they must breathe the unutterable dulness of Eastern life,—not that it is dull to me, a curious spectator, but how the men with nothing on earth to do *can* endure it is a wonder. I went yesterday evening to call on a Turk at El-Karnak; he is a gentlemanlike man, the son of a former mudeer who was murdered,

—I believe, for his cruelty and extortion. He has a thousand feddáns (acres, or a little more) of land, and lives in a mud house, larger, but no better, than that of a Fellah, and with two wives, and the brother of one of them; he leaves the farm to his Fellaheen altogether, I fancy. There was one book, a Turkish one; I could not read the title-page, and he did not tell me what it was. In short, there were no means of killing time but the nargheeleh; no horse, no gun,—nothing; and yet they don't seemed bored. The two women are always clamorous for my visits, and very noisy and schoolgirlish; but apparently excellent friends, and very good-natured. The gentleman gave me a kuffeeyeh (thick head-kerchief for the sun), so I took the ladies a bit of silk I happened to have. You never heard anything like his raptures over M——'s portrait. " Máshá-alláh! it is the will of God! and, by God, he is like a rose." But I can't take to the Turks; I always feel that they secretly dislike and think ill of us European women, though they profess huge admiration and pay *personal* compliments, which an Arab very seldom attempts.

I heard Seleem Efendi and Omar discussing

English ladies one day lately, while I was inside the curtain with Seleem's slave-girl, and
they did not know I heard them. Omar described J——, and was of opinion that a man
who was married to her could want nothing
more. "By my soul, she rides like a Bedawee, she shoots with the gun and pistol, rows
the boat; she knows many languages and what
is in their books; works with the needle like
an Efreet, and to see her hands run over the
teeth of the music-box (keys of the piano)
amazes the mind, while her singing gladdens
the soul. How, then, should her husband ever-
desire the coffee-shop? Walláhee! she can
always amuse him at home. And as to *my* lady,
the thing is not that she does not know. When
I feel my stomach tightened, I go to the divan and say to her, 'Do you want anything—
a pipe or sherbet or so-and-so?' and I talk till
she lays down her book and talks to me, and I
question her and amuse my mind; and, by
God! if I were a rich man and could marry one
English hareem like these, I would stand before her and serve her like her memlook. You
see I am only this lady's servant, and I have
not once sat in the coffee-shop, because of the

sweetness of her tongue.　Is it not true, therefore, that the man who can marry such hareem is rich more than with money?"

Seleem seemed disposed to think a little more of good looks, though he quite agreed with all Omar's enthusiasm, and asked if J—— were beautiful.　Omar answered, with decorous vagueness, that she was "a moon;" but declined mentioning her hair, eyes, etc.　(It is a liberty to describe a woman minutely.)　I nearly laughed out at hearing Omar relate his manœuvres to make me "amuse his mind."　It seems I am in no danger of being discharged for being dull.　On the other hand, frenchified Turks have the greatest detestation of *femmes d'esprit.*

The weather has set in so hot that I have shifted my quarters out of my fine room to the south-west, into a room with only three sides, looking over a lovely green view to the north-east, and with a huge sort of solid verandah, as large as the room itself, on the open side; thus I live in the open air altogether.　The bats and swallows are quite sociable; I hope the serpents and scorpions will be more reserved.　"El-Khamáseen" (the fifty days) has begun, and the wind is enough to mix up heaven and earth, but it is not distressing, like the Cape south-easter, and though hot, not choking like the khamáseen in Cairo and Alexandria. Mohammad brought me some of the new wheat just now. Think of harvest in March and April! These winds are as good for the crops here as a "nice steady rain" is in England. It is not necessary to water as much when the wind blows strong.

As I rode through the green fields along the dyke, a little boy sang, as he turned round on the musically-creaking Sákiyeh (the water-wheel turned by an ox), the one eternal Sákiyeh tune. The words are *ad libitum*, and my little friend chanted:—"Turn, O Sákiyeh, to the right, and turn to the left; who will take care of me if my father dies? Turn, O Sákiyeh, etc. Pour water for the figs and the grapes, and for the water-melons. Turn," etc. etc. Nothing is so pathetic as that Sákiyeh song.

I passed the house of the Sheykh-el-Abab'-deh, who called out to me to take coffee. The moon rose splendid, and the scene was lovely: the handsome black-brown sheykh in dark.

robes and white turban, Omar in a graceful white gown and red turban, the wild Abab'deh with their bare heads and long black ringlets, clad in all manner of dingy white rags, and bearing every kind of uncouth weapon in every kind of wild and graceful attitude, and a few little brown children quite naked, and shaped like Cupids. And there we sat and looked so romantic, and talked quite like ladies and gentlemen about the merits of Sákneh and Almás, the two great rival women singers of Cairo. I think the sheykh wished to display his experience of fashionable life.

The Copts are now fasting, and cross; they fast fifty-five days for Lent (old style, no Coptic style); no meat, fish, eggs, or milk, no exception of Sundays, no food till after twelve at noon, and no intercourse with the hareem. The only comfort is plenty of arakee; and what a Copt can carry discreetly is an unknown quantity; one seldom sees them drunk, but they imbibe awful quantities. They always offer me wine and arakee, and can't think why I don't drink it; I believe they suspect my Christianity, in consequence of my preference for Nile water. As to that though, they scorn

all heretics (*i. e.* all Christians but themselves
and the Abyssinians) more than they do the
Muslims, and dislike them more. The procession of the Holy Ghost question divides us
with the Gulf of Jehannum.

The gardener of this house is a Copt, such
a nice fellow! and he and Omar chaff one another about religion with the utmost good
humour; indeed they seldom are touchy with
the Muslims. There is a pretty little man
called Meekaeel, a Copt, wakeel to M. M——;
I wish I could draw him, to show you a perfect
specimen of the ancient Egyptian race; his
blood must be quite unmixed. He came here
yesterday to speak to Alee Bey, the mudeer of
Kiné, who was visiting me (a splendid, handsome Turk he is); so little Meekaeel crept in
to mention his little business under my protection, and a few more followed, till Alee Bey
got tired of holding a Durbar in my divan,
and went away to his boat. You see the
people think the kurbáj is not quite so handy
in the presence of an English spectator.

The other day Mustafa Agha got Alee Bey
to do a little job for him;—to let the people
in the Gezecreh (the island), which is Mus-

tafa's property, work at a canal there, instead of at the canal higher up, for the Pasha. Very well; but down comes the Názir (the mudeer's *sub*), and kurbájes the whole Gezeereh; —not Mustafa, of course, but the poor Fellahs who were doing his *corvée* instead of the Pasha's, by the mudeer's order. I went to the Gezeereh, and thought that the first-born in every house were killed as of yore, by the crying and wailing; when up came two fellows, and showed me their bloody feet, which their wives were crying over, as if for their death.

Wednesday.—Last night I bored Sheykh Yoosuf with Antara and Aboo-Zeyd, maintaining the greater valour of Antara, who slew ten thousand men for the love of Ibla; (you know Antar.) Yoosuf looks down on such profanities, and replied, " What are the battles of Antara and Aboo-Zeyd, compared with the combats of our Lord Moses with Og, and other infidels of might; and what is the love of Antara for Ibla, compared to that of our Lord Solomon for Balkees (Queen of Sheba), or their beauty and attractiveness to that of our Lord Joseph?" And then he related the combat of Seyyidna Moosa with Og, and I thought, " Hear, O ye Puritans !" and learn how religion and romance are one, to those whose manners and ideas are the manners and ideas of the Bible, and how Moses was not at all a gloomy fanatic, but a gallant warrior. There is a Homeric character in the religion here: the " Nebee," the Prophet, is a hero like Achilles, and like him, directed by God,—Allah instead of Athene. He fights, prays, teaches, makes love, and is truly a man, not an abstraction ; and as to wonderful events, instead of telling one to shut one's eyes and gulp them down, they believe them and delight in them, and tell them to amuse people. Such a piece of deep-disguised scepticism as *credo quia impossibile* would find no favour here; " What is impossible to God?" settles everything. In short, Mohammad has somehow left the stamp of romance on the religion, or else it is in the blood of the people, though the Koran is prosy and " common-sensical," compared to the Old Testament. I used to think Arabs intensely prosaic, till I could understand a little of their language ; but now I can trace the genealogy of Don Quixote straight up to some Sheykh-el-Arab.

A fine handsome woman with a lovely baby came to see me the other day. I played with the baby, and gave it a cotton handkerchief for its head. The woman came again yesterday, to bring me a little milk and some salad as a present, and to tell me my fortune with date-stones. I laughed, so she contented herself with telling Omar about his family, which he believed implicitly. She is a clever woman evidently, and a great Sibyl here; no doubt, she has faith in her own predictions. Superstition is wonderfully infectious here, especially that of the evil eye; which, indeed, is shared by many Europeans, and even by some English. The fact is, that the Arabs are so impressionable and so cowardly about inspiring any illwill, that if a man looks askance at them it is enough to make them ill; and as calamities are by no means unfrequent, there is always some mishap ready to be laid to the charge of somebody's "eye." A part of the boasting about property, etc., is politeness,—so that one may not be supposed to be envious of one's neighbour's nice things. My Sakka (water-carrier) admired my bracelets yesterday as he was watering the verandah floor, and instantly told me of all the gold necklaces and earrings he had bought for his wife and daughters,—that I might not be uneasy and fear his envious eye. He is such a good fellow! For two shillings a month, he brings up eight or ten huge skins of water from the river a day, and never begs or complains, is always merry and civil; I shall enlarge his baksheesh.

A number of camels sleep in the yard under my verandah; they are pretty and smell nice, but they growl and swear at night abominably. I wish I could draw you an Egyptian farmyard,—men, women, and cattle. But what no one can draw is the amber light,—so brilliant and so soft; not like the Cape sunshine at all, but equally beautiful,—hotter and less dazzling. There is no glare in Egypt as in the south of France, and I suppose, in Italy.

Thursday.—I went yesterday afternoon to the island again, to see the crops and farmer Omar's house and Mustafa's village; of course we had to eat, and did not come home till the moon had long risen. Mustafa's brother, Abd-er-Rahmán, walked about with us,—a noble-looking man, tall, spare, dignified, and active; grey-bearded and hard-featured, but as lithe and bright-eyed as a boy; scorning any conveyance but his own feet, and quite dry, while we ran down with perspiration. He was like Boaz, the wealthy gentleman-peasant; nothing except the Biblical characters give any idea of the rich Fellah. We sat and drank new milk in a " lodge in a garden of cucumbers " (the lodge is a neat hut of palm-branches), and saw the moon rise over the mountains and light up everything like a softer sun. Here you see all colours as well by moonlight as by day; hence it does not look as brilliant as the Cape moon, or even as I have seen it in Paris, where it throws sharp black shadows and white light. The night here is a tender, subdued, dreamy sort of enchanted-looking day. Ya Leyl! ya Leyl! ya Leyl, etc.

My Turkish acquaintance from El-Karnak has just been here, and he boasted of his house at Damascus, and invited me to go with him after the harvest here; also of his beautiful wife in Syria, and then begged me not to mention her to his wives here. It is very hot now; what will it be in June ? It is now 86° in my shady room at twelve o'clock, noon; it will be hotter at two or three. But the mornings and evenings are delicious. I am shedding my clothes by degrees,—stockings are unbearable,—I feel much stronger, too; the horrible feeling of exhaustion has left me: I suppose I must have salamander blood in my body to be made lively by such heat.

Saturday.—This will go by Mr. B—— and Mr. C——, the last winter swallows. We went together yesterday afternoon to the Tombs of the Kings on the opposite bank; the mountains were red-hot, and the sun went down into Amenti all on fire. We met Herr Dümmichen, the German who is living in the Temple of Ed-Deyr-el-Bahree, translating inscriptions, and went down Belzoni's tomb. Herr Dümmichen translated a great many things for us which were very curious, and I think I was more struck with the beauty of the drawing of the figures than last year. The face of the goddess of the western shore, Amenti,—Athor or Hecate,—is ravishing, as she welcomes the king to her regions; Death was never painted so lovely. The road is a long and most wild one, truly through the valley of the shadow of death; not an insect nor a bird.

Our moonlight ride home was beyond belief beautiful. The Arabs who followed us were extremely amused at hearing me interpret between German and English, and at my speaking Arabic. One of them had droll theories about " Amellica"—as they always pronounce it;—*e. g.* that the Americans are the Fellaheen of the English; " they talk so loud." " Was the king very powerful, that the country was called El Melekeh" (the queens)? I said, "No, all are kings there; you would be a king like the rest." My friend disapproved of that utterly; " If all are kings, they must all be taking away every man the other's money;"—a delightful idea of the kingly vocation.

I wish I could send you my little Ahmad, just of R——'s size, who "*takes care* of the Sitt" when riding or walking. He is delicious, so wise and steady, like a good little terrier. When we landed on the opposite shore, I told him to go back in the ferry-boat which had brought over my donkey; a quarter of an hour after I saw him by my side. The guide asked why he had not gone as I told him. " Who would take care of the lady?" said he. Of course he got tired, and on the way home, seeing him lagging, I told him to jump up behind me *en croupe*, after the fellah fashion. I thought the Arabs would never have done laughing, and saying "Wallah" and "Másháalláh."

Sheykh Yoosuf talked about the excavations; he is shocked at the way in which the mummies are kicked about; he said one boy told him, as an excuse, that they were not Muslims. Yoosuf rebuked him severely, and told him it was "harám" (accursed) to do so to any of the children of Adam.

The harvest is about to begin here, and the crops are splendid this year; Old Nile pays his damages. I went to Mustafa Agha's farm two nights ago to drink new milk, and saw the preparations for harvest,—baking bread, and selecting a young bull to be killed for the reapers,—all just like the Bible. I reckon it will be Easter here in a fortnight. All eastern Christendom adheres to the old style; the Copts, however, have a reckoning of their own —probably that of ancient Egypt.

It is not hot to-day; only 84° in a cool room.

The dust is horrid; with the high wind everything is gritty, and it obscures the sun; but
the wind has no evil quality in it.

I am desired to eat a raw onion every day
during the Khamáseen, for health and prosperity. This too must be a remnant of ancient
Egypt.

LETTER XXXIX.

El-Uksur, April 6, 1864.

I INTENDED to write by some boats now going down;—the very last, with a party of Poles. Hekekian Bey much advises me to stay here the summer, and get my disease " evaporated." Since I wrote last the great heat has abated, and we now have 76° to 80° with strong north breezes up the river,—glorious weather! neither hot nor chilly at any time.

The evening before last, I went out to the threshing-floor to see the stately oxen treading out the corn, and supped there with Abd-er-Rahmán on roasted corn, sour cream, and eggs, and saw the reapers take their wages,—each a bundle of wheat, according to the work he had done; a most lovely sight! The graceful half-naked brown figures, loaded with sheaves; some having earned so much that their mothers or wives had to help them to carry it; and little fawn-like stark-naked boys trudging off so proud of their small bundles of wheat or of hummuz (a sort of vetch, much eaten, both green and roasted). The Sakka, who has brought water for the men, gets a handful from each, and drives home his donkey with empty water-skins and a heavy load of wheat; and the barber, who has shaved all these brown heads on credit for this year past, gets his pay, and every one is cheerful and happy in their gentle, quiet way: here there is no beer to make men sweaty, and noisy, and vulgar. The harvest is the most exquisite pastoral you can conceive: the men work seven hours in the day (*i.e.* eight, with half-hours to rest and eat), and seven more during the night; they go home at sunset to dinner, and to sleep a bit, and then to work again,— " these lazy Arabs!" The man who drives the oxen on the threshing-floor gets a measure and a half for his day and night's work (of threshed corn, I mean). As soon as the wheat, barley, addas (lentils), and hummuz are cut, we shall sow durah of two kinds—common maize and

Egyptian—and plant sugar-cane," and, later, cotton. The people work very hard, but they eat well; and being paid in corn, they get the advantage of the high price of corn this year. In Lower Egypt there is really a famine, I fear.

I told you how my purse had been stolen, and the proceedings thereanent. Well! Mustafa asked me several times what I wished to be done with the thief, who has spent twenty-one days here in irons. With my absurd English ideas of justice, I refused to interfere at all; and Omar and I had quite a tiff, because he wished me to say, "Oh! poor man, let him go; I leave the affair to God." I thought Omar absurd;—it was I who was wrong. The authorities concluded that it would oblige me very much if the poor devil were punished with "a rigour beyond the law;" and had not Sheykh Yoosuf come and explained to me the nature of the proceedings, the man would have been sent up to the mines in Feyzoghloo *for life*, out of civility to me. There was no alternative between my forgiving him " for the love of God," or sending him to certain death by a climate insupportable to these people. Mustafa and Co. tried hard to prevent

Sheykh Yoosuf from speaking to me, for fear I should be angry and complain at Cairo, if my vengeance were not wreaked on the thief; but he said he knew me better, and brought the *procès-verbal* to show me. Fancy my dismay. I went to Seleem Efendi and to the Kádee with Sheykh Yoosuf, and begged the man might be let go and not sent to Kiné at all. Having settled this, I said that I had thought it right that the people of El-Karnak should pay the money I had lost, as a fine for their bad conduct to strangers, but that I did not require it for the sake of the money, which I would accordingly give to the poor of El-Uksur in the mosque and in the church (great applause from the crowd). I asked how many were Muslim and how many Nasránee, in order to divide the three napoleons and a half according to the numbers. Sheykh Yoosuf awarded one napoleon to the church, two to the mosque, and the remaining half to the water-drinking place, the Sebeel, which was also applauded. I then said, "Shall we send the money for the Nasránee to the Bishop?" but a respectable elderly Copt said, "Máleysh, máleysh (never mind), better give it all to Sheykh Yoosuf;

he will send the bread to the church." Then the Kádee made me a fine speech, and said I had behaved like a great Emeerch and one that feared God; and Sheykh Yoosuf said he knew the English had mercy in their stomachs, and that I especially had Muslim feelings (as we say, Christian charity).

Did you ever hear of such a state of admistration of *justice?* Of course, sympathy here, as in Ireland, is mostly with the " poor man" in prison,—" in trouble," as we say. I find that accordingly a vast number of disputes are settled by private arbitration, and Yoosuf is constantly sent for to decide between contending parties, who abide by his decision rather than go to law; or else, five or six respectable men are called upon to form a sort of amateur jury, and to " settle the matter." In criminal cases, if the prosecutor is powerful, he has it all his own way; if the prisoner can bribe high, he is apt to get off. All the appealing to my compassion was quite *en règle.*

Another trait of Egypt;—the other day we found all our water-jars empty, and our house unsprinkled; on inquiry, it turned out that the Sakkas had all run away, carrying with them their families and goods, and were gone no one knew whither, in consequence of " some persons having authority," (one, a Turkish ka-wás), having forced them to fetch water for building purposes at so low a price that they could not bear it. My poor Sakka is gone without a whole month's pay,—two shillings, —the highest pay by far given in El-Uksur.

I am interested in another story. I hear that a plucky woman here has been to Kiné, and threatened the Mudeer that she will go to Cairo, and complain to Efendeena himself of the unfair drafting for soldiers;—her only son is taken, while others have bribed off. She will walk in this heat all the way, unless she succeeds in frightening the Mudeer, which, as she is of the more spirited sex in this country, she may possibly do. You see these Saeedees are a bit less patient than the Lower Egyptians: the Sakkas can *strike*, and a woman can face a Mudeer.

Provisions get dearer and scarcer here daily. Food here is now about at London prices; this does not distress the Fellaheen, as they sell the corn dear; but in the large towns it must be dreadful.

You would be amused at the bazaar (Es-Sook) here: there is a barber, and on Tuesdays some beads, calico, and tobacco are sold for the market-people. The only artisan is a jeweller. We spin and weave our own brown woollen garments, and have no other wants; but gold necklaces and nose- and earrings *are* indispensable: it is the safest way of hoarding, and happily combines saving with ostentation. Can you imagine a house without beds, chairs, tables, cups, glasses, knives,—in short, with nothing but an oven, a few pipkins and water-jars, and a couple of wooden spoons, and some mats to sleep upon? Yet people are happy and quite civilized who live so. An Arab cook, with his fingers and one cooking-pot, will serve you an excellent dinner quite miraculously. The simplification of life possible in such a climate is not conceivable, unless one has seen it.

The Turkish ladies whom I visit at El-Karnak have very little more. They are very fond of me, and always want me to stay, and sleep in my clothes on a mat, on a mud-divan,—poor spoiled European that I am; but they are full of pity and wonder at the absence of my

" master."　I made a sad slip of the tongue, and said my " husband " (Góz), before Abd-er-Rafeea, the master of the house.　The ladies laughed and blushed tremendously, and I felt very awkward; but they turned the tables on me in a few minutes by some questions they asked quite coolly.　They have lived all their lives within less than a quarter of a mile of the ruins of El-Karnak, and never have seen them, or wished to see them.

The dragoman of the Polish boats has just come to desire that my letters be ready in the morning, as his people do not stay here; so I must say farewell.　I hardly know what I shall have to do.　If the heat does not turn out overpowering, I shall stay here; if I cannot bear it, I must go down.　Mustafa Agha, I believe, goes to England; I wish I could send you Sheykh Yoosuf as a specimen of a genuine Arab gentleman.　Mustafa is somewhat Europeanized.

I asked Omar if he could bear a summer here—so dull for a young man fond of a little coffee-shop and gossip; for that if he could not, he might go down for a time and join me again, as I could manage with some man here.

He absolutely cried, and kissed my hands, and declared he was never so happy as with me; and he could not rest if he thought I had not all that I wanted. "I am your memlook, not your servant; your memlook." I really do believe that these people sometimes love their English masters better than their own people. Omar certainly loves Cyril Graham like a very dear relation, and he certainly has shown the greatest fondness for me on all occasions.

Suleyman, the Coptic gardener, has given me a little old Coptic cross of silver, rude but pretty, as a charm; I will send it to R—— when I have a good chance.

Sheykh Yoosuf is to write my name in Arabic, which I shall get engraved on a signet at Cairo. It is the only valid signature here.

LETTER XL.

April 7, 1864.

HARVESTING is going on, and never did I see, in any dream, a sight so lovely as the whole process;—the brown reapers, the pretty little naked boys helping and hanging on the stately bulls at the threshing floor. An acquaintance of mine, one Abd-er-Rahmán, is Boaz; and as I sat with him on the threshing-floor, I felt quite puzzled as to whether I were really alive, or only existing in imagination in the Book of Ruth. It is such a *keyf* one enjoys under palm-trees with such a scene. The harvest is magnificent here; I never saw such heavy crops. There is no cattle disease, but a good deal of sickness among the people; I have to practise very extensively, and often feel very anxious, as I cannot refuse to go to the poor souls and give them medicine, though with sore misgivings all the while.

The more I see of my teacher, Sheykh Yoosuf, the more pious, amiable, and good he appears to me; he is intensely devout, and not at all bigoted—a difficult combination;—and moreover he is lovely to behold, and has the prettiest and merriest laugh possible. It is quite curious to see the mixture of a sort of learning, and such perfect high breeding and beauty of character, with utter ignorance and great superstition.

I want dreadfully to be able to draw or photograph. The group at the Sheykh-el-Abab'deh's a few nights ago was ravishing; all but my ugly hat and self: the black ringlets, and dingy white drapery, and obsolete weapons of the men—the graceful splendid Sheykh, " black, but beautiful," like the Shulamite—I thought of Antar and Aboo-Zeyd.

The Khamáseen here is pleasant rather than not—only the dust is horrid; but the wind is not stifling, as it is down stream.

Thursday, April 14, 1864.

We have had a tremendous Khamáseen

wind, and now a strong north wind, quite fresh and cool; the thermometer was 92° in the Khamáseen, but it did me no harm. Luckily I am very well, for I am worked hard, as a strange epidemic has broken out, and I am the Hakeemeh of El-Uksur. The Hakeem Bashi from Cairo came up and frightened the people, telling them it was catching; and Yoosuf forgot his religion so far as to beg me not to be all day in the people's huts. But Omar and I despised the danger, I feeling sure it was not infectious, and Omar saying, " Min Alláh." The people have stoppage of the bowels, and die in eight days, unless they are physicked. All who have sent for me *in time* have recovered; thank God that I can help the poor souls! It is harvest, and the hard work, and the spell of intense heat, and the green corn, beans, etc. etc., which they eat, bring on the sickness. Then the Copts are fasting from all animal food, and full of green beans, and salad, and green corn. Mustafa tried to persuade me not to give physic, for fear those who died should pass for being poisoned; but both Omar and I thought this only an excuse for selfishness. Omar is an excellent assistant.

The Bishop tried to make money by hinting that if I forbade my patients to fast, I might pay for their indulgences.

One poor peevish little man refused the chicken broth, and told me that we Europeans had our heaven in *this* world. Omar let out a " Kelb!" (dog!) But I stopped him, and said, " O my brother, God has made the Christians of England unlike those of Egypt, and surely will condemn neither of us on that account; mayest thou find a better heaven hereafter than I now enjoy here!" Omar threw his arms round me, and said, " O thou good one! surely our Lord will reward thee for acting thus with the *meekness of a Muslimeh,* and kissing the hand of him who strikes thy face. (See how each religion claims humility as its peculiar characteristic!) Suleyman was not pleased at his fellow-Christian's display of charity. It does seem strange that the Copts of the lower class will not give us the blessing, or thank God for our health, as the Muslimeen do. Most of my patients are Christians, and some are very nice people indeed.

The people have named me Sitti Noor-âlâ-

Noor. A poor woman, whose only child, a young man, I was happy enough to cure when dreadfully ill, kissed my feet, and asked by what name to pray for me. I told her my name meant "noor" (light, *lux*); but as that was one of the names of God, I could not use it. "Thy name is Noor-âlâ-Noor," said a man who was in the room; that means something like "God is upon thy mind," or "Light from the light;" and "Noor-âlâ-Noor" it remains: a combination of the names of God is quite proper, like Abdallah, Abd-er-Rahmán, etc. etc.

I begged some medicines of a Polish Countess, who went down the other day. When all is gone, I don't know what I shall do. I am going to try to make castor-oil: I don't know how; but I shall try, and Omar fancies he can manage it. The cattle disease has also broken out desperately up in the Mudeeriat of Esneh, and we see the dead beasts float down all day; of course, we shall soon have it here.

Sunday, April 17.

The epidemic seems to be over, but there is still a great deal of gastric fever, etc., about.

The hakeem from Kiné has just been here,—
a pleasing, clever young man, speaking Italian
perfectly, and French extremely well; he is
the son of some fellah, of Lower Egypt, sent
to study at Pisa, and has not lost the Arab
gentility and elegance by a Frangee education.
We fraternized greatly, and the young hakeem
was delighted at my love for his people, and
my high opinion of their intelligence. He is
now gone to inspect the sick, and is to see me
again and give me directions. He was very
unhappy that he could not supply me with
medicines; none are to be bought above Cairo,
except from the hospital-doctors, who sell the
medicines of the government, as the Italian at
Asyoot did; but Alee Efendi is too honest for
that. The old Bishop paid me a visit of three
and a half hours yesterday, and, *pour me tirer
une carotte*, he sent me a loaf of sugar; so I
must send a present " for the church,"—to be
consumed in arakee. The old man was not
very sober, and asked for wine; I coolly told
him that it was " harám" (forbidden) to us to
drink during the day,—except with our dinner.
I never will give the Christians drink here;
and now they have left off pressing me to

drink spirits at their houses. The Bishop offered to alter the hour of prayer for me, and to let me into the "Heykel" (where women must not go) on Good Friday, which will be eighteen days hence; all of which I refused, and said I would go on the roof of the church, and look down through the window, with the other hareem. Omar kissed the Bishop's hand, and I said, "What! do you kiss the hand of a Copt?" "Oh yes," he answered, "he is an old man, and a servant of my God;—but dreadful dirty," added Omar, —and it was too true. His presence diffused a fearful monastic odour of sanctity. A bishop must be a monk, as the priests are married.

Monday.—To-day Alee Efendi el-Hakeem came again to tell me how he had been to try to see my patients, and failed; all the families declared they were well, and would not let him in. Such is the deep distrust of everything connected with the Government. They all waited till he was gone away, and then came again to me with their ailments. I scolded, and they all said, "Wallah! ya Sitt, ya Emeereh, that is the Bash Hakeem, and he will send us off to the hospital at Kiné, and there they would poison us; by thy eyes, do not be angry with us, or leave off having compassion on us, on this account." I said, Alee Efendi is an Arab, and a Muslim, and an Emeer (gentleman), and he gave me good advice, and would have given more, etc. etc. All in vain! He is the Government doctor, and they had rather die, and will swallow anything from the Sitt Noor-âlâ-Noor. Here is a pretty state of things!

I gave Sheykh Yoosuf four pounds for three months' daily lessons in Arabic last night, and had quite a contest to force it upon him. "It is not for money, O lady!" and he coloured crimson. He had been about with Alee Hakeem, but could not get the people to see him. The Copts, I fear, have a religious prejudice against him, Alee, and indeed against all heretics. They consider themselves and the Abyssinians as the only true believers; if they acknowledge us as brethren, it is for money. I speak only of the low class, and of the priests,—of course the educated merchants think very differently. I had two priests, two deacons, and the mother of one of them here to-day, for physic for the woman. She was very pretty and pleasing, miserably weak, and reduced, from the long fast; I told her she must eat meat, drink a little wine and take cold baths, and gave her quinine. She will take the wine and the quinine, but neither eat nor wash. The Bishop tells them they will die if they break the fast, and half the Christians are ill from it. The one priest spoke a little English; he fabricates false antiques very cleverly, and is tolerably sharp.

But, oh heaven! it is enough to make one turn Muslim, to compare these greasy rogues with high-minded charitable Shurafa (noblemen) like Sheykh Yoosuf. A sweet little Copt boy, who is very ill, will be killed by the stupid bigotry about the fast. My friend Suleyman is much put out, and backs my exhortations to the sick to break it. He is a capital fellow, and very intelligent, and he and Omar are like brothers; it is the priests who do all they can to keep alive religious prejudice,—luckily they are only partially successful.

Mohammad has just heard that seventy-five head of cattle are dead in El-Mootaneh. Here only a few have died as yet, and Alee Hakeem thinks the disease less virulent than in Lower Egypt. I hope he is right; but the dead beasts float down the river all day long.

Saturday, April 23.

Happily the sickness is going off. I have just heard Suleyman's report as follows:—Hasan Aboo-Ahmad kisses the Emeereh's feet, and the *bullets* have cleaned his stomach, and he has said the Fat'hah for the lady. The two little girls who had diarrhœa are well. The Christian dyer has vomited his powder, and wants another. The mother of the Christian cook who married the priest's sister has got dysentery. The Hareem of Mustafa Aboo-Obeyd has two children with bad eyes. The Bishop had a quarrel, and scolded and fell down, and cannot speak or move; I must go to him. The young deacon's jaundice is better. The slave girl of Khursheed Agha is sick, and Khursheed is sitting at her head, in tears; the women say I must go to her too. Khursheed is a fine young Circassian, and very good to his hareem.

That is all. Suleyman has nothing on earth

to do, and brings me a daily report; he likes the gossip and the importance. The Reyyis of a cargo-boat brought me up your Lafontaine and almanac yesterday, and some newspapers and books from Hekekian Bey; the papers were very welcome, also a letter from P——. I am very sorry he had not time to come here, and study the splendid forms of the reapers and camel-drivers. Sheykh Yoosuf is going down to Cairo, to try to get back some of the lands which Mohammad Alee took away from the mosques and the Ulema without compensation. He asked me whether R—— would speak for him to Efendeena or to Haleem Pasha: what are the Muslimeen coming to? As soon as I can read enough, he offers to read in the Koran with me,—a most unusual proceeding, as the " noble Koran " is not generally put into the hands of heretics. But my " charity to the people in sickness " is looked upon by Abd-el-Wáris, the Imám, and by Yoosuf, as a proof that I have " received direction," and am of those Christians of whom Seyyidna Mohammad has said, " that they have no pride, that they rival each other in good works, and that God will increase their reward." There is no *arrière-pensée* of conversion,—that they think hopeless.

Next Friday is the Gumha el-Kebeer (Great or Good Friday) with the Copts, and the prayers are in the daytime, so I shall go to the church. Next moon is the great Bairam, el-Eed el-Kebeer with the Muslimeen,—the commemoration of the sacrifice of Isaac or Ishmael (commentators are uncertain which); and Omar will kill a sheep for the poor, for the benefit of his baby, according to custom.

I have at length compassed the destruction of mine enemy, though he has not written a book. A fanatical Christian dog (quadruped), belonging to the Coptic family who live on the opposite side of the yard, hated me with such virulent intensity, that not content with barking at me all day long, he howled at me all night, even after I had put out my lantern and he could not see me in bed. Sentence of death has been recorded against him, as he could not be beaten into toleration. Meekaeel, his master's son, has just come down from El-Mootaneh, where he is the wekeel of M. M——. He gives a fearful account of the sickness there among men and cattle; eight or ten deaths of men a day. Here we have only four a day, at the most, in a population of, I guess, some two thousand. Two hundred and fifty head of cattle have died at El-Mootaneh. Here a few calves are dead, but as yet no full-grown beasts, and the people are healthy again. I really think I did some service by not showing any fear, and Omar behaved manfully. Some one tried to put it into Omar's head that it was " harám " to be too fond of us heretics; but he consulted Sheykh Yoosuf, who promised him a reward hereafter for good conduct to me, and who told me of it as a good joke, adding that he was " rágil emeen," the highest praise for fidelity,—the *sobriquet* of the Prophet. Omar kisses the hands of the Seedee el-Kebeer (the great master), and desires his best salám to the little master and the little lady, whose servant he is. He asks if I too do not kiss Iskender Bey's hand in my letter, as I ought to do as his hareem; or whether I make myself " big before my master," like some Frangee ladies he has seen. Yoosuf is quite puzzled about European women, and a little shocked at the want of respect to their husbands they display. I told him that the outward respect shown us by our men was *our veil*, and explained how superficial the difference was. He fancied that the law gave us the upper hand.

Omar reports yesterday's sermon,—" On Toleration," it appears. Yoosuf took the text of " Thou shalt love thy brother as thyself, and never act towards him but as thou wouldst that he should act towards thee." I forget the chapter and verse, but it seems he took the bull by the horns, and declared *all men* to be brothers,—not Muslimeen only,—and desired his congregation to look at the good deeds of others, and not at their erroneous faith ; for God is all-knowing (*i. e.* He only knows the heart), and if they saw aught amiss, to remember that the best men need say " Astaghfir Allah " (I beg pardon of God) seven times a day.

I wish the English could know how unpleasant and mischievous their manner of talking to their servants about religion is. Omar confided to me how bad it felt to be questioned and then to see the Englishman laugh, or put up his lip and say nothing. " I don't want to talk about his religion at all, but if he talks about mine, he ought to speak of his own too. You, my lady, say when I tell you things, ' that is the same with us,' or, that is different, or good or not good, in your mind; and that is the proper way,—not to look like thinking, *all nonsense.*"

LETTER XLI.

Esneh, Saturday, April 30, 1864.

On Tuesday evening, as I was dreamily sitting on my divan, who should walk in but my cousin A—— T——, on his way all alone, in a big dahabeeyeh, to Edfoo!—so I offered to go too, whereupon he said he would go on to Aswán and see Philæ, as he had company; and we went off to Mustafa to make a bargain with his Reyyis for it. Thus, then, here we are at Esneh. I embarked on Wednesday evening, and we have been two days *en route.*

Yesterday we had the thermometer at 110°. I was the only person awake all day in the boat: Omar, after cooking, lay panting at my feet on the deck; A—— went fairly to bed in the cabin; ditto S——. All the crew slept on the deck. Omar cooked amphibiously, bathing between every meal. The silence of noon, with the *white heat* glowing on the river which flowed like liquid tin, and the silent Nubian rough boats floating down without a ripple, was magnificent, and really awful. Not a breath of wind as we lay under the lofty bank. The Nile is not quite low, and I see a very different scene from last year. People think us crazy to go up to Aswán in May, but I do enjoy it, and I really wanted to forget all the sickness and sorrow in which I have taken part. When I went to Mustafa's he said Sheykh Yoosuf was ill, and I said, "Then I won't go." But Yoosuf came in with a sick headache only. Mustafa repeated my words to him, and never did I see such a lovely expression in human face as that with which Yoosuf said, "Eh, ya Sitt." Mustafa laughed and told him to thank me, and Yoosuf turned to me and said in a low voice, "My sister does not need thanks, save from God." Fancy a shereef, one of the Ulema, calling a Frangeeyeh "sister"! His pretty little girl came in and played with me, and he offered her to me for M——. I cured Khursheed's Circassian slave-girl; you would have laughed to see him obeying my directions, and wiping his eyes on his gold-embroidered sleeve. Then the Coptic priest came for me to go to his wife, who was ill; and he was in a great quandary, because, if she died, he, as a priest, could never marry again, as he loudly lamented before her; but he was truly grieved, and I was very happy to leave her convalescent.

Verily, we are sorely visited; the dead cattle float down by thousands. M. M—— buried a thousand at El-Mootaneh alone, and lost forty men. I would not have left El-Uksur, but there were no new cases for four days before, and the worst had been over for full ten days. Two or three poor people brought me new bread and vegetables to the boat, when they saw me going, and Yoosuf came down and sat with us all the evening, and looked quite sad. Omar asked him why, and he said "it made him think how it would seem when, 'Inshá-alláh,' I should be well, and should leave my place empty at El-Uksur, and go back, with the blessing of God, to my own place and my own people;" whereupon Omar grew sentimental too, and nearly cried.

I don't know how A—— would have managed without us, for he had come to Egypt with two Frenchmen who had proper servants, and who left the boat at Girgeh; and he has only a wretched little dirty Cairene Copt, who can do nothing but cheat a little. He has been spoiled by an Italian education and Greek associates, and thinks himself very grand because he is a Christian. I wonder at the patience and good-nature with which Omar does all his work and endures all his insolence. It really is becoming quite a calamity about servants here. But neither he nor the other men would tolerate what they thought an act of disrespect to me. Ramadán half strangled him; Omar called him dog, and asked him if he was an infidel. All the men cursed him. Omar sobbed with passion, saying that I was to him "like the back of his mother," "and how dared Macarius take my name into his dirty mouth?" The Copt afterwards tried to complain of being beaten, but I signified to him that he had better hold his tongue, for that I understood Arabic; upon which he sneaked off. A—— tells me that men not fit to light Omar's pipe asked him £10 a month in Cairo, and would not take less, and he gives his Copt £6. I really feel as if I were cheating Omar to let him stay on at £3 ; but if I say anything, he kisses my hand and tells me " not to be cross."

Everything is enormously dear. The country people do not suffer, but the town people must be dreadfully pinched and starved. Omar often looks grave, when he thinks of what his wife must be paying now for her living in Alexandria. It is really too hot to write, and I feel given up to laziness and to sitting on deck, looking at the river. I have letters from Yoosuf to people at Aswán ; if I should want anything, I am to call on the Kádee. We have a very excellent boat and a good crew, and are very comfortable. When the El-Uksur folks heard the " son of my uncle" was come, they thought it must be my husband. A—— has been all along the Suez Canal, and seen a great many curious things ; the Delta must be very unlike Upper Egypt, from what he tells me.

The little Káfileh for Mecca left El-Uksur about ten days ago ; it was a pretty and touching sight—three camels, five donkeys, and about thirty men and women, several with babies on their shoulders, all uttering the

Zagháreet (cry of joy). They will walk to Kuseyr (eight days' journey with good camels), babies and all. It is the happiest day of their lives, they say, when they have scraped money enough to make the hájj. This minute a poor man is weeping beside our boat over a pretty heifer decked with many Hegábs (amulets) which have not availed against the sickness. It is heartrending to see the poor beasts and their unfortunate owners.

Some dancing-girls came to the boat just now for cigars which A—— had promised them, and to ask after their friend El Maghrabeeyeh, the good dancer at El-Uksur, who, they said, was very ill. Omar did not know anything about her, and the girls seemed much distressed; they were both very pretty, one an Abyssinian. I must leave off to send this to the post. It will cost a fortune, but you won't grudge it.

LETTER XLII.

El-Uksur, May 15, 1864.

WE returned to El-Uksur the evening before last, just after dark. The salute which Omar fired with your old horse-pistols brought down a host of people, and there was a chorus of "El-hamdu-lilláh Sálimeh ya Sitt!" and such a kissing of hands, and " Welcome home to your place!" and " We have tasted your absence and found it bitter!" etc. etc. Mustafa came with letters for me, and Yoosuf, beaming with smiles; and Mohammad, with new bread made of new wheat, and Suleyman with flowers, and little Ahmad rushing in wildly to kiss hands. When the welcome had subsided, Yoosuf, who stayed to tea, told me all the cattle were dead. Mustafa lost thirty-four, and had three left; and poor farmer Omar lost all—fifty-seven head. The people are pretty well here; but the distress in Upper Egypt will now be fearful. Within six weeks all our cattle are dead. They are threshing the corn with donkeys, and men are turning the sákiyehs, and drawing the ploughs, and in many places dying by scores, of overwork and want of food. The whole agriculture depended on the oxen, and they are all dead. At El-Mootaneh, and the nine villages around Haleem Pasha's estate, 24,000 head have died, and four beasts were left when we were there, three days ago.

Well, I will recount my journey. We spent two days and nights at Philæ. It *was* hot; the basaltic rocks which enclose the river all round the island were burning. S—— and I slept in the Osiris chamber, on the roof of the temple, on our air-beds. Omar lay across the doorway, to guard us; and A—— and his Copt, with the well-bred sailor Ramadán, were sent to bivouac on the Pylon. Ramadán took the Hareem under his especial and most respectful charge, and waited on us devotedly, but never raised his eyes to our faces, or spoke till spoken to. Philæ is six or seven miles from Aswán, and we went on donkeys through the beautiful village of the Cataract, and the noble place of tombs of Aswán. Great was the amazement of every one at seeing Europeans so out of season; we were like swallows in January to them. I could not sleep for the heat in the room, and threw on an abbayeh, and went and lay on the parapet of the temple. What a night! what a lovely view! the stars gave as much light as the moon in Europe, and all but the Cataract was still as death, and glowing hot, and the palm-trees were more graceful and dreamy than ever. Then Omar woke, and came and sat at my feet, and rubbed them, and sang a song of a Turkish slave. I said, "Do not rub my feet, O brother! that is not fit for thee," (it is below the dignity of a free Muslim altogether to touch shoes or feet): but he sang in his song, "The slave of the Turk may be set free by money, but how shall one be ransomed who has been paid for by kind actions and sweet words?"

Then the day broke deep crimson, and I went down and bathed in the Nile, and saw the girls on the island opposite in their summer fashions, consisting of a leathern fringe round their slender hips,—divinely graceful!

—bearing huge saucer-shaped baskets of corn on their stately young heads; and I went up and sat at the end of the colonnade, looking up into Ethiopia, and dreamed dreams of "Him who sleeps in Philæ," until the great Amun-Ra kissed my northern face too hotly, and drove me into the temple to breakfast and coffee, and pipes and keyf; and in the evening three little naked Nubians rowed us about for two or three hours on the glorious river in a boat made of thousands of bits of wood, each a foot long, and between whiles they jumped overboard and disappeared, and came up on the other side of the boat. Aswán was full of Turkish soldiers, who came and took away our donkeys, and stared at our faces most irreligiously. We returned from Philæ to our boat the third morning; and S—— fainted after we got back, from a combination of heat, fatigue, and cucumber for supper. Omar came in, and cried over her bitterly,—frightened out of his senses at seeing a faint. She was all right again, next day; but I was ill, and lay in bed; and Omar did sick-nurse, and brought me pigeons boiled with rice, which are esteemed medicinal.

When I refused to eat, he proceeded to pull off tit-bits with his fingers, and to feed me with them. I wished it had happened to "a particular" Englishwoman just arrived. I have got to prefer food with fingers—Arab fingers I mean, which are washed fifty times a day. I got well again directly, but did not go ashore at Kóm Omboo or El-Káb,—only at Edfoo, where we spent the day in the temple, and at Esneh, where we tried to buy sugar, tobacco, etc., and found nothing at all, —even at Esneh, which is a *chef-lieu*, with a mudeer. It is only in winter that there is anything to be got for the travellers. We had to get the Názir in Edfoo to order a man to sell us charcoal. People do without sugar, and smoke green tobacco, and eat beans, etc.; and soon we must do likewise, for our stores are nearly exhausted. We stopped at El-Mootaneh and had a good dinner in the M——s' handsome house there, and they gave us a loaf of sugar.

Madame M—— described Rachel's stay with them for three months at El-Uksur, in my house, where they then lived. Rachel hated it so that, on embarking to leave, she turned back and spat on the ground, and cursed the place inhabited by savages, where she had been *ennuyée à mort.*

French women generally do not like the Arabs, who, they say, are not at all " galants." As I write this, I laugh to think of *galanterie* and Arab in one sentence, and glance at " my brother" Yoosuf, who is sleeping on a mat, quite overcome with the Simoom, which is blowing, and the fast which he is keeping to-day as the eve of the Eed el-Kebir.

This is the coolest place in the village; the glass is only $98\frac{1}{2}°$ now at 11 A.M., in the darkened divan. The Kádee, the Maohn, and Yoosuf came together to visit me, and when the others went, Yoosuf lay down to sleep; Omar is sleeping in the passage, S—— in her own room. I alone don't sleep; but the Simoom is terrible. A—— runs about sight-seeing and drawing all day, and does not suffer at all from the heat. I can't walk now, as the sand blisters my feet. Last night I slept on the terrace and was very hot. To-day at noon, the north wind sprang up and re-vived us, though it is still 102° in my deewan.

My old great-grandfather (as he calls himself) has come in for a pipe and coffee. He was Belzoni's guide, and his eldest child was born seven days before the French under Bonaparte marched into El-Uksur. He is superbly handsome and erect, and very talkative, but only remembers old times, and takes me for Madame Belzoni. He is grandfather to Mohammad, the guard of this house, and great-great-grandfather to my little Ahmad. His grandsons have married him to a decent old woman, to take care of him. He calls me " my lady grand-daughter," and Omar he calls Mustafa, and we salute him as " Grandfather." I wish I could paint him, he is so grand to look at.

The Simoom has lasted nine days, and is very trying; the tremendous sweating thins us all. The glass keeps at 98°, which is very pleasant with the north wind, but the Simoom parches one; it is awful,—so dark and depressing.

LETTER XLIII.

El-Uksur, June 12, 1864.

I HAVE had an abominable toothache, which was much aggravated by the Oriental custom, namely, that all' the *beau monde* of Thebes would come and sit with me, and suggest remedies, and look into my mouth, and make quite a business of my tooth. Sheykh Yoosuf laid two fingers on my cheek, and recited verses from the Koran,—I regret to say, with no effect, except that while his fingers touched me the pain ceased. I find he is celebrated for soothing headaches and other nervous pains; I dare say he is an unconscious mesmerizer.

The other day, our poor Maohn was terrified by a communication from Alee Bey (Mudeer of Kiné), to the effect that he had heard from Alexandria, that some one had reported that the dead cattle had lain about in the streets of El-Uksur, and that the place was pestilential. The British mind at once suggested a counter-statement, to be signed by the most respectable inhabitants; so the Kádee drew it up, and came and read it to me, and took my deposition and witnessed my signature; and the Maohn went his way rejoicing, in that "Kalám el-Inkeleezeeyeh" (the words of the Englishwoman) would utterly defeat Alee Bey. The truth is, that the worthy Maohn worked really hard, and superintended the horrible dead-cattle business in person, which is some risk, and very unpleasant. To dispose of three or four hundred dead oxen every day, with a very limited staff of labourers, is no trifle; and if a travelling Englishman smells one a mile off, he abuses the "lazy Arabs." The beasts could not be buried deep enough, but all were carried a mile off from the village. I wish some of the *dilettanti* who stop their noses at us in our trouble, had to see or to do what I have seen and done.

June 17.—We have had four or five days of such fearful heat, with a simoom, that I have been quite knocked up, and literally could not write; besides, I sit in the dark all day, and am now writing in the dark. At night I go out and sit in the Feshah, and can't have candles because of the insects. I sleep out till about six A.M., and then go in-doors till dark again. This fortnight is the hottest time. To-day the drop falls into the Nile at the source, and it will now rise fast and cool the country; it has risen one cubit, and the water is green,—next month it will be blood-colour. We can't sleep now under a roof at all, so now we are as lazy as we can afford to be, and only do what we must. The tooth does not ache now, praise be to God! for I rather dreaded the barber with his tongs, who is the sole dentist here.

I was amused the other day by the entrance of my friend the Maohn, attended by Osmán Efendi, and his kawás and pipe-bearer, and bearing a saucer in his hand, and wearing the look, half sheepish, half elate, with which elderly gentlemen in all countries announce what he did; *i.e.* that his Gariyeh (black slave-girl) was three months gone with child, and longed for olives; so the respectable magistrate

had trotted all over the bazaar, and to the
Greek corn-dealers, to buy some, but for no
money were they to be had. So he hoped I
might have some, and that I would forgive the
request, as I of course knew that a man must
beg, or even steal for a woman under these
circumstances. I called Omar, and said, " I
trust there are olives for the honourable hareem of Seleem Efendi; they are needed there."
Omar immediately understood the case, and
exclaimed,—" Praise be to God! a few are
left; I was about to stuff the pigeons for dinner with them; how lucky I had not done it!"
and then we belaboured Seleem with compliments. "Please God, the child will be fortunate to thee!" said I. Omar said, " Sweeten
my mouth, O Efendim, for did I not tell thee
God would give thee good out of this affair,
when thou boughtest her?" While we were
thus rejoicing over the possible little mulatto, I
thought how shocked a white christian gentleman of our colonies would be at our conduct.
To make such a fuss about a black girl; *he*
give her sixpence! (under the same circumstances, I mean,) he'd see her"—etc., and my
heart warmed to the kind old Muslim sinner (?)

as he took his saucer of olives, and walked with them openly in his hand along the street. Now the black girl is free, and can only leave Seleem's house by her own goodwill; and probably after a time she will marry, and he will pay the expenses. A man cannot sell his slave after he has made known that she is with child by him, and it would be considered unmanly to detain her if she should wish to go. The child will be added to the other eight who fill the Maohn's quiver at Cairo, and will be exactly as well looked on, and have equal rights, if it is as black as a coal.

A most quaint little half-black boy, a year and a half old, has taken a fancy to me, and comes and sits for hours gazing at me, and then dances to amuse me; he is Mohammad, our guard's son, by a jet-black slave of his, and is brown-black, and very pretty. He wears a bit of iron-wire in one ear, and iron rings round his ankles, and nothing else; and when he comes up, little Ahmad, who is his uncle, " makes him fit to be seen " by emptying a pitcher of water over his head, to rinse the dust off, in which, of course, he had been rolling. That is equivalent to a clean pinafore. You would want to buy little Saeed, I know; he is so pretty and jolly; he sings and dances, and jabbers baby-Arabic, and then sits like a quaint little idol, cross-legged, quite still for hours.

I am now writing in the kitchen, which is the coolest place where there is any light at all. Omar is diligently spelling words of six letters, with a wooden spoon in his hand, and a cigarette in his mouth; S—— lying on the floor. I won't describe our costume; it is two months since I have worn gloves or stockings, and I think you would wonder at the " Fellahah" who "owns you,"—so deep a brown are my face, hands, and feet. One of the sailor's in A——'s boat said, " See how the sun of the Arabs loves her; he has kissed her so hotly that she can't go home among her own people."

Poor Suleyman's little boy is dead of small-pox; luckily it has not spread. The fact is, that vaccination is far more general here than in Europe; very few neglect it. Suleyman is grievously altered, so pale and thin. He talked just like a Muslim. " Allah! Min Allah! Maktoob!" (it is written!) You would not know a Christian here at all by his talk, or his feelings on religious matters.

I went last night to look at El-Karnak by moonlight; the giant columns were overpowering,—I never saw anything so solemn. On our way back we met the Sheykh-el-Beled, who ordered me an escort of ten men home. Fancy me on my humble donkey, guarded most superfluously by ten tall fellows, with, oh! such spears and venerable matchlocks! At Mustafa's house we found a party seated before the door, and joined it. There was a tremendous Sheykh-el-Islám from Tunis, a Maghrabee, seated on a carpet, in state, receiving homage. I don't think he liked the heretical woman at all; even the Maohn did not dare to be as polite as usual to me, but took the seat above me, which I had respectfully left vacant, next to the holy man. Mustafa was in a perplexity,—afraid not to do the respectful to me and fussing after the sheykh. Just then Yoosuf came fresh out of the river, where he had bathed and prayed; and then you saw the real gentleman. He salámed the great sheykh, who motioned to him to sit before him, but Yoosuf quietly came round and sat *below* me on the mat, leaned his elbow on my cushion, and made more demonstrations of regard for me than ever; and when I went, came and helped me on my donkey. The holy Sheykh went away to pray, and Mustafa hinted to Yoosuf to go with him, but he only smiled, and did not stir; he had prayed an hour before down at the Nile. It was as if a poor curate had devoted himself to a Papist under the nose of a scowling Low Church Bishop.

Then came Osman Efendi, a young Turk, with a poor devil accused in a distant village of stealing a letter with money in it, addressed to a Greek money-lender. The discussion was quite general,—the man of course denying all; but the Názir had sent word to beat him. Then Omar burst out,—"What a shame to beat a poor man on the mere word of a Greek money-lender, who eats the people! The Názir should not help him." There was a Greek present who scowled at Omar, and the Turk gaped at him in horror. Yoosuf said with his quiet smile, "My brother, thou art talking English," with a glance at me; and we all laughed, and I said, "Many thanks for the compliment."

All the village is in good spirits. The Nile is rising fast, and a star of most fortunate character has made its appearance,—so Yoosuf tells me,—and portends a good year, and an end to our afflictions. I am much better. I, too, feel the rising Nile; it puts new life into all things. The last fortnight or three weeks have been very trying, with the simoom and intense heat. I suppose I look better, for the people here are for ever praising God about my amended looks.

LETTER XLIV.

June 26, 1864.

I HAVE just paid a singular visit to a political *détenu*, or exile rather. Last night Mustafa came in with a man in great grief, who said his boy was very ill on board a kangeh, just come from Cairo, and going to Aswán. The watchman on the river-bank had told him that there was an English "Sitt, who would not turn her face from any one in trouble," and advised him to come to me for medicine. So he went to Mustafa, and begged him to bring him to me, and to beg the kawás (policeman) in charge of El-Bedrawee (who was being sent in banishment to Feyzoghloo), to wait a few hours. The kawás (may he not suffer for his humanity!) consented. The poor father described his boy's symptoms, and I gave him a dose of castor-oil, and said I would go to the boat in the morning. El-Bedrawee was a Cairo merchant, but living at Khartoom; he poured out his sorrow in true Eastern style. "Oh! my boy, and I have none but he! and how shall I come before his mother, O lady, and tell her, 'Thy son is dead'?" So I comforted him, and went this morning early to the boat. It was a regular old Arab kangeh, lumbered up with corn-sacks of matting, live sheep, etc. etc.; and there I found a sweet graceful boy, of fifteen or so, in a high fever. The oil had not acted, so I sent for my medicine-chest, and gave what I thought best. The symptoms were the usual ones of the epidemic. His father said he had visited a certain Pasha on the way, and evidently meant that he had been poisoned, or had the evil eye. I assured him it was only the epidemic, and asked why he had not sent for the doctor at Kiné. The old story,—he was afraid: "God knows what a Government doctor might do to the boy!"

Then Omar came in, and stood before El-Bedrawee, and said, "O my master, why do we see thee thus? I once ate of thy bread when I was of the soldiers of Saeed Pasha, and

I saw thy riches and thy greatness; and what has God decreed against thee?" So El-Bedrawee, who is (or was) one of the wealthiest men of Lower Egypt, and lived at Tanta, related how Efendeena (Ismail Pasha) sent for him to go to Cairo to the citadel, to transact some business; and how he rode his horse up to the citadel, and went in, and there the Pasha at once ordered a kawás to take him down to the Nile, and on board a common cargo-boat, and to go with him, and to take him to Feyzoghloo. Letters were given to the kawás to deliver to every Mudeer by the way, and another dispatched by land to the governor of Feyzoghloo, with orders concerning El-Bedrawee. He begged leave to see his son once more before starting, or any of his family. " No, he must go away at once, and see no one." But luckily a Fellah, one of his relations, had come after him to Cairo, and had £700 in his girdle; he followed El-Bedrawee to the citadel, and saw him being walked off by the kawás, and followed him to the river, and on board the boat, and gave him the £700 which he had in his girdle. The various Mudeers had been civil to him, and friends in different places had given him clothes and food. He had not got a chain round his neck, nor fetters, and was allowed to go ashore with the kawás, for he had just been to the tomb of Abu-l-Haggág, and had told that dead sheykh all his afflictions, and promised, if he came back safe, to come every year to his Moolid (*fête*), and pay the whole expenses (*i. e.* feed all comers). Mustafa wanted him to dine with him and me; but the kawás could not allow it, and so Mustafa sent him a fine sheep, and some bread, fruit, etc. I made him a present of some quinine, rhubarb pills, and sulphate of zinc for eye-lotion.

Here, you know, we all go upon a more than English presumption, and believe every prisoner to be innocent, and a victim. As he gets no trial, he *never* can be proved guilty. Besides, poor old El-Bedrawee declared he had not the faintest idea what he was accused of, or how he had offended Efendeena. I listened to all this in extreme amazement; and he said, "Ah, I know you English manage things very differently. I have heard all about your excellent justice." He was a stout, dignified-looking, fair man, like a Turk, but talking broad Lower Egypt Fellah talk, so that I could not understand him, and had to get Mustafa and Omar to repeat his words. His father was an Arab, and his mother a Circassian slave-girl, which gave the fair skin and reddish beard. He must be over fifty, fat, and not healthy. Of course, he is meant to die up in Feyzoghloo, especially going at this season; he was much overcome with the heat even here. He owns (or owned, for God knows who has it now!) twelve thousand feddáns of fine land between Tanta and Sámánnood, and was enormously rich. He consulted me a great deal about his health, and I gave him certainly very good advice. I cannot write what drugs a Turkish doctor had furnished him with, to *strengthen* him in the trying climate of Feyzoghloo. I wonder, were they intended to kill him, or only given in ignorance of the laws of health equal to his own? After awhile, the pretty boy became better, and recovered consciousness; and his poor father, who had been helping me with trembling hands and swimming eyes, cried for joy, and said, " By God the Most High, if ever I find any of the English poor or sick or afflicted up in Feyzoghloo, I will make them know that I, Aboo-Mohammad, never saw a face like the pale face of the English lady bent over my sick boy;" and then El-Bedrawee and his Fellah kinsman, and all the crew, blessed me; and the captain and the kawás said it was time to sail. So I gave directions and medicine to Aboo-Mohammad, and kissed the pretty boy, and went out.

El-Bedrawee followed me up the bank, and said he had a request to make,—"Would I pray for him in his distress?" I said, "I am not of the Muslimeen;" but both he and Mustafa said, "Máleysh!" (never mind) for it was quite certain I was not of the Mushrikeen, as they hate the Muslimeen, and their deeds are evil; but, blessed be God, many of the English begin to repent of their evil, and to love the Muslims, and abound in kind actions." So we parted in much kindness. It was a strange feeling to me to stand on the bank and see the queer savage-looking boat glide away up the stream, bound to such far more savage lands, and to be exchanging kind farewells, quite in a *homely* manner, with such utter "aliens in blood and faith." "God keep thee, lady!" "God keep thee, Mustafa!" Mustafa and I walked home very sad about poor El-Bedrawee.

Friday, July 7.—It has been so intensely hot that I have not had pluck to go on with my letter, or indeed to do anything but lie on a mat in the passage, with a minimum of clothes quite indescribable in English. "El-hamdu-lilláh!" laughs Omar, "that I see the clever English people do just like the lazy Arabs." The worst is, not the positive heat, which has not been above 104°, and as low as 96° at night, but the horrible storms of hot winds which are apt to come on at night, and prevent one's even lying down till twelve or one o'clock. Thebes is bad in the height of summer, on account of its expanse of desert, and sand and dust. The Nile is pouring down gloriously, but *really* as red as blood—more crimson than a Herefordshire lane; and in the far distance the reflection of the pure blue sky makes it deep violet. It had risen five cubits a week ago; we shall soon have it all over the land here. It is a beautiful and inspiriting sight to see the noble old stream as young and vigorous as ever. No wonder the Egyptians worshipped the Nile; there is nothing like it.

We have had all the plagues of Egypt this year, only the lice are commuted for bugs, and the frogs for mice; the former have eaten me, and the latter have eaten my clothes. We are so ragged! Omar has one shirt left, which he has to wash every night. The dust, the drenching perspiration, and the hard-fisted washing of Mohammad's slave-woman destroy everything. Then I cannot wear stockings or any close-fitting garments; I go about in slippers and a loose dress, and that is worn out.

I have just received a letter from you and one from J——. Who could have imposed upon her credulity by the story of Ulema at a ball? Why, the bench of bishops in the opera stalls would be more probable. An Alim can't see dancing or hear music, and if the Pasha forced them to go he has sinned fearfully; it would be an abomination. Do you know that if a Muslim " sins with his eye," it is as bad as if he had sinned altogether? He must bathe all over before he can eat or pray. I don't say all do it, but the Ulema would not expose themselves to sin and scandal;—the chief merchants and police people, *à la bonne heure*,—but the Ulema, who are " the men of the law," no! Mustafa intends to give you a grand fantasia if you come, and to have the best dancing-girls down from Esneh for you.

I have been "too lazy Arab," as Omar calls it, to go on with my Arabic lessons, and Yoosuf has been very busy with law business connected with the land and the crops. Every harvest brings a fresh settlement of the land. Wheat is selling at one pound the ardebb here on the threshing-floor, and barley at a hundred and sixteen piastres; I saw some Nubians pay Mustafa that. He is in comic perplexity about such enormous gains. You see it is rather awkward for a Muslim to thank God for dear bread; so he compounds by lavish almsgiving. He gave all his Fellaheen clothes the other day,—forty calico shirts and drawers.

Do you remember my describing an *emancipirtes Fräulein* at Asyoot? Well, the other day I saw, as I thought, a nice-looking lad of sixteen selling corn to my opposite neighbour, a Copt. It was a girl. Her father has no sons, and is infirm, so she works in the fields for him, and dresses and does like a man; she looked very modest, and was quieter in her manner than the veiled women often are.

I can hardly bear to think of another year without seeing the children. However, it is lucky for me that "my lines have fallen in pleasant places;" so long a time at the Cape, or any colony, would have become intolerable. If I can afford it, I will go down to Cairo with the Big Nile next month, or in September, and await you there. Omar desires his salám to his great master, and to that gazelle, Sittch R——.

LETTER XLV.

El-Uksur, August 13, 1864.

For the last month we have had a purgatory of hot wind and dust, such as I never saw,—impossible to stir out of the house; so, in despair, I have just engaged a return boat, a *Gelegenheit*, and am off to Cairo in a day or two, where I shall stop till, "Inshalláh!" you come to me.   November is the pleasant time in Cairo.

I am a "stupid, lazy Arab" now, having lain on a mat in a dark stone passage for six weeks or so; but my chest is no worse,—better, I think,—and my health has not suffered at all, only I am stupid and lazy.   I had a pleasant visit lately from a great doctor from Mecca, a man so learned that he can read the Koran in seven different ways, and also from a physician of European *hekmeh*. Fancy my wonder when a great Alim in gorgeous Hejazee dress walked in and said, "Madame, tout ce qu'on m'a dit de vous fait tellement l'éloge de votre cœur et de votre esprit, que je me suis arrêté pour tâcher de me procurer le plaisir de votre connaissance." A number of El-Uksur people came in, to pay their respects to the great man, and he said to me that he hoped I had not been molested on account of my religion, and if I had I must forgive it, as the people here were so ignorant, and *barbarians were bigots everywhere.* I said, "The people of El-Uksur are my brothers;" and the Maohn said, " True, the Féllaheen are like oxen, but they are not such swine as to insult the religion of a lady who has served God among them like this one. She risked her life every day." " And if she had died," said the great theologian," her place was made ready among the martyrs of God, because she showed more love to her brethren than to herself." Now, if this was humbug, it was said in Arabic before eight or ten people, by a man of great religious authority. Omar was " in heaven " to hear his " Sitt " spoken of " in such a grand way for the religion." I believe that a great change is taking place among the Ulema; that Islam is ceasing to be a mere party-flag, just as occurred with Christianity; and that all the moral part is being more and more dwelt on. My great Alim also said I had practised the precepts of the Koran; and then laughed and said, "I suppose I ought to say, the Gospel; but what matters it? The truth (el Hakk) is one, whether spoken by our Lord Eesa or by our Lord Mohammad."

He asked me to go to Mecca next winter for my health, as it is so hot and dry there. I found he had fallen in with El-Bedrawee and the Khartoom merchant at Aswán. The little boy was well again, and I had been out-rageously extolled by them. I have suffered horribly from prickly heat, till I thought it would end in erysipelas; but the Arabian doctor told me to do nothing to it, to bear it patiently, as he believed it would do my lungs good; and I am sure he was right.

We are now sending off all the corn. I sat the other evening on Mustafa's doorstep, and saw the Greeks piously and zealously attending to the divine command, to spoil the Egyptians. Eight months ago, a Greek bought up corn at sixty piastres the ardebb; (he foresaw the Coptic tax-gatherer, like a vulture after a crow;) now wheat is a hundred and seventy piastres the ardebb here; and the Fellah has paid three and a half per cent. per month besides,—reckon the profit! Two men I know are quite ruined, and have sold all they had. The cattle disease forced them to borrow at these ruinous rates, and now, alas! the Nile is sadly lingering in its rise, and people are very anxious.

Poor Egypt! or rather, poor Egyptians! Of course I need not say that there is great improvidence in those who can be fleeced, as they are fleeced. Mustafa's household is a pattern of muddling hospitality, and Mustafa is generous and mean by turns. But what chance have people like these, so utterly ignorant of all that we call civilization, and so isolated as the Upper Egyptians, against Europeans of unscrupulous character? I now know the Fellaheen pretty well, I think. I can't write more in the wind and dust; I will write again from Cairo. If you lived in "constant simoom," you would be as lazy.

LETTER XLVI.

Cairo, October 21, 1864.

I RECEIVED your letter yesterday; I hope you have heard I am better. My illness turned out to be continued fever, not intermittent, and ended in congestion of the liver, of course aggravating the cough; but I am now " all right" again, only rather weak. However, I ride my donkey, and the weather has suddenly become glorious, dry, and cool. (I rather shiver with the thermometer at 79°; absurd, is it not? but I got so used to real heat.)

I could not write about my departure from El-Uksur, or my journey, for our voyage was quite tempestuous after the first three days, and I fell ill as soon as I was in my house. I hired a boat for six purses (£18), which had taken Greeks up to Aswán, selling groceries and strong drinks; but the Reyyis would not bring back their return-cargo of black slaves to dirty the boat, and picked us up at El-Uksur.

We sailed at daybreak, having waited all the day before, because it was an unlucky day. As I sat in the boat, people kept coming to ask very anxiously whether I should return, and bringing fresh bread, eggs, and other things, as presents; and all the *quality* came to take leave, and hope, " Inshalláh !" I should soon " come home to my village" safe, and bring the Master, please God, to see them; and then to say the Fat'hah, for a safe journey and my health.

In the morning, the balconies of my house were filled with a singular group, to see us sail;—a party of wild black Abab'deh, with their long Arab guns and flowing hair, a Turk, elegantly dressed, Mohammad, in his decorous brown robes and snow-white tur-ban, and several Fellaheen. As the boat moved off, the Abab'deh blazed away with their guns, and Osman Efendee with a sort of blunderbuss; and as we dropped down the river there was a general firing, even Todoros (Theodore), the Coptic Ma'allim, popped off his

American revolver, Omar keeping up a return with A——'s old horse-pistols, which are much admired here on account of the excessive noise they make. Poor old Ismaeen, who always thought I was Madame Belzoni, and wanted to take me to meet my husband up at Aboo-Sembel, was in dire distress that he could not go with me to Cairo. He declared he was still "shedeed,"—strong enough to take care of me, and fight. He is ninety-seven, and only remembers what occurred fifty or sixty years ago, in the old wild times; a splendid old man, handsome, and erect. I used to give him coffee, and listen to his long stories, which had won his heart. His grandson, the quiet and rather stately Mohammad, who is guard of the house I lived in, forgot all his Muslim dignity, broke down in the middle of his set speech, flung himself on the ground, and kissed and hugged my knees, and cried. He had got some notion of impending ill-luck, I found, and was unhappy at our departure, and the baksheesh failed to console him. Sheykh Yoosuf was to come with me, but a brother of his just then wrote word that he was coming back from the Hejaz, where he had been with the troops in which he is serving his time. I was very sorry to lose his company. Fancy, how dreadfully irregular for one of the Ulema and a heretical woman to travel together! What would our bishops · say to a parson who did such a thing?

We had a lovely time on the river for three days, and such moonlight nights! so soft and lovely; and we had a sailor, who was as good as an Alatee, or professional singer. He sang religious songs, which, I observe, excite these people more than love songs. One, which began, " Remove my sins from before thy sight, O God," was really beautiful and touching, and I did not wonder at the tears which streamed down Omar's face. A very pretty profane song ran thus;—" Keep the wind from me, ·O Lord! I fear it will hurt me" (*wind* means *love*, which is like the simoom). " Alas! it has struck me, and I am sick! Why do ye bring the physician? O physician, put back thy medicine in the canister, for only *he* who has hurt can cure me."

N.B. The masculine pronoun is always used instead of the feminine in poetry, out of decorum; sometimes even in conversation.

23rd October.

I must send my letter to-day or to-morrow. Yesterday I met a Saeedee, a friend of the brother of the Sheykh of the wild Abab'deh, and as we stood hand-shaking and kissing our fingers in the road, some of the Anglo-Indian travellers gazed with fierce disgust; the handsome Hasan, being black, was such a flagrant case of a " native."

It is really heart-breaking to see *what* we are sending to India now. The mail days are dreaded; we never know when some brutal outrage may possibly excite " Mussulman fanaticism." They try their hands on the Arabs, in order to be in good training for insulting Hindoos. The English tradesmen here complain as much as any of the natives; and I, who, to use the words of the Kádee of El-Uksur, am "not outside the family" (of Ishmael, I presume), hear what the Arabs really think. There are also crowds, " like lice," as one Mohammad said, of low Italians, French, etc.; and I find my stalwart Hasan's broad shoulders no superfluous "*porte-respect*" about the Frangee quarter. Three times I have been followed and insolently stared at (*à mon âge!!*), and once Hasan had to speak. Imagine how dreadful to Muslims! I have come to hate the sight of a hat in this country.

Was I not a true prophet in what I wrote from the Cape? . . . It seems that rumours of the disputes in our Church have reached a few people even here. They hope it will end favourably; *i. e.* in our conversion to the true faith (Islám). If God will, we shall yet " tear off our outer garments in a mosque, and confess there is no God but God." How curious it is to meet with precisely the same sentiment attaching itself to hostile creeds!

The dearness of all things is fearful here; all is treble at least what it was in 1862–63; but wages have risen in proportion. A sailor, who got 60 piastres a month, now gets 300. All is at the same rate—clothes, rents, everything. Cairo is dearer than London, and Alexandria dearer still, I believe,—at all events, as to rent.

I can't write more now, though I have much more to tell, but my eyes are very weak still.

Omar begs me to give you his best salám, and say, Inshalláh, he will take great care of your daughter, which he most zealously and tenderly does. Lady ——'s Italian courier despised Omar's heathenish ignorance in preferring to stay with me for half the wages he could have got elsewhere. It quite confirmed him in his contempt for the Arabs.

Let me say, by the bye, that I advise nobody to bring a retinue to this country. Italian couriers and French cooks are a perfect torment in Egypt; they hate the country, make difficulties, and find fault with everything. A good English servant, of either sex, gets along well; and, next best, a German. The Arabs like and respect them, but they despise the southern Europeans, whose faults are an exaggeration of their own, and who are vulgar into the bargain. Mind, I speak from the Arab *point de vue* entirely. Also, people who " make themselves big " must expect to pay for it, and must not be out of humour at the cost.

LETTER XLVII.

On the Nile, Friday, December 23, 1864.

HERE I am again between Benee-Suweyf and Minyeh, and already better for the clear air of the river and the tranquil boat-life; I will send you my Christmas salám from Asyoot. Many thanks for your baksheesh of the wine, which is very acceptable indeed. While —— was with me I had as much to do as I was able to accomplish, and really could not write, for I had not recovered from the fever, and there was much to see and talk about. I think he was amused, but I fear he felt the Eastern life to be very poor and comfortless, and was glad to get back to European ways in Alexandria. I have got so used to *having nothing*, that I had quite forgotten how it would seem to a new-comer. The real evil is the enormous cost of everything. Cairo is twice as dear as London in many things, and I expect to find even El-Uksur very expensive. There are very few travellers this year, partly, no doubt, in consequence of the cost of everything. I am quite sorry to find how many of my letters must have been lost from El-Uksur; in future I will trust the Arab post, which certainly is safer than English travellers.

Please to tell Dean Stanley that his old dragoman, Mohammad Gazowee, cried with pleasure when he told me he had seen "Sheykh Stanley's" sister on her way to India, and the little ladies "knew his name," and shook hands with him, which evidently was worth far more than the baksheesh. I wondered who "Sheykh Stanley" could be, and Mohammad (who is a darweesh, and very pious) told me he was the Gasees (priest) who was Imám (spiritual guide) to the son of our Queen; "and, in truth," said he, "he is really a Sheykh, and one who teaches the excellent things of religion. Why, he was kind even to his horse; and it is of the mercies of God to the English, that such a one is the Imám of your Queen and Prince."

"I said," laughing, "how dost thou, a dar-

weesh among Muslims, talk thus of a Nazarene priest?" "Truly, O Lady," said he, "one
who loveth all the creatures of God, him God
loveth also; there is no doubt of that."

Is any one bigot enough to deny that Dr.
Stanley has done more for real religion in the
mind of that Muslim darweesh, than if he had
baptized a hundred savages out of one fanatical faith into another? There is no hope
of a good understanding with Orientals until
Western Christians can bring themselves to
recognize what there is of common faith contained in the two religions; the real difference
consists in all the class of notions and feelings
(very important ones no doubt) which we de-
rive, not from the Gospels, but from Greece
and Rome, and which of course are altogether
wanting here.

—— will tell you how curiously Omar illustrated the patriarchal feelings of the East
by entirely dethroning me, to whom he is so
devoted, in favour of the "Master," whom he
had never seen. "*That our Master;* we all eat
bread from his hand and he work for *us*." Omar
and I were equal before *our* "Seedee." He can
sit at his ease at my feet, but when the Master

comes in he must stand reverently, and gives me to understand that I too must be respectful.

I have got the boat of the American Mission at an outrageous price—£60, but I could get nothing under; the consolation is that the sailors profit, poor fellows! and get treble wages. My crew are all Nubians; such a handsome Reyyis and steersman, brothers! and there is a black boy of fourteen or so, with legs and feet so sweetly beautiful as to be quite touching; at least I always feel those lovely round young innocent forms to be somehow affecting.

Our old boat of last summer (A—— T——'s) is sailing in company with us, and the stately old Reyyis, Mubárak, hails me every morning with the blessing of God and the peace of the Prophet; and Alee Kubtán, my steamboat captain, will announce our advent at Thebes. He passed us to-day. The boat is a fine sailer, but iron-built, and therefore noisy, and not convenient. The crew encourage her with "Get along, father of three!" because she has three sails, whereas two is the usual number. They are active, good-humoured fellows, my men, but lack the Arab courtesy and *simpatiche*

ways.   And then I don't like not understanding their language, which is pretty, and sounds
like Caffre, rather bird-like and sing-song, instead of the clattering, guttural Arabic.   This
latter language I now speak tolerably for a
stranger, *i. e.* I can keep up a conversation;
I understand all that is said to me much better than I can speak, and follow about half
what people say to each other.   I bought a
very tolerable dictionary in Cairo, which is
a great help and comfort.   When I see you,
Inshalláh, Inshalláh, next summer, I shall be
a good scholar, I hope.

                    Asyoot, December 29, 1864.

In haste.   I am remarkably well, and the
weather very fine, though the wind is fitful
God bless you

LETTER XLVIII.

El-Uksur, January, 1865.

I DISPATCHED a letter for you by the Arab post at Girgeh, as we had passed Asyoot with a good wind; I hope you will get it. My crew worked as I never saw men work; they were paid to get to El-Uksur, and for eighteen days they never rested nor slept, day or night, and were all the time quite merry and pleasant. It shows what powers of endurance these "lazy Arabs" have when there is good money at the end of a job, instead of the favourite panacea of "stick."

We arrived at midnight, and next morning my boat had the air of being pillaged: a crowd of laughing, chattering fellows ran off to the house laden with loose articles snatched up at random,—loaves of sugar, pots and pans, books, cushions,—all helter-skelter. I feared breakages, but all was housed safe and sound; the small boys, of an age licensed to penetrate into the cabin, went off with the oddest cargoes of dressing things and the like; of baksheesh not one word. " El-hamdu-lilláh salámeh" (thank God, thou art in peace), and "Ya Sitt, ya Emeereh," till my head went round. Old Ismaeen fairly hugged me, and little Ahmad clung close to my side. I went up to Mustafa's house while the unpacking took place, and breakfasted there, and found letters from all of you, from my dear mother, to my darling R——. Sheykh Yoosuf was charmed with her big hand-writing, and said he thought the news in that letter was the best of all. The weather was intensely hot the two first days. Now it is heavenly, a fine fresh air and gorgeous sunshine. I brought two common Arab lanterns for the tomb of Abu-l-Hajjáj, and his Moolid is now going on. Omar took them and lighted them up, and told me he found several people who called on the rest to say the Fat'hah for me.

I was sitting out yesterday with the people

on the sand, looking at the men doing fantasia on horseback for the Sheykh, and a clever dragoman of the party was relating about the death of a young English girl whom he had served, and so, *de fil en aiguille*, we talked about the strangers buried here, and how the bishop had extorted £100. I said, "Máleysh, (never mind,) the people have been hospitable to me while living, and they will not cease to be so if I die, but will give me a tomb among the Arabs." One old man said, "May I not see thy day, O Lady! and, indeed, thou shouldst be buried as a daughter of the Arabs, though we should fear the anger of thy Consul and thy family; but thou knowest that, wherever *thou* art buried, thou wilt assuredly lie in a Muslim grave."—"How so?" said I.—"Why, when a bad Muslim dies, the angels take him out of his tomb, and put one of the good from among the Christians in his place." This is the popular expression of the doctrine that the good are sure of salvation. Omar chimed in at once: "Certainly, there is no doubt of it; and I know a story that happened in the days of Mohammad Alee Pasha which proves it." We demanded the story, and Omar began.

"There was once a very rich man of the Muslims, so stingy, that he grudged everybody even so much as ' the bit of the paper inside the date ' (Koran). When he was dying, he said to his wife, ' Go out and buy me a lump of pressed dates;' and when she had bought it, he bade her leave him alone. Thereupon he took all his gold out of his sash, and spread it before him, and rolled it up, two or three pieces at a time, in dates, and swallowed it, piece after piece, until only three were left, when his wife came in and saw what he was doing, and snatched them from his hand. Presently after he fell back and died, and was carried out to the burial-place and laid in his tomb. When the Kádee's men came to put the seal on his property, and found no money, they said, ' O woman, how is this? We know thy husband was a rich man, and behold, we find no money for his children and slaves, nor for thee.' So the woman told what had happened, and the Kádee sent for three other of the Ulema, and they decided that after three days she should go herself to her husband's tomb and open it, and take the money from his stomach. Meanwhile a guard was put over the tomb, to keep away robbers. After three days, therefore, the woman went, and the men opened the tomb, and said, 'Go in, O woman, and take thy money.'

" So the woman went down into the tomb alone. When there, instead of her husband's body, she saw a box (coffin) of the boxes of the Christians, and when she opened it she saw the body of a young girl, adorned with many ornaments of gold, necklaces, and bracelets, and a diamond Kurs on her head, and over all a veil of black muslin, embroidered with gold. So the woman said within herself, ' Behold, I came for money, and here it is; I will take it, and conceal this business for fear of the Kádee.' So she wrapped up the whole in her meláyeh (a blue-checked cotton sheet, worn as a cloak), and came out, and the men said, ' Hast thou done thy business?' and she said, ' Yes,' and returned home. In a few days, she gave the veil she had taken from the dead girl to a dellal (broker) to sell for her in the bazaar, and the dellal went and showed it to the people, and was offered a hundred piastres. Now there sat in one of the shops of the merchants a great Ma'allim (Copt clerk), belonging to the Pasha, and he saw the veil, and said, 'How much askest thou?' and the dellal said, 'O Hadrat-el-Ma'allim! (your Honour the clerk,) whatever thou wilt.' Then the Ma'allim said, 'Take from me these five hundred piastres, and bring the person that gave thee the veil to receive the money.' So the dellal fetched the woman, and the Copt, who was a great man, called the police, and said, 'Take this woman, and fetch my ass, and we will go before the Pasha;' and he rode in haste to the palace, weeping and beating his breast, and went before the Pasha, and said, 'Behold, this veil was buried a few days ago with my daughter, who died unmarried; and I had none but her, and I loved her like my eyes, and would not take from her her ornaments; and this veil she worked herself, and was very fond of it; and she was young and beautiful, and just of the age to be married; and behold, the Muslims go and rob the tomb of the Christians, and if thou wilt suffer this, we Christians will leave Egypt, and go and live in some other country, O Efendeena! (our Lord,) for we cannot endure this abomination.' Then the Pasha turned to the woman, and said, 'Woe to thee, O woman! art thou a Muslimeh, and doest such wickedness?' And the woman spoke, and told all that happened, and how she sought money, and finding gold, had kept it. So the Pasha said, 'Wait, O Ma'allim, and we will discover the truth of this matter;' and he sent for the three Ulema, who had desired that the tomb should be opened at the end of three days, and told them the case; and they said, 'Open now the tomb of the Christian damsel,' and the Pasha sent his men to do so; and when they opened it, behold it was full of fire, and within it lay the body of the wicked and avaricious Muslim. Thus it was manifest to all that on the night of terror the angels of God had done this thing, and had laid the innocent girl of the Christians among those who have received direction, and the evil Muslim among the rejected."

Admire how rapidly legends arise here! This story, which every body declared was quite true, is placed no longer ago than in Mohammad Alee Pasha's time.

There are hardly any travellers this year; instead of a hundred and fifty or more boats,

perhaps twenty.   A youth of fourteen, of Is-
raelitish race, has just gone up, travelling like
a royal prince in one of the Pasha's steamers,
having all his expenses paid, and crowds of
attendants.   "All that honour to the money
of the Jew!" said an old Fellah to me, with a
tone of scorn.   He has turned out his dragoman, a respectable elderly man who is very
sick, paid him his bare wages, and given him
the munificent sum of six pounds to take him
back to Cairo.   On board his boat he had
a doctor and plenty of servants, and yet he
abandons the man here on.Mustafa's hands!

As I regret whatever tends to strengthen
prejudices, especially religious ones, I am very
sorry anything should occur to make the name
of Yahoodee stink yet more than it does in
the nostrils of the Arabs.   I have brought Er-
Rasheedee, the sick man, to my house, as poor
Mustafa is already overloaded with strangers.

Mr. Herbert, the painter, went back to Cairo
from Farshoot below Kiné.   So I have no
"Frangee" society at all; but Sheykh Yoosuf
and Sheykh Ibraheem, the Kádee, drop in to
tea very often, and as they are very agreeable
men, I am quite content with my company.

So far as manners go, no company can possibly be better. Indeed, I must confess that since I have become accustomed to the respectful ways of well-bred Arabs to hareem, I feel quite astonished at the manners of Englishmen. And yet all the people here call me "O sister!" and the poorest sit and talk quite freely and easily, without any embarrassment or constraint.

By the bye, I will tell you what I have learned as to the tenure of land in Egypt, which people are always disputing about, as the Kádee laid it down for me.

The *whole* land belongs to the Sultan of Turkey, the Pasha being his wekeel (representative), nominally, of course, as we know. Thus there are no owners, only tenants, paying from a hundred piastres tareef (£1) down to thirty piastres yearly per feddán (near about an acre), according to the quality of the land, or the favour of the Pasha when granting it. This tenancy is hereditary to children, but not to collaterals or ascendants, and it may be sold, but in that case application must be made to the Government ("el-meena"). If the owner or tenant dies childless, the land reverts to the

Sultan, *i. e.* to the Pasha; and *if the Pasha chooses to have any man's land, he can take it from him, with payment—or without.* Don't let any one tell you that I exaggerate, I have known it happen: I mean the *without;* and the man received feddán for feddán of desert in return for his good land, which he had tilled and watered.

To-morrow night is the great night of Sheykh Abu-l-Hajjáj's moolid, and I am desired to go to the mosque for the benefit of my health, etc., and that my friends may say a prayer for my children. The kind, hearty welcome I found has been a real pleasure, and every one was pleased, because I was glad to come home to my "Beled—Beledee;" and they all thought it so nice of my "master" to have come so far to see me, because I was sick; all but one Turk, who clearly looked with pitying contempt on so much trouble taken after a sick old woman.

I received your letter here. I did indeed feel with you; I have never left off the habit of thinking how I shall tell my father this and that, and how such things would interest him, and what he would say. The thought comes, and with it the sadness, more often than I can tell.

. . . .

I have left my letter a long while. You will not wonder, for after some ten days' fever, my poor guest, Mohammad Er-Rasheedee, died to-day. Two Prussian doctors gave me help for the last four days, but went last night. He sank to sleep quietly at noon, with his hand in mine. A good old Muslim sat at his head on one side, and I on the other. Omar stood at his head, and his black slave-boy Kheyr at his feet. We had laid his face towards the Kibleh, and I spoke to him to see if he were conscious, and when he nodded, the three Muslims chanted the Islamee, "La Iláha," etc. etc., till I closed his eyes. The "respectable men" came in by degrees, took an inventory of his property, which they delivered to me, and washed the body; and within an hour and a half we all went out to the burial-place; I following among a troop of women who joined us, to wail for "the brother who had died far from his place." The scene, as we turned in between the broken colossi and pylones of the temple to go to the mosque, was overpowering.   After the prayer in the mosque we went out to the graveyard, —Muslims and Copts helping to carry the dead, and my Frankish hat in the midst of the veiled women; all so familiar and yet so strange!

After the burial the Imám, Sheykh Abd-el-Waris, came and kissed me on the shoulders; and the Shereef, a man of eighty, laid his hands on my shoulders and said:—" Fear not, my daughter, neither all the days of thy life, nor at the hour of thy death, for God leadeth thee in the right way (sirát mustakeem)." I kissed the old man's hand, and turned to go, but numbers of men came and said, " A thousand thanks, O our sister, for what thou hast done for one among us!" and a great deal more. Now the solemn chanting of the Fikees, and the clear voice of the boy reciting the Koran in the room where the man died, are ringing through the house.   They will pass the night in prayer, and to-morrow there will be the prayer of deliverance in the mosque.   Poor Kheyr has just crept in here for a quiet cry. Poor boy! he is in the inventory, and to-morrow I must deliver him up to " *les autorités*," to be forwarded to Cairo with the rest of the property. He is very ugly with his black face wet and swollen, but he kisses my hand and calls me his mother, "quite natural like." You see colour is no barrier between human beings here.

The weather is glorious this year, and spite of some fatigue and a good deal of anxiety, I think I am really better. I never have felt the cold so little as this winter, since my illness; the chilly mornings and nights don't seem to signify at all now, and the climate seems more delicious than ever.

I am very sorry that the young traveller I spoke of was so hard to Er-Rasheedee, and that his French doctor refused to come and see the dying man; such conduct naturally makes bad blood here. The German doctors, on the other hand, were *most* kind and helpful. Tell young Mr. S——,* if you see him, it was his dragoman who died in my house.

The Festival of Ábu-l-Hajjáj was quite a fine sight; not splendid at all,—*au contraire*, but spirit-stirring; the flags of the Sheykh borne by his family, chanting, and the men

* See page 196.

with their spears tearing about on horseback in mimic fight. My acquaintance of last year, Abd-el-Mutowwil, the fanatical sheykh from Tunis, was there. At first he scowled at me; then some one told him how Er-Rasheedee had been left by his master, upon which he held forth about the hatred of all unbelievers, Jew or Christian, to the Muslims, and ended by asking where the sick man was. A quiet little smile twinkled in Sheykh Yoosuf's soft eyes, and curled his silky moustache, as he said demurely, " Your honour must go and visit him at the house of the English lady." I am bound to say that the Pharisee " executed himself" handsomely, for in a few minutes he came up to me and took my hand, and even hoped I should visit the tomb of Abu-l-Hajjáj with him!!

Ramadán, February 7.

Since I wrote last I have been rather poorly, —more cough and most wearing sleeplessness.

A poor young Englishman has died here, at the house of the Austrian consular agent. I was too ill to go to him; but a kind, dear young Englishwoman, Mrs. Walker, who was here with her family in a boat, sat up with him three nights, and nursed him like a sister. A young American lay sick at the same time in the house; he is now gone down to Cairo, but I doubt if he will reach it alive. The Englishman was buried on the first day of Ramadán, in the place where they bury strangers, on the site of a former Coptic church. Archdeacon Moore read the service; Omar and I spread my old English flag over the bier, and Copts and Muslims helped to carry the poor stranger.

It was a most impressive sight: the party of Europeans—all strangers to the dead, but all deeply moved; the group of black-robed and turbaned Copts, the sailors from the boats, the gaily-dressed dragomans, several brown-shirted Fellaheen, and the thick crowd of children— all the little Abab'deh stark naked, and all behaving so well; the expression on their little faces touched me most of all. As Muslims, Omar and the boatmen laid him down in the grave; while the English prayer was read the sun went down in a glorious flood of light over the distant bend of the Nile. "Had he a mother? he was young!" said an Abab'deh woman to me, with tears in her eyes, and pressing my hand in sympathy for that poor far-off mother of such a different race.

I regret that so many of my letters have been lost, but I can't replace them; I tried, but it felt like committing a forgery. Passenger steamers come now every fortnight, but I have had no letters for a month, except one of the 10th January, from ——, which had been sent by private hand, and went to Aswán, and then back by post. I have no almanack, and have lost count of European time; to-day is the 3rd of Ramadán, that is all I know.

The poor black slave was sent back from Kiné—God knows why; because he had no money, and the Mudeer could not "eat off him," as he could off the money and goods, he believes. In order to compensate me for what he eats, he proposed to wash for me; and you would be amused to see Kheyr, with his coal-black face and filed teeth, doing laundry-maid out in the yard. He fears Er-Rasheedee's family will sell him, and hopes he may fetch a good price "for his boy" (his master's son); only, on the other hand, he would so like me to buy him, and so his mind is disturbed: meanwhile, the having all my clothes washed clean is a great luxury.

The steamer is come, and I must finish in haste.

LETTER XLIX.

February, 1865.

M. Prévost-Paradol is here for a few days, and I am enjoying " a great indulgence of talk," as heartily as any nigger. He is a delightful person. This evening he is coming with Arakel Bey, his Armenian companion, and I will invite a few Arabs to show him. A little good European talk is a very agreeable interlude to the Arab prosiness, or rather *enfantillage*, on the part of the women.

M. Paradol is intoxicated with Egypt, yet Egypt is not itself this year. All the land here, which last year glowed in emerald verdure, is now a dreary expanse of dry mud, brown and desolate! The Nile is lower already than it was at lowest Nile last July; it all ran away directly this year, so that in many places there will be no crops whatever.

There have been very few travellers this year; indeed, none but a few Americans: one Californian parson was a very nice fellow.

I paid Fadl Pasha a visit in his boat, and it was just like a scene in the Middle Ages. In order to amuse me, he called upon a horrid little black boy of about four to do tricks like a dancing dog, which ended in a performance of the Muslim prayer. The little wretch was dressed in a Stamboolee dress of scarlet cloth.

All the Arab doctors come to see me now as they go up and down, and to give me a help if I want it; some are very pleasant men. Murad Efendi speaks German exactly like a German. The old Sheykh-el-Beled of Erment, who visits me whenever he comes here, and has the sweetest voice I ever heard, complained of the climate of Cairo. "There is no sun there at all; it is no lighter or warmer than the moon." What do you think *our* sun must be, now that you know what that of Cairo is? We have had a glorious winter, like the finest summer at home, only so much finer.

The black slave, who was returned upon my hands by the Mudeer of Kiné, is still here; it seems no one's business to take him away, as the Kádee did the money and goods; and so it looks as if I should quietly inherit poor ugly Kheyr, who is an excellent fellow, and of a degree of ugliness quite transcendant. His teeth are filed sharp, " in order to. eat people," as he says; but he is the most good-humoured creature in the world. It is evidently not my business to send him to be sold in Cairo, so I wait the event; meanwhile, he is a kind of lady's-maid to me, and a very tolerable laundryman. If nobody claims him, I shall keep him at whatever wages may seem fit, and he will subside into liberty. *Du reste*, the Maohn here says he is legally entitled to his freedom.

I fear my plan of a dahabeeyeh of my own would be too expensive. The wages of common boatmen are three napoleons a month.

I am very popular here, and the only Hakeem. I have effected some brilliant cures, and get lots of presents—eggs, turkeys, etc. It is quite a pleasure to see the poor people; instead of trying to spunge on one, they are anxious to make a return for kindness. These country-people are very good; a nice ycung Circassian sat up with a dying Englishman, a stranger, all night, because I had doctored his wife.

I have also a pupil, Mustafa's youngest boy, a sweet intelligent lad, who is pining for an education. He speaks very well, and reads and writes indifferently, but I never saw a boy so wild to learn. I quite grieve, too, over little Ahmad, forced to dawdle away his time and his faculties here.

LETTER L.

February 7th, 1865.

WE have delicious weather, and have had all along. There has been no cold at all this winter.

I have sought about for shells, and young Mr. C—— tells me he has brought me a few from the Cataract; but of snails, I can hear no tidings, nor have I ever seen one; neither can I discover that there are any shells at all in the Nile mud. At the first Cataract they are found sticking to the rocks. The people here are very stupid about natural objects that are of no use to them. As with French *badauds*, the small birds are all sparrows; and wild flowers there are none, and only about five varieties of trees in all Egypt. The Red Sea shells, I know, are beautiful.

This is a sad year; all the cattle are dead. The Nile is *now* as low as it was last July; and the song of the men, watering with the shadoofs, sounds sadly true, as they chant, "Ana ga'án," etc., "I am hungry, I am hungry for a piece of dura bread," sings one; and the other chimes in, "Meskeen, meskeen!" (Poor man! poor man!), or else they sing a song about Seyyidna Eiyoob, "our Lord Job," and his patience. It is sadly appropriate now, and rings on all sides, as the shadoofs are greatly multiplied for lack of oxen to turn the sákiyehs (water-wheels). All is terribly dear, and many are sick from sheer weakness, owing to poor food; and then I hear fifty thousand men are to be taken to work at the canal from Geezeh to Asyoot, through the Fyoom. The only comfort is the enormous rise of wages, which however falls heavily on the rich.

If the new French Consul "knows not Joseph," and turns me out, I am to live in a new house, which Sheykh Yoosuf is now building, and of which he would give me the terrace, and build three rooms on it for me.

If the Consul will let me stay on here, I

will leave my furniture, and come down straight to Alexandria, *en route* for Europe. I know all Thebes would sign a round-robin in my favour, if they only knew how. I will leave El-Uksur in May, and get to you towards the latter part of June.

The Abab'deh have just been here, and propose to take me, two months hence, to the Moolid of Sheykh Abu-l-Hasan el-Shad'lee (the coffee saint), in the Desert, three days' journey from Edfoo. No English have ever been there, they think, and all the wild Abab'deh and Bishareeyeh go with their women and their camels. It is very tempting, for I sleep very ill, and my cough is harassing, and perhaps a change like that might do me good.

LETTER LI.

March 13, 1864.
Therm. 89° in my deewan at 4 P.M.

I HOPE your mind has not been disturbed by any rumour of " battle, murder, and sudden death " in our part of the world. A week ago we heard that a Prussian boat had been attacked, all on board murdered, and the boat burnt; then that ten villages were in open revolt, and that Efendeena (the Viceroy) himself had come up and " taken a broom and swept them clean;" *i. e.* exterminated the inhabitants.

The truth now appears to be, that a crazy darweesh has made a disturbance; but I will tell the story as I heard it.

He did as his father likewise did thirty years ago, made himself " ism " (name) by repeating one of the appellations of God, such as " ya Lateef," three thousand times every night for three years, which rendered him invulnerable. He then made friends with a Jinn, who taught him many more tricks; among others, that practised in England by the Davenports, of slipping out of any bonds. He then deluded the people of the Desert, giving himself out as " El-Mahdi " (he who is to come with the Lord Jesus, and to slay Antichrist at the end of the world), and proclaimed a revolt against the Turks. Three villages below Kiné, Gow, Rahaeneel, and Bedu, took part in the disturbance, upon which Fadl Pasha came up with troops in steamboats, shot about a hundred men, and devastated the fields. At first, we heard a thousand were shot, now it is a hundred. The women and children will be distributed among other villages. The darweesh, some say, is killed, others that he is gone off into the Desert with a body of Bedawees, and a few of the Fellaheen from the three ravaged villages. Gow is a large place,—as large, I think, as El-Uksur. The darweesh is a native of Salameeyeh, a village close by here; and yesterday his brother, one Mohammad et-Teiyib, a very quiet man, and his father's father-in-law, old Hajji Sultan, were carried off prisoners to Cairo or Kiné, we don't know which. It seems that the boat robbed belonged to Greek traders, but none were hurt, I believe, and no European boat has been molested. Baron K—— was here yesterday with his wife, and they saw all the sacking of the villages, and said no resistance was offered by the people, whom the soldiers were shooting down as they ran, and they saw the sheep and cattle driven off by the soldiers.

You need be under no alarm about me. The darweesh and his followers could not pounce on us, as we are eight good miles from the Desert, *i. e.* the Mountain. So we must have timely notice; and we have arranged that if they appeared in the neighbourhood, the women and children of the outlying huts, and also any travellers in boats, should come into my house, which is a regular fortress; and we muster little short of seven hundred men, able to fight (including El-Karnak). Moreover, Fadl Pasha and the troops are at Kiné, only forty miles off.

Three English boats went down stream to-day, and one came up. Baron and Baroness K—— went up the river last night; I dined with them and with the Copt who is their consular agent here. She is very lively and pleasant. A little boy here has fallen desperately in love with her (he is twelve, and quite a boyish boy, though a very clever one). He had put on a turban to-day, on the strength of his passion, to look like a man, and had neglected his dress otherwise, as he said young men do when they are sick of love. The lady is, I imagine, about thirty. The fact is, she was kind and amiable, and tried to amuse him, as she would have done to a white boy, which inflamed his susceptible heart. He asked me if I had any medicine to make him white; he little knows how very pretty he is with his brown face. As he sat cross-legged on the carpet at my feet, with his white turban and blue shirt, reading aloud, he was quite a picture.

My little Ahmad, who is donkey-boy and general little slave, the smallest, slenderest, quietest little creature, has implored me to take him with me to England, or to any " beled Frangee," wherever I go. I wish R—— could see him; she would be so surprised at

his dark, brown little face, so "*fein,*" and with
eyes like a dormouse. He is a true little
Arab; can run all day in the heat, sleeps on
the stones, and eats anything; quiet, gentle,
and noiseless, and fiercely jealous. If I speak
to any other boy, he rushes at him and drives
him away; while black Kheyr was in the
house, Ahmad suffered a martyrdom, and the
kitchen was the scene of incessant wrangle
about the coffee. Kheyr would bring me my
coffee, and Ahmad resented this usurpation of
his functions; of course quite hopelessly, as
Kheyr was a great, stout black of eighteen,
and poor little Ahmad not bigger than R——.
I am really tempted to adopt the vigilant, active little creature. I will send this letter by
a steamer, which came up last night and goes
to-morrow. It brings a party of Russians to
see Thebes in two days!

Sheykh Yoosuf returned from a visit to Salameeyeh last night. He tells me the darweesh, Ahmad et-Teiyib, is not dead; he believes that he is a mad fanatic and a communist. He wants to divide all property
equally, and to kill all the Ulema and destroy
all theological teaching by learned men, and

to preach a sort of revelation or interpretation of the Koran of his own. " He would break up your pretty clock," said Yoosuf, "and give every man a broken wheel out of it; and so with all things."

One of the dragomans had been urging me to go down the Nile, but Yoosuf laughed at any idea of danger. He says the people here have fought the Bedaween, and will not be attacked by such a handful as are out in the mountain now. *Du reste*, the Abu-l-Hajjajee-yeh (family of Abu-l-Hajjáj), the Shurafa, will " put their seal to it " that I am their sister, and answer for me with a man's life. It would be foolish to go down into whatever disturb-ance there may be, alone, in a small country boat, and where I am not known.

The Pasha himself, we hear, is at Girgeh, with steamboats and soldiers; and if the slight-est fear should arise, steamers will be sent up to fetch all the Europeans. What I grieve over is the poor villagers, whose little property is all confiscated; guilty and innocent, all alike are involved in one common ruin.

I hear that there is great and general dis-content. The Pasha's attempt to regulate the price of food has had the usual results of such attempts; and of course the present famine prices are laid to his charge. I don't believe in an outbreak; I think the people too much accustomed to suffer and to obey; besides, they have no means of communication, and the steamboats can run up and down and destroy them *en détail,* in a country which is eight hundred miles long by from one to eight wide, and thinly peopled. Only Cairo could do anything, and everything is done to please the Caireens at the expense of the Fellaheen.

The great heat has lasted these three days; my cough is better, and I am grown fatter again. The Nile is so low that I fancy six weeks or two months hence I shall have to go down in two little boats; even now the dahabeeyehs keep sticking fast continually.

I have promised my neighbours to bring back some seed-corn for them; the best English wheat without a beard. All the wheat here is bearded, and they are very desirous to have some of ours. I long to bring them wheelbarrows and spades and pickaxes. The great folks get steam-engines, but the labourers work with no better implements than their bare hands and a rush basket, and it takes six men to do the work of one who has good tools.

I send you a pretty fragment of a tablet, such as Joseph numbered his master's goods on. It will serve as a paperweight.

LETTER LII.

March, 1865.

" May the whole year be fortunate to thee !"
(The 'compliments of the season.')

Now is Bairam, I rejoice to say, and I have lots of physic to make up for all the stomachs damaged by Ramadán.   I have persuaded the engineer who was with Lord —— to take my dear little pupil, Ahmad Ibn-Mustafa, to learn the business at Fowler's engineering shop at Leeds, instead of idling in his father's house here.   Mr. Fowler has kindly offered to take him without a premium.   I will give the child a letter to you, in case he should go to London.   He is a good and intelligent boy.   It is very good-natured of Lord —— to take him.

He has been reading the Gospels with me

at his own desire. I refused, till I had asked his father's consent. Sheykh Yoosuf, who heard me, begged me by all means to make him read them carefully, so as to guard him against the heretical inventions he might be beset with among the English " of the vulgar sort." What a dilemma for a missionary!

I sent down the poor black lad Kheyr with Arakel Bey; he took leave of me with his ugly face all blubbered, like a sentimental hippopotamus. He said, " for himself he wished to stay with me, but then what would his boy (his little master) do? There was only a stepmother, who would take all the money, and who else could work for the boy?" Little Ahmad was charmed to see Kheyr depart, of whom he chose to be horribly jealous, and to be wroth at all he did for me.

Now the Sheykh-el-Beled of Baidyeh has carried off my watchman, and the Christian Sheykh-el-Hárah, of our quarter of El-Uksur. has taken the boy Yoosuf for the canal; the former I successfully resisted, and got back Mansoor, not indeed " incolumis," for *he* had been handcuffed and bastinadoed, in order to make *me* pay two hundred piastres; but he bore it like a man, rather than ask me for the money, and was thereupon surrendered. But the Copt will be a tough business; he will want more money, and be more resolved to get it. *Veremos.* I must, I suppose, go to the Nazir at the canal (a Turk), and buy off my donkey-boy.

I gave Lord —— an Arab dinner on a grand scale, to meet all the notabilities at El-Uksur. I think he was quite frightened at the sight of the tray, and the Arab fashions and company, and the black fingers in the dishes.

Yesterday was Bairam, and numbers of " hareem" came in their best clothes to wish me a happy year, and enjoyed themselves much with sweet cakes, coffee, and pipes. Khursheed's wife (whom I cured completely) looked very handsome. Khursheed is a Circassian, a fine young fellow, much shot and hacked about, and with a Crimean medal. He is kawás here, and a great friend of mine. He says, if ever I want a servant, he will go with me anywhere, and fight anybody, which I don't doubt in the least. He was a Turkish memlook, and his condescension in wishing to serve a Christian woman is astounding. His fair face, and clear blue eyes, and brisk, neat, soldier-like air, contrast curiously with the brown Fellaheen. He is like an Englishman, only fairer, and, like Englishmen, too fond of the coorbaj. What would you say if I appeared attended by a memlook, with pistols, sword, dagger, carbine, and coorbaj, and with a decided and imperious manner,—the very reverse of the Arab softness? Such a Muslim too! Prayers five times a day, and extra fasts, besides Ramadán. "I beat my wife," said Khursheed; "oh, I beat her well! she talked so much; and I am like the English, I don't like many words."

I was talking the other day with Yoosuf about people trying to make converts, and I uttered that eternal *bêtise*, "Oh, they mean well!" "True, O lady! perhaps they do mean well, but God says in the noble Koran that he who injures or torments those Christians whose conduct is not evil, merely on account of religion, shall never smell the fragrance of the garden (paradise). Now, when men begin to want to make others change their faith, it is extremely hard for them not to injure or torment them; and therefore I think it better to abstain altogether, and to wish rather to see a Christian a good Christian, and a Muslim a good Muslim."

No wonder a pious old Scotchman told me that the truth which undeniably existed in the Muslim faith was the work of Satan, and the Ulema were his "meenisters." That benign saint, Yoosuf, a "meenister" of Satan! I really think I *have* learnt some "Muslim humility," for I endured this harangue, and did not argue at all. But, as Satan himself would have it, the fikees were just then reading the Koran in the hall; and Omar, who gave a khatmeh that day at his own expense, came in and politely offered the Scotchman some sweets prepared for the occasion.

I have been really amazed at several instances of English fanaticism this year. Why do people come to a Muslim country with such hatred "in their stomachs" as I have witnessed three or four times?

I often feel quite hurt at the way in which the people here thank me for what the poor at home would turn up their noses at. I think hardly a dragoman has been up the river since Er-Rasheedee died, but has come to thank me as warmly as if I had done himself some great

service, and many to give me some little present.
While the man was ill, numbers of the Fellaheen
brought eggs, pigeons, etc.,—even a turkey;
and food is worth money now, not as it used
to be (*e. g.*, butter is three shillings a pound).
I am quite weary, too, of hearing, " Of all the
Frangee, I never saw one like thee!" Was
no one ever at all humane before? For, remember, I give no money, only a little physic
and civility. How the British cottager would
" thank you for nothing!" and how I wish my
neighbours here could afford to do the same!

After much wrangling, Mustafa has got back
my boy Yoosuf, but the Christian Sheykh El
Hárah has made his brother pay two pounds,
whereat Mohammad looks very rueful. Two
hundred men are gone out of our village to
the works, and of course the poor hareem have
not bread to eat, as the men had to take all
they had with them.

LETTER LIII.

El-Uksur, March, 1865.

I DINED with Baroness —— one day, and after dinner we invited several Arab Sheykhs to come for coffee. The little Baronin won all hearts by her pleasant vivacity, and to see the dark faces glittering with merry smiles as they watched her, was very droll.

Mustafa also gave us a capital dinner; the two Abab'deh Sheykhs, the Sheykh of El-Karnak, the Maohn, and Sheykh Yoosuf dined with us. The Sheykh of El-Karnak took off the lamb's head, and handed it to me in token of the highest respect. He performed miracles of eating, and I complimented him, in the words of the popular song, on "doing deeds that Antar did not." After dinner, Baroness —— showed the Arabs how ladies curtsey to the

Queen of England, upon which the Abab'deh acted the ceremonial of presentation at the Court of Darfoor, where you have to rub your nose in the dust at the king's feet. Then we went out with lanterns and torches, and the Abab'deh danced the sword-dance for us. It is performed by two men with round shields and great straight swords. One dances a *pas seul* of challenge and defiance, with prodigious leaps and pirouettes, and Hah! Hah's! Then the other enters, and a grand fight ensues. When the handsome Sheykh Hasan bounded out, the scene was really heroic. All his attitudes were alike grand and graceful.

They wanted Sheykh Yoosuf to play the Arab single-stick—"en-Nebboot," and said he was the best man hereabouts at it; but as his sister died lately, he would not. One of them expressed a great desire to learn "the fighting of the English." He little knows how he would get pounded by English fists.

Another night I went to tea in Lord ——'s boat. Their sailors gave a grand fantasia, curiously like a Christmas pantomime. One danced like a woman (Columbine), and there was a regular Pantaloon, only "more so," and a sort of Clown in sheepskins and a pink mask, who was duly tumbled about, and distributed *claques* freely with a huge wooden spoon.

I am so used now to our poor, shabby life, that it makes quite a strange impression on me to see all the splendour which English travellers manage to bring with them on board their boats,—splendour which, two or three years ago, I should not even have remarked. And thus, out of my " inward consciousness " (as Germans say), many of the peculiarities and faults of the people of Egypt are explained to me and accounted for.

The weather is now very unpleasant; the winds have begun, and as all which last year was green is now arid, the dust is beyond all belief. I must move down as soon as I can.

Sheykh Hasan Abab'deh is going down in his boat with a party, in twenty days or so, and suggests that I should travel under his escort, in case there should be any straggling robbers about. I am not afraid, but if I hear in time that no dahabeeyeh has been bought for me, I may as well join Hasan. His party will be six or eight guns, I believe. If there is no dahabeeyeh and I do not go with Hasan, I will send to Kiné for two small boats, each with one cabin, so as to avoid the constant "*sitzen bleiben*" of a large boat in this extraordinarily low Nile. It is now many cubits lower than it was last year at its lowest, three months later.

I intended, as I told you, to go this year to the moolid of Sheykh-el-Shád'lee, out in the Bisharee desert; but I fear it would delay me too long, for the descent of the Nile will be very tedious for want of water and consequently of current, and from the violent north winds having set in two months before their time. "Inshallah, next year!" say my friends.

The Hajjees have just started from hence to Koseir, some with camels and donkeys, but most on foot. They are in very great numbers this year. The women drummed and chanted all night on the river-bank, and it was fine to see fifty or sixty men in a line praying after their Imám, with the red glow of the sunset behind them. The prayer in common is quite a drill, and very stately to see. There are always quite as many women as men. One wonders how they stand the march and the hardships.

My little Ahmad grows more pressing with

me to take him. I will take him to Alexandria, I think, and leave him in J——'s house, to learn more home service. He is a dear little boy, and very useful. I don't suppose his brother will object, and he has no parents.

Ahmad Ibn-Mustafa also coaxes me to take him with me to Alexandria, and try again to get his father to send him to England. I wish most heartily I could. He is an uncommon child in every way, full of ardour to learn and do something, and yet childish and winning and full of fun. His pretty brown face is quite a pleasure to me. His remarks on the New Testament teach me as many things as I can teach him. The boy is pious, and not at all ill taught; he is much pleased to find so many points of resemblance between the teaching of the Koran and the "Engeel." He wanted me, in case Omar did not go with me, to take him to serve me. Here there is no idea of its being derogatory for a gentleman's son to wait on an oldish person; and on one who teaches him, it is positively incumbent. He does all " menial offices" for his mother in Alexandria, and always hands coffee, waits at table, or helps Omar in anything, if I have company; nor will he eat or smoke before me, or sit till I tell him. It is like service in the Middle Ages.

Mustafa asks whether the boy could be put to school and kept in England for a hundred a year. Of course it must be a school where no conversion would be attempted. Mustafa is a strong Muslim, though so fond of the English.

LETTER LIV.

El-Uksur, April 3rd, 1865.

In my last letter to ——, I told how one Ahmad et-Teiyib, a mad darweesh, had raised a riot at Gow, below Kiné, and how a boat had been robbed, and how we were all rather looking out for a razzia and determined to fight Ahmad and his followers. Then we called them " harámee," and were rather blood-thirstily disposed towards them, and resolved to keep order and protect our property. But *now* we say " nás mesákeen," and can only bewail the misery which this outbreak has brought on the unfortunate villagers. The truth, of course, we shall never know. I can only send you the rumours which reach me. No doubt there is another version of this miserable story current at Cairo and Alexandria, and it may be that there are facts of which I have not heard. But I live among the oppressed race, and I cannot help it if the profound compassion inspired by their fate makes me lean to their side.

It seems that a Greek boat was plundered, and the steersman killed; but I cannot make out that anything was done by the "insurgents" beyond going out into the desert to listen to the darweesh's nonsense, and see "a reed shaken by the wind." The party that robbed the boat was, I am told, about forty strong. The most horrid stories are current among the people, of the cruelties committed on the wretched villagers by the soldiers; and unhappily, past experience makes them but too credible.

The worst thing is that every one believes that the Europeans aid and abet, and all declare that the Copts were spared to please the Frangees. Mind, I am not telling you facts; I only repeat what the people are saying. One Mohammad, a most respectable, quiet young man, sat before me on the floor the other day, and told me the horrible details he had heard from those who had come up the river. "Thou knowest, O our lady, that we are people of peace in this place; and behold, now, if one madman should come, and a few idle fellows go out to the Mountain (desert) with him, Efendeena will send his soldiers to destroy the place, and spoil our poor little girls, and hang us: is that right, O lady? And Ahmad-el-Berberee saw Europeans with hats in the steamer with Efendeena and the soldiers. Truly, in all the world none are miserable like us Arabs. The Turks beat us, and the Europeans hate us and say 'quite right.' By God, we had better lay our heads in the dust (die), and let the strangers take our land and grow cotton for themselves. As for me, I am tired of this miserable life, and of fearing for my poor little girls." Mohammad was really eloquent, and when he threw his meláyeh over his face and sobbed, I am not ashamed to say that I cried too.

I know very well that Mohammad was not quite wrong in what he says of the Europeans. I know the cruel old platitudes about governing orientals by fear; I know all about " the stick" and " vigour," and all that. But I " sit among the people," and I know too that Mohammad feels just the same as John Smith or Tom Brown would feel in his place, and that men who were exasperated against the rioters in the beginning are now in much the same humour as free-born Britons might be under similar circumstances.

What *is* characteristic of this country and people is, that a thing happening within a few weeks and within sixty miles already assumes a legendary character.

According to the popular belief the affair began thus:—A certain Copt had a Muslim slave-girl, who had read the Koran and who served him. He wanted her to be his concubine, and she would not, and went to Ahmad et-Teiyib, who offered money for her to her master. He refused it and insisted on his rights, backed by the government, whereupon Ahmad proclaimed a revolt, and the people, tired of taxes and oppressions, said "we will go with thee." But Ahmad et-Teiyib is not dead, and where the bullets hit him he shows little marks like burns. He still sits in the island, invisible to the Turkish soldiers, who are still there. This is the only bit of *religious* legend connected with the business.

Now for a little fact. The boat which brought up the prisoners from Gow stopped a mile above El-Uksur. I saw it, but the prisoners were all below. The Sheykh of the Abab'deh here has had to send a party of his men to guard them through the desert. When we came near the boat my companion went on as far as the point of the island; I turned back, after only looking at it from the bank, and smelling the smell of a slave-ship. It never occurred to me, I own, that the Bey on board had fled before a solitary woman on a donkey, but so it was. He had given orders not to let me come on board, and told the captain to go a mile or two further, which he did; the boat stopped three miles above El-Uksur, and its dahabeeyehs had all their things carried to that distance. There were on board " a hundred prisoners less two " (ninety-eight). Amongst them, the Mudeer of Soohág, a Turk, in chains and wooden hand-cuffs like the rest. The poor creatures are dreadfully ill-used by the men who guard them. There has been some disturbance up at Esneh, and twelve men are gone down in chains to Kiné, four of them having been concerned in the riots, the rest only because they are related to Ahmad et-Teiyib.

From Salaneeyeh, two miles above El-Uksur, it is said that every man, woman, and child in any degree akin to Ahmad et-Teiyib has been taken in chains to Kiné, and no one here expects to see one of them return alive. Some are remarkably good men, I hear; and I have heard men say, " If Haggee Sultan is killed and all his family, we will never do a good action any more, for we see it is of no use."

It is more curious than you can conceive, to hear all that the people say. It is just like going back four or five centuries at least, but with the admixture of the heterogeneous element of steamers, electric telegraphs, etc.

There was a talk, I find, among the three or four Europeans here, at the beginning of the rumours of the revolt, of organizing a defence amongst Christians only. Conceive what a silly and gratuitous provocation! Religion had nothing whatever to do with the affair; and of course, the proper person to organize defence was the Maohn; he and Mustafa and others had indeed talked of using my house as a castle, and defending that in case of a visit from the rioters. I have no doubt the true cause of the disturbance is the usual one—hunger,—the high price of food. It was like our Swing or bread riots,—nothing more, and a very feeble affair too.

It is curious to see the travellers' gay dahabeeyehs passing just as usual, and the Europeans as far removed from all care or knowledge of these distresses as if they were at home. When I go and sit with the English, I feel almost as if they were foreigners to me too,—so completely am I now "Bint el-Beled" (daughter of the country).

Altogether, we are most miserable here,—all we Fellaheen. The country is a waste for want of water, the animals are skeletons, the people are hungry, the heat has set in like June, and there is some sickness, and, above all, the massacres at Gow have embittered all hearts. There is no Zaghareet to be heard, and all faces are sad and gloomy. I shall not be surprised if there are more disturbances. At first, as I told you, every one was furious against Ahmad-et Teiyib and the insurgents; but since they have been so frightfully dealt with, of course we pity them and their poor women and children. These " vigorous measures " will cause the evil they are meant to punish. You know I don't buy or sell, or lend money, or even give it. So no one has any interest in concealing his true feelings from me, and the people talk to me wherever I go. I wish " Efendeena " could hear a little of what I hear. I have no doubt he is ignorant of much that is done in his name.

I have just seen a man who was at Gow, and who tells me fourteen hundred men were decapitated, and a hundred were sent to Feyzoghloo in the steamer. Ahmad et-Teiyib has escaped. I think my informant is quite a truthful man. He says that all these cruelties were perpetrated by the local Pashas, and that the Viceroy ordered the massacre to be stopped as soon as he knew of it.

LETTER LV.

El-Uksur, Good Friday,
14th April, 1865.

*   *   *   *   *

THE version of the massacre here, current at Alexandria, is quite curious to us.

I know well the Sheykh-el-Arab who helped to catch the poor people, and I know also a young Turk who stood by while Fadl Pasha had the men laid down by ten at a time, and *chopped* with the pioneers' axes. He quite admired the affair (though a very good-natured young fellow), and expressed a desire to do likewise. The lowest computation of men, women, and children killed is sixteen hundred. M. M—— reckons it at *above* two thousand.

I have seen *with my eyes* a second boat-load of prisoners. I wish fervently the Viceroy knew.

the deep exasperation which his subordinates are causing. I do not like to repeat all that I hear. What must it be, to force from all the most influential men and the most devout Muslims such a sentiment as this?—" We are Muslims, but we should thank God to send Europeans to govern us." The feeling is against the Turks, and not against Christians.

A Coptic friend of mine here has lost all his uncle's family at Gow. All were shot down, Copt and Arab alike.

As to Hajji Sultan, who lies in chains at Kiné, a better man never lived, nor one more liberal to Christians. Copts ate of his bread as freely as Muslims. He lies there because he is distantly related by marriage to Ahmad et-Teiyib; or, to give the real reason, because he is wealthy, and some enemy covets his goods. All this could be confirmed to you by M. M——. Perhaps I know even more of the feelings of the people than he. I sit every evening with some party or other of decent men, and they speak freely before me.

I assure you I am in despair at all I see, and if the soldiers do come, it will be worse than the cattle disease. Are not the Cavasses bad enough? Do they not buy in the market at their own prices, and beat the Sakkas in sole payment for the skins of water they take from them by force?

Who denies it here? At Cairo things are " kept sweet;" but here—Allah kereem! Of course Efendeena hears the " smooth prophecies" of the tyrants whom he sends up here. When I wrote before, I knew nothing certain; but now I have the testimony of eye-witnesses. It is certain that an order from the Viceroy did stop the slaughter of women and children which Fadl Pasha was about to perpetrate.

THE END.